DEAD SLOW

DOUGLAS PRATT

MANTA
PRESS

*For Ashlee
who has my back at every turn*

1

My skin had a warm, sticky sensation from the salt water. I grabbed the tail of the main halyard and pulled it back, releasing it from the capstan. Now freed, the line zipped around the winch as the mainsail dropped down the mast, settling in folds in the lazy jack cradle atop the boom.

Carina's forward motion slowed when the sheet fell. The engine rumbled beneath my feet.

"I personally don't mind, but we'll be getting into the marina soon," I told Amanda, who was stretched out on the starboard bench in the cockpit. Her bronze nude form made it hard for me to focus on the waterway, and she pulled the cat's eye sunglasses down off the bridge of her nose to peer over at me.

"Are you suggesting I put clothes on?" she inquired.

Shaking my head, I countered, "Never. I think you've found the perfect state to be in."

She grinned at me. "It's been too lovely of a day to end it dressed."

"I'm not the one who has a thirty-six-hour shift tomorrow morning," I reminded her.

"Want me to call out?" she asked.

"If you were going to do that, you should have done it before we pulled up anchor," I advised. "Now we're already back. And who will save all those lives if you don't go to work?"

"You make me sound like I'm important. If I'm lucky, we'll have a few chest pains and some guy who will have inserted his dick into something he shouldn't have."

"Story of my life," I quipped. "You are the sexiest paramedic in all of South Florida."

"Only South Florida?"

"I'd have to do a more thorough study to determine that answer."

Amanda smiled a wistful grin. "Chase Gordon, you are paramount to scientific research."

"We all need a passion," I pointed out.

"You have three days to do your research," she teased. "Then I'm off for a week."

"I can do a lot in three days," I warned her.

"Fair warning, I will shack up with fifteen firemen and three other paramedics during that same time."

I smiled at her. "It would take fifteen firemen to equal one Marine."

She sat up, reaching for a towel to cover her breasts. "Don't get all territorial," she scolded. "You know the rules."

The rules were uncomplicated, as was our status. We didn't have any. In the few months that I'd been seeing Amanda, she'd dodged any attempt at monogamizing our relationship. Yet, she'd devoted almost all her free time to me.

With the Perkins diesel churning the screw, I steered

toward the entrance of the Tilly Marina where *Carina* and I called home. Above the masts and fishing towers, the historic Tilly Inn peered down at the collection of boats. The hotel, built in the mid-1930s, had stood sentry on the shores of Lake Worth for almost a century.

Amanda wrapped the oversized beach towel around her body. I stuck my bottom lip out in a pout, and she leaned toward me to kiss my lips. Her breath tasted like beer, but not in a bad way. It was a subtle reminder of our last few days on the water.

We ventured out Friday, crossing the Gulf Stream to Bimini, where we stayed for three days, anchored out in an isolated reef. We spent most of our days lounging on deck, swimming and snorkeling, or making love. None of which required a lot of clothes—except the snorkeling. I wasn't about to offer up my bits to an errant jellyfish. That kind of thing might make a great story at the bar a few years from now, but the immediate reaction was far more negative.

"I'm going below," Amanda announced. "Do you need me to help you dock it?"

"I can handle it," I assured her.

Amanda and I had spent the last four months seeing each other, even if our relationship remained somewhat undefined and murky. She'd been the paramedic who treated me when I was on the wrong end of a knife fight. Of course, calling it a knife fight was generous since only one of us had a blade, and it wasn't me.

As I passed the fuel dock, Randy, the harbormaster, gave me a wave. I offered him a two-finger salute. The old Michigan native ambled along the pier. If I knew the codger, he'd be at my slip before me to throw the dock lines to me.

We'd pushed the daylight to its brink, and dusk crept across the sky, casting an orange-red glow over the horizon.

The pylon at the end of my pier sported a stenciled image of a grim reaper spray-painted on the concrete post. The warning underneath the robed figure read "Dead Slow," a reminder to boaters to keep their speed at the bare minimum.

Something bobbed just under the surface near the pylon. I cast my eyes at it, but refocused on *Carina*'s bow. I spun the wheel all the way to port, making a wide swing out so I could go straight into the slip.

Amanda reappeared in the companionway. She was wearing a thin t-shirt with nothing underneath and a pair of simple shorts.

"What is that?" she asked, motioning behind us.

Without turning around, I knew she must be talking about the same bobbing object I saw. "I don't know," I admitted as I trained my focus on sliding the bow into my berth.

As soon as the bowsprit entered the slip, I reversed the engines. The resistance against *Carina*'s inertia matched, and she came to an almost complete stop. I shifted back into neutral, allowing the creeping forward motion to edge me into the slip.

"Heads up!" Randy called at the front.

"I got it," Amanda declared, climbing forward to catch the bowline as the grizzled dockmaster tossed it to her.

As she looped a hitch knot around the forward starboard cleat, I hooked the stern line with my boat hook, dragging it over to me. In under two minutes, we tied up, and I reconnected the shore power.

"Chase, how was your weekend?" Randy asked, casting a side-eye at Amanda, who was tidying the lines at the front.

"Pretty nice," I admitted.

The older man flashed a shit-eating grin my way. "I bet it was," he remarked.

"Don't be a creep, Randy," I scolded as Amanda sidled up next to me. She smiled at Randy, who blushed slightly.

"No need to worry, Chase," she replied. "Randy's just stating the obvious. We had perfect weather, dolphins, and a ton of fucking."

The dockmaster's face turned crimson. "I—uh—I mean, I didn't—"

"It's okay, Randy," she said, grinning. "I'm messing with you."

"Right," he stammered. "I got a delivery coming in a bit."

"Hey," I called as he started to turn. "There's something snagged on the pylon back there."

"Oh?" he asked, lifting his hand to his brow as if that offered him superior vision. "Yeah, it is. Looks to be a few feet under the surface. I'll try to get over there in a few minutes and pull it up. Don't want it getting loose at night. Some fool will come in here in the dark and foul his prop."

"Shit, we don't need that again," I remarked, remembering a Beneteau that snagged a crab pot that floated into the marina last month. Before he could clear the fouled propeller, his boat drifted into a Hatteras and a PDQ.

A horn honked, causing Randy to look up. "That's the UPS guy," Randy said.

"I'll take the tender and run over there if you want," I offered. "It'll be dark before you get him squared away."

"Thanks, Chase," he replied as he rushed toward the land.

"Need some help?" Amanda offered.

"Yeah, grab a mask and snorkel," I suggested. The water around the Tilly Marina was like almost every marina—dirty. There seemed to be a film of oil and particulates perpetually floating on the surface. While I had been in it plenty of times, I invariably came out searching for a shower almost immediately. Still, if this flotsam had snagged on something, it might take some work to get it unattached.

Amanda ducked into the cabin as I climbed onto the dock. She returned, holding my mask on her arm. I helped her onto the pier before we hurried to the Tilly's tender, a ten-foot flat-bottomed boat with a nine-horsepower outboard. Most of its use was for Randy or one of the dockhands to make repairs or retrieve lost objects before Poseidon claimed them forever.

"Another boat ride already," Amanda joked. "We could try to rock this boat before we call it a day."

I curled my lip. "We'd be the talk of the marina," I remarked.

"Oh, I bet your boss would love that," she jabbed.

I cast a playful warning glance her way as I started the outboard. Amanda, who had become adept at rope work, untied the dock line, tossing the end into the bottom of the boat. With the tiller on the outboard, I steered us through the maze of dock fingers and piers until we reached the pylon.

Now that the sun had set, the marina had an eerie evening glow. Amanda stood up in the bow as I nudged up against the post. Her hand caught the concrete just under the grim reaper's scythe.

"Nothing to tie onto," she pointed out.

"Let me see what we got," I said, leaving the outboard idling in neutral. "I should have grabbed a light."

"Sorry, Chase."

"Don't be sorry," I told her as I leaned over the gunwale on the tender. "What is that?"

"I can't see," Amanda replied.

My right hand dunked below the surface. All I could make out was a bright red blob. I sensed Amanda behind me, looking into the dark waters.

"Chase," she said in a serious tone.

I glanced back at her, experiencing the same sickening sensation. "Hand me the hook," I said.

She grabbed a boat hook attached to the starboard gunwale, and I reached below the surface with it until it prodded the object. I didn't like the way it felt, but I dragged the hook along its surface until I felt it give some resistance. After testing it with a couple of tugs, I pulled at it.

"It's caught," she pointed out.

"Can you hold the pylon?" I asked.

"You're going in?"

"Something is holding it there."

"Do you want me to do it?" she asked. "I've recovered plenty."

"No, I can handle it," I assured her as I donned my mask.

Rather than rolling onto my back, I slid into the warm salt water. Whatever remnants of daylight remained seemed to vanish when I went under the water.

Even with diminished light, I could make out the body. The red I'd seen was a leather jacket. It was about four feet below the surface. With a long exhale, I descended a few feet until I found the filament line holding the corpse to the pylon. The thin wire snapped when I jerked against it, and the figure sank a few inches.

My fingers grabbed dead leather collar and pulled it toward the surface. My head broke through the water with a gasp.

"I got you," Amanda said as her fingers caught my shirt.

"Can you hold on to this?" I asked, pulling the body up to the top. Amanda placed her hand next to mine on the collar, allowing me to let go. I swam under the hull to the other side and pulled up on the gunwale.

After rolling into the tender, I sat up and reached over the side to help Amanda heave the corpse into the boat. Despite being dead weight, the corpse was small. As soon as it flopped into the bottom of the dinghy, I knew it had been dead for a bit.

To be honest, that was a relief. When I first realized it was a body, I worried that it had just drowned while I was docking. But she—and it was definitely a woman—had been down for hours.

In the waning daylight, I examined the body. The leather jacket I'd used to haul her to the surface was a short-cropped type. Under it, she wore only a tank top that had the bottom six inches cut off and a pair of red panties that matched the jacket.

Just above her pelvis on the right side, I noticed a tattoo of a wolf wearing a crown. A simple anklet with what looked like emeralds hung on her right foot.

As I looked at her face, I noticed one other thing: she hadn't drowned. Without asking Amanda's professional opinion, I determined the cause of death was the knife wound across her throat. Someone had murdered her.

2

———

"You have to be kidding me," Missy complained as she marched down the dock.

"You can't come through here," a Palm County sheriff's deputy warned her.

"The hell I can't," she countered. "I own this damned marina."

The deputy turned to look at his superior, a detective named Carlson. Carlson had replaced Jay Delp, my best friend. Jay left Palm County several months ago to return home to Mississippi to care for his ailing father. Had he still been around, Jay would likely be the one investigating this murder.

Carlson had only said four words to us so far: "I'll get to you."

We were still waiting to be gotten to, and I was ready to take a shower and wash off the marina grime.

Once Amanda and I got the corpse to the dock, we called the police. Randy, always an exemplary employee, notified his boss, Missy. Technically, she was my boss, too, since I worked as a bartender in the Manta Club.

"When I heard there was a body in the water, I knew you'd be here," she said to me as she approached us, though her gaze never wandered toward Amanda.

"I didn't put her there," I pointed out. "Just found her."

"I guess I'm going to go back to the boat," Amanda said. She stood up and walked away.

It was a wise move, and it was hard to miss how diplomatic Amanda was around Missy. Missy, on the other hand, was the opposite.

Missy Seine and I had a sordid history. To be honest, we hadn't resolved it yet. While she was unhappily married, we'd carried on a less-than-clandestine relationship. Since Amanda had shown up, our situation had evolved into something more complicated. Missy, who had never been willing to abandon her husband to be with me, had grown jealous of my budding connection with Amanda.

Of course, Amanda, like Missy, was unwilling to commit to a relationship—although, in fairness, Missy was in a committed relationship with her asshole husband. Her explanation for never leaving him was that he provided a certain status for her. Apparently, a Jewish lawyer held more social standing than a boat bum from the Ozarks.

"Missy, you don't have to be rude," I told her after Amanda left.

"Is this coming from the guy who has threatened my husband on more than one occasion?"

"Fair, but remember when I saved his life? That should count for something," I reminded her. "Besides, he has always started it."

She shook her head. "What the hell, Chase?"

"That statement covers a lot, Miss."

Missy glanced at the dock. "You and what's-her-name seem happy."

"Jealousy doesn't look good on you," I pointed out.

She sneered at me. "I don't like being passed up."

"Join the club," I retorted.

"It's not the same thing."

I lifted an eyebrow. "You made it clear we weren't going anywhere."

"You know why."

"I'm not disagreeing with you."

"Whatever, Chase," she groaned. "What the hell happened here?"

"The cops will give you better details, but I fished a girl out of the water. Someone cut her throat."

"Here at the marina?"

I shrugged. "Not sure. She might have drifted in. I found her about four feet down, snagged on that pylon."

"Fuck me," she muttered. "This will play great on the news."

"There's no such thing as bad publicity," I reminded her.

"Unless you're running a high-end hotel with a high-end murder rate."

"The waterway is public," I pointed out.

"Tell that to the guests who already wonder why they're staying in West Palm Beach instead of Palm Beach."

"It's not hoity-toity over here."

"Pshaw," she spat. "Doesn't stop everyone from expecting Mar-a-Lago."

"That's a special clientele," I remarked. "They wouldn't recognize real five-star service. They just believe the island is nicer than West Palm."

"It is on the ocean side."

"Meh, whatever. We have a better bar."

Missy shook her head, smiling despite herself. "How long are the cops going to be here?"

"Beats me," I responded. "Carlson has only said one thing to me."

"I miss Jay," she commented.

"At least we agree on that," I told her.

Missy rolled her eyes at me. "Are you working tonight?" she questioned, changing the subject to something more professional.

"Tomorrow," I informed her.

Her eyebrows lifted. "Good."

"Mr. Gordon?" Carlson called out as he meandered toward us down the pier.

"Detective," I replied.

"Who are you?" he asked Missy once he stopped in front of us.

"Melissa Seine. I own the Tilly."

"Oh, right. Nice to meet you," he said, his demeanor shifting as he realized she was the woman in charge. "We'll try to get out of your way as soon as we can."

"It's fine, Detective," Missy assured him. "Do you think someone killed her here?"

"I can't say, Ms. Seine."

"Like, you don't know?"

He shook his head.

"Understood," Missy said. "I just want to be ahead of the guests' questions."

"I don't suspect the killer is sticking around," Carlson offered.

"Chase said someone cut her throat. That's terrible."

Carlson nodded. "Yes. Not a fun way to die."

"Think she was still alive when she went into the water?" I asked.

The detective cocked his head. "Probably," he admitted. "How did you find her?"

"I was coming in on *Carina* when I saw something floating under the surface."

Carlson furrowed his brow. "Who is Carina?"

"*Carina* is my boat."

He nodded. "Right. I'm not a boat guy."

"I thought everyone down here was," Missy remarked. "Maybe you need to spend time out there."

"Ms. Seine, I don't have a boat to do that."

"Call me Missy," she retorted with a coy smile. "We have a center console here for tours. We could go out sometime."

I glanced at Missy, saying nothing.

The detective replied with a boyish grin. "That could be fun," he said.

Of course it could be fun. Missy was gorgeous, and someone like Carlson would love to spend an afternoon on the water where she almost always wore a bikini or, if we sailed out far enough, nothing at all.

"How about this week?" she suggested.

Carlson's head bobbed as he pulled out a spiral notebook. "I need to jot down your contact information, anyway. That way, I can keep you apprised of the case."

"That would be good," she replied.

Missy took the notebook and jotted down her phone number, adding a little smiley face after it with her name. I noticed it was her cell phone, too. She returned the notebook to him.

"Mr. Gordon, why didn't you call us right away instead of pulling her out?" Carlson asked.

"I didn't realize it was body until I got on top of it. Part of me worried she'd just gone in the water."

Carlson nodded. "What did you find?"

"She'd gotten tangled in some filament line. Probably

another crab pot that broke loose. The line caught on the concrete."

"Your dockmaster said you were trying to help clear what you thought was flotsam."

I wasn't sure if he was asking a question or restating Randy's words. Either way, I nodded. "We were worried it was something that might tangle in someone's prop."

Carlson looked up. "That's a big problem?"

"Down here, yes," I answered. "This is a busy waterway, and a lot of trash floats through here. A fouled prop can cause problems."

"He's right," Missy acknowledged, as if her statement confirmed my own. "We had one last month that caused thousands of dollars in damages."

Carlson's head bobbed as she spoke. He continued to look at her as he spoke to me. "Sounds like you were just trying to help. You live here and work here?"

"I do," I replied.

"Chase is our bartender up at the Manta Club, but he helps Randy down here some, too."

"That's convenient," he noted.

"Very," Missy said snidely. "Most of the time."

"We're going to get out of here soon," he assured Missy. "I'm leaving a couple of unis to canvass for any witnesses. But with the body submerged, the medical examiner has to establish a time of death. When that happens, we might need to come back."

"Please do," she offered. "We're available for anything you want."

"Thanks, Ms. Seine."

"Missy," she corrected.

"Missy."

I leaned over toward her. "Missy, why don't you let Detective Carlson finish up here?"

"Right," she said. "I hope to hear from you, Detective."

"Jake," he told her.

"Chase is all yours," she informed the detective before leaving me there with him.

"She's something," he remarked with a half-grin on his face.

"That she is," I agreed.

"I'm guessing you two have something going on?"

"It's complicated," I answered.

"Oh?"

"We have history, but I still work for her."

"But you aren't currently with her?"

I don't know what I am to her. That wasn't what I said, but it was how I felt. Missy and I hadn't been together in months, something that, until a few months ago, only happened when I was cruising. But with Amanda not wanting to settle into an exclusive relationship, it didn't mean Missy and I were all done.

Besides, Missy was still married. That was a fact I chose not to point out to the detective. Better to let her tell him, or he could use his deduction skills to learn that on his own.

"I don't guess I am," I answered after a minute.

The problem was that I loved Missy, and a few months ago, she could have talked me into selling *Carina* and settling down. Deep down, I'd have been miserable, but I wanted it. Or I'd convinced myself that I did.

Carlson pursed his lips. "Did you recognize the girl?" he asked, shifting back into investigative mode.

I shook my head. "No. She looked pretty young, though. If she was twenty, I'd be surprised. But it's hard to tell at this point."

"That's true."

"She had a tattoo," I pointed out.

"We noted that."

"It might mean nothing," I added.

Carlson regarded my observation with only a hint of annoyance. "It will help us identify her."

"That's all I saw before we got her back to the dock and called you."

Carlson nodded. "If I need to talk to you again, do you have a number?"

I shook my head. "I don't have a phone."

His face scrunched up. "You don't have a phone?"

"Nope."

"How does anyone get in touch with you?"

"With any luck, they don't," I replied with a smile. "But you can call the Manta Club. I get my messages there."

He shook his head. "That's weird, man."

"I spent a lot of years tethered to others in the Corps. Now I like the freedom of not having any connections. Plus, I'm going to be cruising the islands half the time, and a phone won't work there."

"They have satellite phones," Carlson pointed out.

"Right," I said sardonically. "I'm sitting on a beach in Jamaica, just wishing my mom would call to interrupt me."

"You don't talk to your mother, either?"

"I didn't say that," I said. "However, I do limit it."

"Geez, what kind of guy are you?"

With a smirk, I replied, "An enlightened one, I hope."

"I'm sure I'll be in touch."

He flipped his notebook closed just like Joe Friday before sticking it in his pocket. Like my friend and his predecessor, Jay, Carlson wore tan khakis and a short-sleeved polo shirt. It was simply too hot most of the year to wear a cheap suit and tie. Although, I suspected that the dressiest Jay ever got was in his dress blues.

The night sky showed a few brighter stars fighting through the light pollution along the eastern seaboard of South Florida. I found Amanda in *Carina*. She was stretched out in the v-berth, wearing nothing. Two cold Kaliks we'd picked up in Bimini rested on the shelf. She leaned forward and handed me one.

"Figured you might need to relax after that ordeal," she said with a smile.

I turned up the bottle, gulping down several swallows. "I like the way you think," I told her.

"Is Missy still mad at you?"

"We don't have to talk about her," I pointed out.

"You know I don't want to cause any problems."

"How about we just worry about these beers and how to entertain ourselves? After all, you'll be working over the next few days."

"Then get up here, sport, and plant your flag," she ordered, grabbing my hand and pulling me up on the bed before she kissed me.

3

After what turned into an all-nighter with Amanda last night, I slept most of the morning away. She'd slipped off *Carina* around five in the morning, which gave her an hour to get home and shower before reporting to the fire station for her roll call at seven.

When I blinked awake later, my internal clock told me it was half past noon. I was usually a little more accurate with it than that, but it was close.

I rolled onto my back to stare at the ceiling. While I loved *Carina*, the forty-foot Tartan sailboat offered little space. It was roomy enough for one, but add another person, and the square footage shrank exponentially.

Though I'd gotten used to being alone, I knew I would miss Amanda this week. My plan before I'd met her was to work for a few months and earn some money for my cruising kitty. But now, I wasn't sure when I was going to head back out to the islands for an extended time.

And I realized I didn't care.

My stomach and my bladder reminded me to get up.

Plus, I'd never taken a shower after dipping into the water. I'd gotten distracted. Amanda should be commended for her willingness to be that close to me after that.

My boat came with a shower, and when I'm anchored in some far-off bay, it's perfect for me. However, the bathroom at the marina has virtually unlimited hot water and enough elbow room to wash my back.

I grabbed a pair of shorts I kept hanging on a hook next to the head. It might surprise some people how many times I had to dress in a hurry. Sadly, it wasn't always for the same reason.

As I climbed out of the companionway, I stopped, staring at two green and yellow cowboy boots standing at my eye level on the dock.

"Fuck me, Gordon," Scar moaned. "Can't you get dressed before you step outside?"

I peered up at the second most powerful man in the South Florida cocaine trade. Esteban Velasquez was the number-two man to Julio Moreno, the head of the Cuban cartel in Miami. The first time I met the hitter, he was only recognizable by the large, jagged scar across his cheek. Still, I couldn't shake my nickname for him from my brain, and since Esteban was not an individual with a refined sense of humor, I didn't call him that to his face.

"Esteban, this is technically my back porch," I pointed out. "Besides, I'm heading to the shower."

As I climbed up on the dock, Scar said, "There were whispers you had an incident here last night."

"Incident?" I inquired. "That's one way to put it. Do you have any part in it?"

"It was a girl, no?" he asked.

I nodded. "Young, too."

Scar shook his head slowly. "No, that's not my style."

"You don't kill women or girls?"

The Cuban just flashed a bright grin. It might have been the first time I'd seen his smile. I had a fleeting thought that he had some very white teeth.

"What's your concern, then?" I asked.

"Mr. Moreno has been struggling with some competition lately."

"Oh?" I commented, raising my eyebrows with piqued curiosity.

"Mostly squabbles, but it could be part of that. Sounds like their—how do you say it? Motive?"

"MO?"

"*Sí*. MO."

"Killing girls?" I questioned. "That's your competitor's MO?"

"Señor Moreno doesn't trade in people," he told me.

I pursed my lips and angled my head to study him. It wasn't something I kept abreast of at all; however, I would have been surprised to learn that Moreno ran prostitutes. While he was a murdering drug dealer, Moreno and Scar had some odd sense of respectability to them. Even a degree of honor. I doubted I'd let either babysit my kid, but they rarely lied to me.

"Are you suggesting that she was a prostitute?" I asked.

"Safe bet," he replied. "I doubt she's on any missing person list, though."

"Why not?"

"They pluck their girls from poor neighborhoods in rural areas. Dope them up and put them on the streets," he explained. I sensed the disgust in his tone, and I wondered if it had anything to do with the idea that this girl was someone's daughter. I was one of the few people Scar trusted with his daughter's identity, and he worked to keep that secret safe for her own well-being.

Unlike my own father, Scar behaved like the most traditional dad, and he would do anything to protect his girl. Since learning that fun tidbit about the hitter, I'd found him a lot softer. Although, I was willing to admit that my bias might be circumstantial and based on pure emotions.

"What's the deal, Esteban?" I asked. "Why did Julio send you here to talk to me?"

"He thinks these people are dangerous and *astutos*. Tricky."

"Julio thought I could do something about it?"

"You have a friend who is a detective, do you not?"

"Not anymore," I replied.

"Oh?" Scar's face twisted. "I'm sorry."

"He's not dead or anything," I countered. "He just moved to Mississippi."

Scar curled his lip. "Why?"

"Family stuff."

"So you don't know the detective?"

"I met him, but I don't think if I go up and say, 'Hey, the number-one drug dealer in Florida suggests that the girl was a hooker,' he's going to do much with that information. In fact, he probably knows she was a hooker."

"I doubt it," Scar replied.

"Who are these competitors?"

"*Les Loups Noirs.*"

"By now, you should realize I don't speak Spanish," I pointed out.

Scar shook his head in disgust. "How do you live in South Florida and not speak the language?"

"It's on my to-do list, but I never get around to it."

"Even I know there's an app," the Cuban advised.

"I don't have a phone, either," I reminded him.

"I forget you're a strange one, Gordon."

As I pressed my lips together, I sighed. "Could it be that I'm the only enlightened one?"

"Unlikely," Scar noted. "It's a Haitian gang. Translates to 'The Black Wolves.'"

"Wolves?" I repeated.

Scar nodded.

"She had a tattoo of a wolf on her hip," I recalled.

Scar gave me a satisfied expression. "Something to share with your detective."

"Not my detective," I reminded him.

He grinned again. "Certainly not mine."

"I'm not sure what to do with that information," I told him.

"I know you, Gordon," Scar replied. "You'll be up to your asshole in this before too long."

Before I could say another word, Scar gave me a two-finger salute, similar to the one I'd given Randy last night as I sailed into the Tilly. He left me standing on the finger as he walked away. If there was one thing the man thrived at, it was his sexy indifference. Not that I found him all that sexy, but he certainly had swagger.

As the cartel hitman strolled back to shore, I took my towel under my arm and started for the shower. Randy came out of his office and waved.

"Crazy shit yesterday," the old harbormaster noted. "Cops tell you anything?"

I shook my head. This would be the talk around the Tilly for the rest of the week. It wasn't the most exciting thing to happen here. That award might go to the gunmen who took a hit out on Missy's lawyer husband. But the marina and the hotel had a history of such things.

"Me either," he replied. "They said she was real young."

"Hard to say, Randy," I confessed. "In that state, everything looks off."

"No doubt," he agreed. "Makes me wish it had been another dead manatee or a dolphin instead."

"I don't know, Randy. A dead dolphin might get us canceled."

"Good point, Chase. No one wants that, do they?"

"Right," I concurred.

"Chase, can I pry?"

"Into what?"

"Our boss," he answered.

"What about her?"

"I know you and her have a thing," he started.

"Let me stop you there, Randy. That's not really any concern of anyone's."

"No, I get that. And, well, personally, I don't care. Someone was poking around, though. Asking questions about her."

"What questions?" I inquired.

"Did she visit anyone down here? Was she seeing anyone? Stuff like that," he explained. "I didn't tell them anything. Gave them the whole, 'What are you talking about?' response."

"Did you get his name?"

"No, and I didn't push it, either."

"Probably smart," I acknowledged. "Did the cameras catch him?"

"Maybe," he answered. "I'll go back and check. Should I tell Missy?"

I shook my head. "No, not yet. See if you can find a picture of the guy first. No reason to worry her for nothing."

"You got it, Chase," he responded.

As I walked to the shower, the overload of information hit me. First Scar, and now Randy. It was a lot to process as I washed off the grime.

4

"Chase, what the hell is going on around here?" Wilson Peterson asked as I dropped off the espresso martini he'd ordered.

Peterson was the mayor of West Palm and a regular at the Manta Club. He popped in every Friday like clockwork, and in turn, a gaggle of bureaucratic hangers-on showed up. It gave Fridays an early evening rush before the dinner crowd arrived.

"You talking about the body?" I asked.

"Damn straight. Makes for terrible news coverage."

I cocked my head and raised my eyebrows. Everyone appeared concerned with the media's reaction to a murder. It seemed callous, but I might be biased since I'd found the girl. Her lifeless eyes reminded me that at one time, they should have been full of life.

Maybe. If what Scar had told me held any truth, the girl's death could have been a release from the grind and toil of slavery. Like most people, I'd read the placards posted in the train stations and airports about stamping out human trafficking. I'd witnessed it firsthand, but even I wanted to believe that what I'd encountered was an outlier and not the norm.

That wasn't true, though. Almost every prostitute was a victim, and the rest of us tended to ignore that. Like most things, we equated it to not being something we had to face. Humans, as a whole, had an excellent talent for ignoring matters that didn't affect us.

"Wilson, do you know much about the gang activity around here?" I asked.

"Oh, do you think it's connected?"

I shrugged. "Someone mentioned that there was a new gang out of Miami pimping girls along the coast."

"Not sure," Wilson replied. "Like any big metropolitan area, we have those issues. I don't keep up with all the factions."

"This girl looked very young," I remarked to him.

"How young?"

"I couldn't say, but a teenager, I'd bet."

"Sick," he grumbled.

"She had a tattoo," I informed him. "It seemed odd, given her age."

"Yeah, for sure."

"I bet the detective will look into it. Just have to wonder what a young girl would have to do to get her throat cut and dumped in the sea."

The mayor bobbed his head thoughtfully. For Wilson, the most important thing was optics. He would want someone arrested to show how determined the city and county administration were to protect their constituents.

Not that I thought Wilson didn't care about the poor girl's death, but his every waking moment focused on how things appeared to the public. He'd use whatever empathy he had for the victim to decry the violence. Hopefully, the little nuggets I'd dropped in his ear made it to the sheriff himself.

That was all I wanted to deal with, though. Not unlike the rest of the world, I didn't want to be embroiled in a murder involving gangs or really anyone. I'd served my country in the Corps, and since getting out, I'd helped the CIA out with a global nuclear threat. Right now, I only wanted to earn some money and take Amanda for an extended cruise down island.

A comptroller for the city flagged me down from across the bar. I didn't recall his name, but he came in most Fridays when Wilson did. The other clientele, for the most part, were similar officials who used the happy hour at the Manta Club as the place to make behind-the-scenes deals.

"I need a dirty martini," he said. "Can I get the blue cheese-stuffed olives?"

"No, we're out," I told him.

"You made them for me last time," he reminded me.

I nodded. "Yes, and you stiffed me on the bill."

"No, I didn't," he barked.

"Yeah, you did," I countered. "If I recall, you were in here with a young woman. I assumed you didn't do it maliciously, though, which is why you're still allowed in here."

"That's ridiculous," the comptroller argued.

"Then I guess you can leave," I told him.

Laughter erupted from the gentleman next to the asshole. "He's right, Gary. You totally bailed on that. Jeanette paid your tab that night."

Gary blushed as he looked at the guy reprimanding him. "I don't recall that, Sammy."

Sammy shook his head. "Of course not. You were trying to slide into that intern's panties."

Gary flushed. "Chase, I'm sorry," he told me. "It was an accident."

I shrugged. "I told you I assumed as much. You were the one getting hostile."

"Yeah, my bad," Gary replied. "Can I still have a martini?"

"Sure," I said. "Do you have a card to put down for the tab?"

He nodded, pulling an American Express card from his wallet and handing it to me.

"Thanks, Gary," I mumbled, reminding myself to remember his name now that I'd heard it. It still didn't help me understand what a comptroller was, though.

While I hadn't remembered Gary's name from his last visit, I recalled his vodka preference was Tito's. He probably drank the house vodka in the well when he wasn't around his coworkers.

As I mixed the ingredients in the shaker tin, I saw Missy come in from the lobby. She was with Detective Carlson. When I poured the martini into the frosted glass, ice crystals floated on top.

"Thanks, Chase," Gary said bashfully as I set the glass in front of him.

Missy and Carlson took a couple of seats at the other end of the bar. I didn't want to be egotistical, but I was certain she'd brought him in to parade him before me.

"What can I get you?" I asked as I approached the pair.

"How about one of your apple martinis?" Missy replied.

I turned to Carlson, who asked, "Do you have Buffalo Trace?"

"Sure do," I told him.

"Can you do an old fashioned?"

"Of course."

"I'll take one of those," he decided.

When I dropped off their drinks, I commented, "Detective, I assume you aren't here on the investigation."

"Not entirely," he admitted. "But I needed to speak with Missy here."

"Oh?" A subtle press to his statement.

He nodded without offering me any information. My clumsy ploy had failed in a miserable fashion.

"With any luck, you've at least identified her," I remarked. "The mayor was asking me about it just a few minutes ago."

"The mayor?" Carlson inquired, looking up from his old fashioned.

"Yeah, he's over there," I told him, jerking my head to the far side of the bar.

Missy eyed me, aware that I was name-dropping on purpose. I was a bartender, after all. It was part of my job to know everything worth knowing. Customers frequently asked inane questions about history, politics, or crime in the area. Once customers learned I was a former Marine, there was always a slew of inquiries about the military or terrorists. People thought bartenders were nothing more than treasure troves of information. In fact, that was often true. I heard more gossip about city hall during our Friday happy hour than anyone could get from the local news.

"Don't worry," I assured him. "He thinks you're doing a fine job."

That was, of course, a lie. Wilson hadn't mentioned if he even had a clue who the detective on the case was, much less his approval of the guy. But, again, I was a bartender, and making people feel better should be in my job description.

"All right, but we still don't have an ID on her," he

remarked, then gestured toward Missy. "I was hoping Missy could lend an assist, but that came up empty."

"How would she help?" I asked.

Carlson might have realized he'd said more than he'd intended, or he considered the information generic enough to not matter. Plus, he had obviously already talked to Missy about it, so it wasn't privileged.

"We found a couple of hotel keys on her," he explained.

"One was ours," Missy added.

"She was a guest here?" I asked.

Missy shook her head as Carlson replied, "Doesn't look like it."

"What room did the key go to?"

"It was blank," Carlson answered. "Or erased."

"That's easy enough to do," I pointed out. We had at least one or two guests every day who accidentally wiped their keys, often by placing them in the same pocket as a cell phone. The magnetic stripe that held that data was simple to mess up, and while some of the newer card systems solved that problem, the Tilly Inn still had an older setup.

"Where did the other key go to?" I asked.

Carlson shook his head. "I'm not sure yet. It's also blank."

"Something erased both keys?"

"Seems like it."

"Probably her phone," I pointed out.

"But we didn't recover a phone," Carlson claimed.

"What if she's like you, Chase?" Missy noted. "A digital hermit."

"What about a pager?" I wondered.

Carlson shook his head.

"Who carries a pager still?" Missy questioned.

"Prostitutes and drug dealers," Carlson answered. "You think she was a prostitute?"

I shrugged. "It's been the talk of the bar today. Someone mentioned to the mayor that she could possibly be a hooker."

Carlson rolled his eyes. I didn't tell him I was the person who told Wilson that, but the information street worked. Now Carlson had that idea to deal with while Wilson could press the issue with the sheriff. It should be enough to get Carlson to investigate it.

"Yeah, I get it," I conceded. "No one wants the mayor trying to solve crimes, right?"

"We just don't have enough details," he admitted.

"Having two hotel keys is weird," Missy advised. "It's not far-fetched."

"But she doesn't show on your surveillance video coming or going," Carlson reminded her.

That explained what he was doing here. It made sense to check the videos, even if she hadn't had a Tilly Inn room key.

I glanced at Missy. "You didn't find her at all?"

She shook her head. "Nothing. I mean, we only watched through this week's surveillance, but she never stepped foot in the lobby."

"What did the other key look like?" I asked.

"It was plain, without words. Just a bright blue," Carlson said. "My guys are going to the local hotels, trying to find who uses that one."

"What color blue?" I asked.

"Like a neon blue."

I smiled. "You should have asked the bartender."

"You know it?"

"Try the Royal Pelican on the island," I suggested. "That

sounds like their suites. The blue card gets you into the Azure Room."

"I've never heard of it," Carlson confessed.

"Very exclusive," Missy confirmed. "One has to be a VIP at the Pelican and get a personal invite from Clayton Connors."

"The real estate mogul?" Carlson asked.

"Same one," I answered. "He owns the Royal Pelican."

"What happens in the Azure Room?" Carlson wondered.

"Isn't that the question?" I joked. "Rumors abound, but I've never crossed paths with anyone who has been in there."

Carlson's gaze drifted off, and I realized he was mulling over this new information. I asked the question I was betting he was wondering about.

"Why would a teenage girl need access to the ever-exclusive Azure Room?"

"Someone gave it to her," Missy considered.

"Most likely," I agreed. "I don't think this girl was a VIP there."

Carlson turned to Missy. "I hate to do this, Missy. I'm having a great time, but I need to follow up on this."

"As long as I get a rain check," she told him.

"Guaranteed," he assured her. "Thanks so much."

There was an awkward back-and-forth between them as he tried to decide if he would kiss her cheek or shake her hand. He opted for a quick hug before leaving his barely sipped old fashioned.

"Nice, Miss," I remarked when he left.

"What?" she asked with mock innocence across her face.

"You want to make me jealous or something?"

"Nothing like that," she told me. "We were going over the video, and this is the closest bar that I own."

"Fair enough," I conceded.

"Chase, why would she have those key cards?" she asked, her tone serious.

"I suspect she might have been a hooker."

"Yeah, but you knew that before Jake mentioned it."

I smiled. "What makes you say that?"

"I can tell from that smug expression on your face when you are ahead of someone else."

"Scar came by to chat with me," I told her. "He suggested the possibility. Given what I knew, it made sense."

"Why didn't you just tell Jake that?"

"Because advertising to a cop that a leader in the Cuban cocaine cartel liked to feed me information did not seem like the wisest move. Do you want it out that Scar and Moreno have frequented your hotel?"

She curled her lip and wrinkled her nose at the idea.

"Right. Your new boyfriend might question that."

"Not my boyfriend," she countered.

"Did you mention your husband to him yet?" I asked.

"Go fuck yourself, Chase," she snapped before leaving the bar and marching back into the lobby.

5

The night air carried hints of hibiscus from Tilly's patio, the flowers in full bloom. Reclined in my cockpit, I sipped another Kalik beer while Haley Reinhart belted out her version of "Creep" through the speakers I'd added to *Carina*'s dodger frame. I had the volume cranked low to not bother any boat neighbors. Most of the boats on this pier remained empty, but I'd seen Tammy Cox, a liveaboard, at the end of the dock. She resided on a Nordhavn 47 Trawler I guessed had twice the space of *Carina*.

The beer went down easily, and I was glad to be off work. At night, there was this peaceful music that the sea and marina worked to create. Halyard shackles clanged against an aluminum mast somewhere, creating a rhythmic *ting-ting-ting-ting*. In the distance, a horn blared like a trumpet, like announcing a king's arrival. Even the faint voices carrying across the water chimed into the song, adding a certain dimension.

I loved it. Throw in a little "Creep," and it was the perfect place to drift off in thought.

My bare feet rested on the lifeline, allowing the sea breeze to tickle my soles. After eight hours on my feet, this felt like heaven.

Unfortunately, my thoughts came back to that girl. What connection did she have to both the Tilly and the Royal Pelican? Usually, I found the answer was the simplest and most logical. She'd worked as a hooker with appointments in both hotels. The people in five-star hotels didn't want to be seen with hookers. That didn't mean they weren't there, though. If the transaction had occurred with a third party, like a pimp, providing the girl with a key beforehand, that allowed her to get on the elevator and go to the client's room without talking to a hotel employee.

It also implied she should have shown up on camera. I knew the Tilly had full coverage on all public areas. Unless you hid in the restroom, you could count on being watched. If our victim had come into the Tilly, she'd be on film.

That meant she hadn't made it there. Which begged the question, who had she stood up?

Across the water, a woman screamed. Lost in my thoughts, it took a second for the noise to register with me. More shouting echoed off the water's surface, and I sat up.

Sound danced chaotically off water, making it difficult to triangulate the voices. I climbed out of the cockpit onto the dock and scanned around.

"Leave me alone!" a girl wailed.

I tracked the high-pitched cry and saw a woman and man walking along the boardwalk bordering the marina. The wooden walkway got a lot of traffic from the neighboring condominiums and other hotels.

"Get back here!" the man shouted, reaching out to grab the female's arm.

"Dammit," I muttered, stalking toward the pair, careful not to drag my bare feet across the wood planks on the dock.

Part of my unwritten job description for getting a free slip was that I helped police the area at night. Randy would be nestled in his twenty-eight-foot Bertram on the far end of the marina. By this time of night, he was always three tokes into the wind and dozing off his medicinal weed. Most of the time, it was just me asking transients to keep the noise down. On some busy spring break weeks, I might break up a fight over a girl. Otherwise, it was a quiet job.

Tonight didn't bless me. From my vantage point, this argument looked like it was bordering on a domestic situation. Those were historically bad every time.

"You don't just get to leave," the man demanded. "I paid you already."

My ears perked up at that. This had turned from a domestic spat into something different altogether.

"Excuse me," I stated in a deep, stern tone. "What's going on here?"

"This is a personal matter," the man snapped. He was a white, mid-fifties male wearing a sport coat and slacks. His shirt had been hastily rebuttoned, and he'd mismatched the holes.

"Sir, you're making it a matter for everyone."

"Wait... you're the bartender up at the hotel," he noted. "Get lost. I'm a guest."

"At the moment, I'm off-duty," I said. "Since I live here, too, you're now crossing the line."

I took a second to study the woman, who, upon closer inspection, was much younger than I'd thought. Much like the girl I fished from the water yesterday, she didn't seem to be over twenty.

"Are you okay?" I asked.

"Fine," she stated. "Just want to get away from him."

My gaze cut over to the male again. I might have recognized him from the bar, but I wasn't sure. If he'd been at one of the tables, I'd have only seen him on the periphery. Whatever the reason, he only seemed a little familiar.

"What's the issue?" I asked him.

He flushed. "She—uh—stole some money."

"I did not," the girl retorted.

"Let's keep our voices down," I warned. "There are people out here sleeping. Unless you want someone to call the police."

The girl's head hung, and she shook it. I gave the man a hard glare. He confirmed with a head shake that wasn't what he wanted, either.

"Why don't we talk calmly now?" I suggested. "What happened?"

"Look, man," the guy said, "she said she needed some money and... you know how it is."

"Where are you from?" I asked the man, eyeing the gold band on his hand.

"Houston."

"Leave your wife at home?"

The man blushed again. "It's not like that," he stammered.

I turned to face the girl. Her eyes stayed down.

"Right," I replied. "If you want my suggestion, I would tell you to go back to your room. If you cause a scene, someone will call the cops. You may have to explain to your spouse why you got picked up for..." I paused and glanced back at the girl, "...solicitation."

"But my money?" he protested.

"What's your name?"

"Uh..."

"Listen, I don't care what you do," I explained. "My job is to keep the marina safe at night. Since you're a guest, I'm willing to help you stay safe. However, you gotta help me. You know I could go up to the front desk and get your name, anyway."

That part was partly true, but it would take more effort than I wanted to exert.

"Clay Moore," he replied with a reluctant expression.

"Clay, go to your room. I'll make sure she gets out of here safely. None of us want the cops involved, right?"

He nodded.

"Good job, Clay," I replied.

Clay stared at me until I motioned for him to go on.

"Can I go?" the girl asked as Clay walked up the stairs to the hotel.

"Why don't you wait a minute?" I suggested, gesturing to the retreating john. "Give him time to get upstairs."

"I didn't take his money," she argued.

"He gave it to you?"

She nodded.

"What's your name?"

Her brow furrowed.

"Did you hear what he said? I'm the bartender here. That might make me a good guy to know, if you want referrals."

While I didn't make it a habit to direct customers to working girls, it was a question I was asked at least twice a week. Most bartenders in the hotels along Flagler Drive would give a girl's number for the right tip.

"It's Diamond," she told me.

"Diamond, how old are you?"

"Eighteen," she replied in a shaky voice.

"Right," I said. "How much did he give you?"

"Couple hundred."

"How much are you handing off to your... uh... handler?"

"All of it."

"Is he expecting two hundred?" I asked, clarifying my question.

She nodded. "He talked to the guy. Clay."

"Are you working at the Tilly a lot?"

"Mister, I don't have time to chat," she said.

"Sure you do," I corrected her. "Or I can make sure you are flagged at the front desk. You'll never make a call here again."

"I didn't do anything," she barked.

"Just answer a couple of questions," I told her. "We can help each other. If not, I'll call the cops. Want to guess what their response time is here? Because it's not long enough for you to get to the street."

Her face had a look of disgust. "What do you want? A freebie?"

I shook my head. "Did you hear about the girl they found here yesterday?"

Diamond's eyes widened. "No," she lied.

My head cocked as I gave her a stare filled with incredulity. She returned my gaze with unblinking confidence, but never let it be said I couldn't outlast a teenager. We remained motionless until she flinched. Her head dipped, breaking the eye lock.

"Did you know her?" I asked.

"Yeah," Diamond answered.

"What's her name?"

The hooker shrugged.

"C'mon, help me out," I pressed. "You knew her."

Her eyes scanned the area as if she were searching for

someone eavesdropping on our conversation. There was no one in sight.

Finally, her veneer cracked. "Lyla," she whispered.

"Lyla?"

Diamond nodded.

"Is that her real name?"

"It's what I know," Diamond replied. I assumed that Diamond wasn't this girl's real name, either.

"Did she work for the same people as you?"

I got a shrug. "Mister, if you aren't looking for a date, I need to go."

"Okay, Diamond. How about I walk you up to the street?" I offered. "In case Clay is waiting around."

I wasn't worried about that, though. Clay had gotten enough of a fright about the police showing up to argue with the girl anymore.

"'Kay," the girl replied.

As we mounted the steps, I pried a little more about Lyla. Diamond's lips sealed, and I only got head motions in response to my queries. She glanced a couple of times at my bare toes, but she didn't comment.

"Listen, Diamond. I work at the Manta Club. If you need anything, you can reach me there."

She nodded again. Her eyes lingered on my face a little longer.

"If you learn anything that might help catch the man who killed your friend, you can tell me, too."

"She wasn't my friend," Diamond corrected.

"Still, what happened to her could happen to you. Be careful."

"Mister, I can take care of myself," she snapped, her eyes flaring up with heat.

"No doubt," I agreed. "Just offering a shoulder if you need one."

We skirted the Tilly, walking along the concrete path. Solar lights on the black iron handrails illuminated the path. Finally, we reached the curb on Flagler Drive.

"Do you need a ride?" I asked, though I wasn't sure how I could pull off my offer. I didn't have a car, and the best I could do was either borrow the hotel's courtesy car or arrange a ride share.

Before she could answer, a black Lincoln Corsair pulled up to the curb. The passenger door opened, and a bulky black guy stepped out.

"Diamond," he called in a thick Caribbean accent. "Get in."

"Is that your ride?" I asked Diamond under my breath.

"Do you have a problem?" the goon asked me. A glitter of gold flashed from his mouth.

"If she doesn't want to go with you, I do," I retorted.

His eyes narrowed, and he growled something incoherent to the driver, who got out of the car. The lanky man pulled a Ruger SR22, leveling it at me.

"Why don't you get in, too, smartass?" Goldtooth suggested.

"Look, I was just walking the girl up here," I explained. "I don't want any trouble."

"Too late," Goldtooth replied, smiling to reveal a whole mouthful of gold teeth.

"Suppose I don't," I said. "You going to shoot me here? There are cameras right there and there." I pointed at two of the hotel's security cameras that cover the valet circle and curb.

Goldtooth shrugged. "I'll shoot both of you and move on."

"No!" Diamond exclaimed. "I wasn't with him. He just followed me."

"You shouldn't have been followed," he snarled at the young girl.

"Woah, fine," I relented. "She's right. I was tagging along uninvited. The girl didn't want me around."

Diamond continued to nod. Obviously, my fate mattered less to her than her own.

"Both of you get in," the man demanded as the driver motioned with his pistol to the back seat. Goldtooth pointed at me. "You get in the front," he ordered.

I raised my hands and obeyed.

6

The two men were likely Haitian, although we hadn't had a long enough conversation for me to be certain. In the front seat, I could see the tattoos covering the driver. On the back of his right hand, I noticed three long rifle bullets crossed and bound by the stem of a black rose. At least the ink was black; whether the intent had been for the rose to be black or just colored in was hard to determine. Despite the rudimentary style, these weren't regular jailhouse tattoos. The person who had etched them into his skin was an artist.

Along his forearm, I counted six different symbols for the devil and two more simplistic-looking pistols. The name "Tig" stretched across his other arm. The tattoo artist had drawn the tail of a tiger where the tail of the "g" hung down.

"Tig?" I asked.

The driver glared at me.

"Shut up," Goldtooth growled.

I'd seen Goldtooth remove a Glock before getting in the seat behind me. That was incentive for me to behave. There was almost no way to turn and disarm him before he shot me through the seat. My only hope was that the Lincoln Corsair was very new. In fact, it still had the new-car smell. That was a feat, given how both Goldtooth and Tig stank of marijuana.

With any luck, Goldtooth wouldn't want to spray the interior with my guts unless I forced him to.

"Where are you taking me?" I asked.

"He's a cold motherfucker, ain't he, Tig?" Goldtooth remarked.

People like these two thugs thought they had some ice in their veins. They expected people to cower before them because most people did. These two thought they could terrorize the world like wolves in a herd of sheep. When someone like me didn't react the correct way, they had to dig deeper to find the reaction they wanted. Their need for respect or fear—and they didn't recognize the difference— overwhelmed them.

If these two were logical, they wouldn't seek that response from me. They should just recognize my lack of fear and terminate me.

But I counted on that pathology of need. In their world, the only reason anyone respected them was fear. That kind of loyalty wasn't real, but they didn't know any better. I understood loyalty in a way these two never would. Goldtooth would sell out Tig in a heartbeat. Therefore, they needed something to empower them.

I could play to that.

"Guys, I really didn't want any trouble," I said. "I'm just a bartender. That's all I was talking to Diamond about. There are lots of guys looking for girls coming through the bar. It's good to have some connections."

I glanced at the rearview mirror at Goldtooth's eyes. There was some curiosity glimmering in them.

"It's a high-end hotel, so you know money comes through," I added.

Tig said something in what sounded like a mixture of French and something else. Whatever it was, I didn't understand him. Goldtooth replied in the same language. While I didn't understand the words, I read the body language.

The idea of having someone in an expensive hotel offered potential. I could direct them to the right clients.

"We could make this a profitable partnership," I suggested.

"You aren't our partner," Goldtooth barked. "We own you."

"Whatever you say," I replied.

However, he narrowed his gaze at me. I didn't sound scared of him, or contrite enough. That unnerved Goldtooth, who was used to a level of kowtowing I wasn't delivering.

He blinked, and in that motion, I saw him reappraise me. His logical side was warning him that I was dangerous. Before, he'd mistaken me for either stupid or naive. Now, he realized that my nonchalance wasn't an act or some misguided behavior. It was similar to the look a dog gives another when they realize they are about to fight.

Despite that dawning realization, Goldtooth was also evaluating his position. There were two of them and only one of me. While he hadn't searched me, he assumed correctly that he and Tig had weapons while I did not. Had I been smart and grabbed my M45 from *Carina* before interceding with Diamond and Clay, this might have been a different situation entirely.

Instead, I'd walked into a kidnapping unarmed. Not even wearing shoes. At least if I died, I could haunt this place barefoot. That was something.

Tig drove toward the interstate and took the northbound ramp of I-95. In seconds, he sped up to sixty miles per hour. The interstate at this hour was as empty as it ever got. That only meant traffic was flowing, not that it was sparse. This section of 95 never slept—travelers and commuters zipped up and down 95 all the time. It was just a matter of steady traffic, slow traffic, and stand-still traffic. Tonight, it was steady.

Tig moved into the passing lane as he sped up to pass a FedEx Ground box truck. I hadn't fastened my seatbelt, and the dash continued to ding a warning at Tig. It took five minutes of the incessant shrill alert to make Tig turn to me.

"Buckle up, asshole," he ordered.

I watched the driver as I reached behind me and pulled the strap across my chest with my left hand. As I buckled the latch into the release, I snatched the top of the steering wheel, wrenching it toward me. The result was the front of the Lincoln made a sharp right at sixty-three miles per hour in front of the FedEx truck.

Tires screeched as the driver of the box truck tried to smash his brakes down to stop the freight truck. There simply wasn't enough time or space to even slow the impact, and the truck's front bumper slammed into the side of the Corsair as its sudden maneuver to the right shifted the balance of the SUV to the other side. When the FedEx driver collided with us, the inertia shoved us over into a roll.

Time had a way of slowing down in those moments. As the vehicle struck the pavement on the driver's side, all of us flopped toward the floor, only to be slung the opposite way as the car continued rolling.

Neither Goldtooth nor Diamond had buckled their seat belts, and the pair took a beating as we bounced. My head cracked against the passenger's window, shattering the glass, the window having already absorbed the initial impact by spider-webbing.

I blinked, realizing our rollover had ended. My head hung upside down, and I fumbled for the release button on my seatbelt. The pressure on the belt had jammed the button, and when I pressed it, the belt did not release. My hand reached out for a shard of glass, and I started sawing on the fabric around my waist.

No one else moved, but I could hear Diamond moaning. A quick look at Tig told me the man was still breathing. Goldtooth was stretched over Diamond on the roof of the back seat.

My hand worked faster as I cut through the belt. When it released, I dropped to the ceiling. My right hand was already over my head, allowing my forearm to absorb the fall as I rolled out of the seat.

On my hands and knees, I reached up to Tig's waist, where I found his Ruger tucked into his belt at the small of his back. With the weapon in my hand, I found the door handle and pushed.

Nothing happened, but the door frame crumpled under the impact of the box truck. Dropping to my belly, I slithered through the broken glass and onto the asphalt.

"Are you okay?" the truck driver shouted as he ran toward me.

I waved him off, but he skidded to a stop when he saw the gun in my hand.

"It's okay," I assured him as I pushed to my feet. "I'm the good guy."

"What?" the driver stammered.

Without answering him, I hurried to the other side of the car and opened the rear door. Diamond's hand flopped out onto the pavement, and I grabbed her wrist. With one hand, I tugged on the girl until I pulled her free of the wreckage.

She groaned, and I got my hands under her armpits, pulling her to her feet.

"Can you hear me?" I asked.

"Yeah," she grumbled. "What happened?"

"Motherfucker!" Goldtooth shouted from inside the vehicle.

Diamond reacted to his voice, stepping behind me.

"What's going on here?" the FedEx driver demanded.

"Get her out of here," I urged, motioning for the girl to follow the driver.

Diamond stumbled toward the other man as Goldtooth began to fire his Glock out the door. His rounds hit the swinging rear door, and I jumped back. The gangster crawled out the opened door, waving his Glock wildly.

I leveled the Ruger at the man as he struggled to get to his feet. "Put it down," I insisted.

"Who the hell do you think you are?" Goldtooth barked, raising the Glock toward me.

I fired the Ruger. The .22 caliber pistol was much quieter than the Glock, but its bullet had a firm target. It hit Goldtooth in the face. The small round of metal tore through the man's jaw, spewing flecks of gold, teeth, and bone across I-95. The bullet didn't exit his skull, instead bouncing off his cheekbone and angling into the man's brain.

How the .22 slug killed him was probably more complicated, as it had probably sliced through parts of his brain. However, I watched the instant the life left his eyes, and he crumpled to the ground. I stepped back, keeping the gun on Tig, who still hung unconscious in the driver's seat.

"Call the police," I told the truck driver. "Tell them to contact Detective Carlson. He'll want to be here for this."

The driver stared at me, Diamond hiding behind him.

"Hurry," I urged him out of his trance. "Are you okay, Diamond?"

"You could have killed us," she griped.

"Diamond, they planned to kill us," I argued.

She stared at me before turning her attention to the car. A groan emitted from the driver's side. I knelt down on my haunches, staring through the broken window at Tig. He turned slowly to see me aiming the Ruger at him.

In the distance, I heard sirens blaring as they raced northbound on 95. Behind us, vehicles were stacked up in all lanes. We were now responsible for turning the steady flow of cars into a parking lot.

Such was the Florida interstate system.

Tig spat out more French-sounding words. I guessed from the tone and mannerisms that they were curse words.

I was still squatting beside the car when the first officer showed up. Moving slowly, I laid the Ruger on the ground and raised both hands.

7

It turned into a long night. Carlson showed up forty-five minutes after the first officer arrived. The cops separated all of us, sticking Tig and Diamond in separate cars from me. As the minutes ticked past, my body began to complain. The adrenaline that had powered me right after the wreck drained from my system. What resulted was a complete crash, leaving me ready to collapse in bed.

"Gordon, what happened?" Carlson asked.

"I was kidnapped," I answered.

"Who is the girl?"

"A hooker. She was at the Tilly. I escorted her to the street when these two pulled up." I gestured at the covered body of Goldtooth and the other police cruiser where Tig sat.

"They grabbed you?" he asked.

"At gunpoint," I replied. "Don't think they had the best thing planned for me, either."

"Why?"

I shrugged. "Who knows? I'm a delightful person."

"So far, that's not how I'd describe you," he quipped.

"Opinions vary," I said.

"Who were they?"

"I'm guessing some gang members," I commented. "Caribbean accents, and if I were a gambling man, I'd say they were Haitian."

"We'll see. The girl is a ghost. She's refusing to talk to anyone," Carlson explained.

"She knew the other girl," I told him. "Not too intimately, but she gave me a street name. Lyla."

"Lyla? Like the song?"

I furrowed my eyebrows at him. "Song? Do you mean 'Layla?'"

"No, that's Clapton. You know, 'Lyla. She looks like a woman and talks like a man.'"

"That's 'Lola,'" I corrected him. "By The Kinks."

"Oh, not really my kind of music," he remarked.

"Ah," I said, because I had nothing else to say.

"So the girl knew this Lyla," Carlson considered. "Think these guys were the ones who killed her?"

"Maybe," I answered. "I think they planned to take us somewhere and kill us, too."

"Know where they planned to take you?"

I shook my head. "They spoke to each other in another language."

"If they were Haitian, it might have been their Creole."

"It sounded a bit French," I noted.

"It would. What happened in the car?"

"I took issue with them driving me somewhere to put a bullet in my head. Figured I didn't have much to lose."

"You attacked the driver?"

I shook my head. "Just forced the vehicle in front of a box truck."

Carlson's eyes widened. "How?"

"Grabbed the wheel," I said simply.

"You could have killed yourself," Carlson pointed out.

Nodding, I said, "The option was wait until they took me wherever they planned. If a window didn't open, I'd be in trouble. Besides, I was buckled in, and the airbags did the rest."

"Gordon, that's insane," Carlson said in disbelief. "Tomorrow is going to be painful."

"Do you have anything else for me?" I asked.

"Yeah, the techs need to test your gun and your hand."

"For residue?"

He nodded.

"What's the point?" I asked impatiently. "I admitted to shooting the guy."

"I like to cross my T's and dot my I's."

"I'm beat," I told him.

"Bear with me, Gordon. You get to sleep late, don't you?"

I shrugged. "You need to press the girl," I urged. "She's going to be a little worried that they planned to kill her, too."

"Why?" Carlson asked.

"Hell if I know," I said. "My initial thought was that they wanted to eliminate a connection to the victim we found. However, I think they didn't decide to do it until they saw me with her. So, they might have been worried that she told me something."

"How would they know you were involved?"

I raised an eyebrow. Ever since Scar had shown up the next morning with his own concerns, the fact that I'd found the murdered girl was common knowledge. Much like I told

Missy earlier, it didn't seem wise to tell Carlson I had a tight relationship with Julio Moreno and his number-two man.

"I wouldn't put it past them to have some connections in your department. Hell, all they really had to do was keep someone watching the marina. Word of mouth travels fast in the hotel, too. By the next morning, everyone at the Tilly heard about the girl and my role in it."

"Do you think they are targeting you?" Carlson questioned.

I shook my head. "I doubt it, but they might decide to take an opportunity when it's presented."

"'Kay, Gordon, why don't you wait here?" he suggested. "I can send some coffee over if you want."

"That would be nice," I replied.

"I doubt I have any shoes that would fit you," he remarked, eyeing my bare feet. "Care to explain?"

"I never wear shoes on the boat," I explained. "Thought I was just walking up to the street."

"Was the girl seeing someone at the hotel?"

I nodded.

"Do you have a name?"

"For the guy?" I asked.

"Who else?"

"No can do, Detective. He was a guest. Missy wouldn't want me spreading that around."

"I can talk to her," the detective responded.

"That's on you," I informed him. "If she tells me to give him up, then I will. However, I don't think the guy had anything to do with it. He just made a mistake."

"I can probably find out."

"No doubt. Just, it's a waste of your time."

"Gordon, I'll worry about that."

With a shrug, I folded my arms. Carlson began to walk away.

"Carlson, don't forget about me!" I shouted at his back.

He threw me a wave over his shoulder without glancing back.

8

The banging stirred me from my sleep. I rolled over, throwing the blanket off me. The open hatch over my head allowed the breeze to carry through *Carina*. Until the oppressive South Florida heat made it too uncomfortable, I reveled in the fresh air. At some point, the wind, even off the water, would be hot, sticky, and still. Or at least stiller than was normally comfortable in this climate.

"Chase, there's some guy up at the bar," Missy announced.

I blinked a few times and sat up. My head popped up through the hatch to stare at Missy, who stood with her arms crossed on the dock.

"Since when did you start knocking?" I asked.

"Since you started fucking someone else," she shot back. "I didn't want to find you and the little nurse entangled in there."

"She's a paramedic," I corrected.

Missy scoffed.

"Besides, she'd probably welcome you," I remarked with a snide grin.

She rolled her eyes at me. "Come on," she urged.

"You realize what time it is?"

"This guy is just seated at the bar," she informed me.

"At the Manta Club? It's not open."

"No shit," Missy retorted. "Yet, there he is, sitting there."

"I locked it up," I rebutted defensively.

"I think housekeeping left the door unlocked. But he wants to talk to you."

"Give me five minutes."

After climbing out of the v-berth, I stopped in the head to relieve myself. Without looking at the clock, I knew it was only a little past eight. I'd returned to *Carina* last night around five. Or rather, I'd gotten back to the boat around five this morning. It took a minute to clean up and get to bed, but I'd thought I would get to sleep until around noon.

So much for plans.

I slipped into some joggers and a black t-shirt. This time, I donned a pair of flip-flops to trek up to the bar.

"Who is this guy?" I asked.

"I didn't talk to him," Missy told me. "Jacques from security found him in there. He said he was waiting for you to get to work."

I lifted an eyebrow.

"You look worn out," Missy remarked. "Did Perky Tits keep you up?"

"Damn, Miss. You don't wear jealousy well," I remarked. "Besides, I was out with your new friend, Carlson."

"What?" Missy blurted.

"Long story," I said.

"He texted me this morning and didn't mention it."

I shrugged.

"Was it about the girl?"

"Yeah, in a roundabout way," I answered. "You might tell the security team to keep an eye out for trouble."

"What kind?"

"Haitian gang that traffics in girls."

"Geez," Missy whistled as we climbed the last set of steps to the Manta Club's patio.

When we stepped into the bar, I saw Clay Moore seated at the corner. The man had been waiting for a bit, and judging from his eyes, he appeared to have slept less than I had.

"I got it, Missy," I whispered.

"Who is it?"

"Just a guest."

Her brow wrinkled, and I gestured for her to leave. She didn't argue. Instead, she gave Moore a smile and a nod as she walked past him.

"Do you have any idea what time it is, Clay?" I asked as I strolled over and took a seat next to him.

"I didn't sleep at all," Clay admitted.

"Me neither," I remarked in a dry tone. "Someone had me woken up this morning."

"I have to fly out this afternoon," Clay said. "I was expecting you to reach out to me last night."

"Why?" I asked.

"I thought you might have gotten my money back from that bitch," Clay said.

"Let's not call her names," I warned.

Clay furrowed his brow. "But she stole from me," he argued.

"I don't care. It's hateful, so don't do it."

With some reluctance, he nodded in agreement. "What about my money?"

"Sorry, you're out of luck."

"You promised that you'd help me," Clay protested, raising his voice.

"Calm down," I ordered.

"I should have just stayed and gotten it back from her," he groaned.

"How would you do that?" I pressed. "Take it by force? I just met you, but that doesn't seem up your alley."

"Well, I could have done something," Clay countered.

"If you'd have stuck around, you could have chatted about it with her pimps when they showed up."

Now Clay's eyes narrowed. "Her pimps?"

"Yeah, two Haitian guys who didn't care for me talking to her, and all I did was walk her to the street."

"I'll just call the cops," Clay decided. "Or the hotel can refund me."

I pressed my lips together and appraised the bluster Clay Moore was shelling out. It was all a show of force. He thought he had the clout to throw around to accomplish things. Last night, he was out of his realm, and now he wanted to regain control of the situation.

"Clay, I can't speak for the hotel, but I bet I'd get pretty close to how the owner would respond. She'd be more polite, but it would be the classiest "fuck off" you'll ever hear."

The man stared back at me with an incredulous glare.

"Oh, and the cops might have different comments about you soliciting an underage prostitute," I pointed out.

"She wasn't underage," Clay stammered.

"You're an idiot," I scoffed. "I'd guess sixteen, but probably younger."

"She didn't say."

"They don't care because you knew you ordered a hooker. I bet you suspected she was young, too. Although, you seem smart. You might have only alluded to what you were looking for."

Now Clay was aghast. He wanted to keep arguing and defend his actions.

"Consider it a life lesson," I suggested. "You made a costly mistake, and you skated. No jail time, no pimps trying to kill you. Next time, just take your wife with you on the business trip."

His face remained emotionless. After several seconds, he nodded. "I didn't know she was young. It seemed like a fun idea."

"And it almost cost you too much," I pointed out.

He nodded.

"How did you reach her?" I asked.

"There's a website," he explained. "You can go online and see all these ads. Like the classified ads that Craigslist used to have."

I nodded, signaling for Clay to continue.

"I just ordered what I wanted," he said.

"What's the website?"

"Claudette.com," he told me.

"Sounds French," I remarked.

"Maybe," he said. "I don't know. The girls aren't French."

"Did you pay online?"

"Yeah. That's why I was pissed that she took my cash."

"It wasn't like a tip or anything?"

"We hadn't done anything yet," Clay pointed out. "Am I supposed to tip her for showing up?"

I shrugged. "Can't say. I've never paid for a hooker before."

That sent a flush through his cheeks.

"Have you used that site before?"

Clay shook his head. "No. This was my first time."

"How did you find out about it?"

"Found it in a Telegram channel."

This time, I must have made a face. I had no idea what a Telegram channel was.

"It's an online chat room," he explained.

"Oh," I said with a nod. "Someone just gave you the website on there?"

"It's a... special chat room," he said, flushing a little.

"As in, it's for people with certain kinks?"

"Kinda."

"Weird," I remarked. "Did anyone else talk about girls down here?"

He shook his head. "The group is all across the world. Someone mentioned that the site was based down here."

"Look, sorry I couldn't help you with your money," I told him. It seemed like the thing to say to appease him and end this conversation.

"It's irritating," the man sighed.

"At least it wasn't a setup," I pointed out. "Some of those girls lead you to a place where their pimps wait to kill you."

He blanched at that. "Really?"

"I've seen it happen," I said, not adding that something similar happened to me last night after he left.

Clay stood up. "Thanks, I guess."

I smiled at him as he walked up the steps to the lobby. When he was gone, I went to the back room, where we kept the backup liquor and a small desk with an older Dell PC. It tracked the schedule and purchase orders for the Manta Club, and it had internet.

Claudette.com took me to a flowery website with a large button that read, "Enter." Beneath it was an addendum that stated, "You must be 18 years old to use."

When I clicked the bright red button, a new image

popped up. Rows of pictures lined the monitor. Girls adorned with a heavy application of foundation, blush, and eyeshadow stared back with empty eyes. All the women seemed attractive, and while their ages varied, none looked over twenty-nine or under eighteen.

But then I saw Diamond. Her picture also gave off an older vibe, and I could see how Clay assumed she was of legal age. In fact, nothing listed how old she was. Or any of the ages of the other women featured on the site.

I clicked through the pages of images, counting thirty-six faces. On the third page, I found a familiar face, although this one was full of life. Lyla. The young blond girl stared into the camera with a coy expression.

Nothing suggested she was no longer available, but I couldn't pull my eyes from hers. That come-get-me demeanor would never cross her face again.

Who was this girl? Lyla? No way that was her birth name. If she was only a teenager, then who was looking for her?

Florida, and especially South Florida, made an excellent destination for runaways. Miami offered opportunities, and the weather meant one didn't freeze to death on the streets. There were likely numbers from national runaway organizations showing where most teens escaped to. California would be high on that list, followed by the Sunshine State. However, I wasn't familiar enough with that data to actually quote it.

After snapping a screenshot of Lyla's face and meager biography, I sent the image to my email. My email wasn't something I used often, but Missy had insisted on giving me an email address. I repeated the same thing with Diamond's picture. If the people behind Claudette.com got worried, the website might vanish with the click of a button. I didn't want to lose all that information. In fact, I had no idea if one could recover that sort of thing.

I scrolled through a few more pages, staring at the faces. How many had passed through the bar or the Tilly's lobby? How had they gotten involved?

That question turned out to have easy answers. Most had nowhere to turn to, and some benevolent stranger helped them. Or a more sinister asshole like Goldtooth came across them. Once people like that hooked a vulnerable person, it became almost impossible to break free from them.

Goldtooth's leering face lingered in my mind. How did he connect to the Azure Room or the Royal Pelican? In all probability, it was the same way Lyla had ended up with a key to the Tilly. Yet, something about it nagged at me.

Since my sleep had been disrupted already, I decided to head over to the island and check out the Royal Pelican.

9

The Royal Pelican was perched on Ocean Boulevard, overlooking the Atlantic Ocean. Half a mile north of Mar-a-Lago, the Pelican had a better lot. Most of the building sat atop a mound that lifted the structure about fifteen feet above sea level. That wasn't enough to protect the club from the storm surge of a five, but any hurricane below a four was safe enough. Of course, that was the plan. Mother Nature sometimes had different ideas.

The famous owner of the Pelican was the same Clayton Connors I mentioned to Carlson. Connors had bought the failing resort from a conglomerate that wanted to offload the property after a heinous hurricane season that walloped the hotel five times in three months. Connors managed to protect the structure while renovating the 1920s hotel and bringing it into the new millennium. Under his ownership, the Royal Pelican added six pools and bought a golf course across the causeway.

While the resort was restricted to members and guests, it wasn't a challenge to get past that requirement. The security guards were diligent about keeping the riffraff out, but it only took two phone calls to track down a bartender. I could have done it with one call if I'd gotten Pat from Pat's Bar. The old geezer had been working in Palm Beach for decades. He had a connection to everyone.

I guessed that this morning, he was still in bed with some cocktail server he'd picked up after last call. Since Pat's was the place the rest of the service industry hit up after hours, he usually never closed shop until dawn.

When I couldn't get him, I left a message and called the other bartender from Pat's—Gail. She didn't have any connections at the Pelican, but she launched into a story.

"I dated a guy that worked in the Azure Room," she explained. "He told me some stories. Girls just wander the area naked, and orgies are a regular thing there."

"Orgies?" I questioned.

"Yep. Those were usually listed at BBQ buffets."

"BBQ?"

"I shit you not," Gail said. "My guy said he bartended at one, and it was fucking surreal."

"Sounds like a lot of work," I remarked.

"You don't want to get caught in a pile?" she asked with a twinkle in her eye.

"No, thanks," I responded. "I prefer to be really good with one person. More than that, and it gets daunting."

"Coward," she teased. "Sorry I can't help you more. You should talk to Pat."

"He didn't answer."

She laughed for a second before adding, "Try again. He's probably still in bed with some last-minute whore."

"Last-minute whore?" I echoed. "That doesn't sound very enlightened to me."

"Enlightened, my ass," Gail fussed. "There's not a better

term. If someone is still looking for a fuck by the time Pat gets off, she's either desperate or has the hots for Pat. Let me tell you, Pat's not winning any awards for charms, looks, or brains."

"Gail, you're harsh," I scolded.

"I'm honest," she corrected. "What's the deal with the Azure Room, anyhow, Chase?"

"The girl we fished out of the water had a blue card from the Pelican."

"Oh," Gail replied, sounding intrigued. "Doesn't mean she frequented the place. Could have been a one-night thing."

"Probably was," I admitted. "However, it's strange."

"She pretty?"

"By the time I saw her, I wouldn't call her that. But I'd bet she was attractive enough in life."

"I hope someone says as much about me," she joked.

"Gail, you're dangerously hot," I teased.

"Psh, I'm well over the age threshold of your girlfriends."

"Why would you say that?"

"I've seen them," she informed me. "You might be allergic to a woman over forty."

"First, Gail, that's offensive," I retorted.

"Yeah. You wanna grab a drink and find out if tequila makes my clothes fall off?"

"I'm sorta entangled in two quasi-relationships," I explained.

"Sounds like bullshit to me," Gail replied.

The best I could do was give her a shrug, though I knew she couldn't see it. "Someday," I promised.

"Someday, I'll wear that hard ass of yours out."

"It's not only the ass that's hard," I quipped.

She chuckled. "Seriously, though, do you think that girl was connected to the Azure Room?"

"No clue, Gail. Someone didn't want her talking."

"Or some fuckhead is just a sick bastard," she reminded me. "We have our fair share of those."

"True," I acknowledged. "Let me try Pat again."

"Good luck, Chase," Gail remarked. "Don't forget, I'm waiting with bated breath."

I smiled to myself.

"And Chase, if you find out about those orgies and need a companion, I'm all yours."

"Thanks, I'll keep that in mind," I told her before hanging up.

Pat's phone rang three times before a groggy voice answered. "What?" Pat growled into the speaker.

"It's Chase Gordon from over at the Manta." Even though we were friendly with each other, bartenders met hundreds of people. Keeping names straight could be a challenge, especially for someone waking up after a long shift and who knew how many after-work shots.

"Gordon, what's up?" he moaned, and I could almost visualize him sitting up. A murmur came through the phone, and I guessed it was from whoever was sharing his bed this morning.

"Shh," he urged the person making the noise.

"Pat, sorry if I woke you," I told him. "Gail suggested I call you."

"Of course the bitch did," Pat spat. "She's just mad she went home alone."

For a couple of people easily ten years my senior, Pat and Gail acted a bit like college kids. They carried some forever-young gene passed along to rock stars, actors, and bartenders.

"Did you hear about that girl we found at the Tilly?" I asked.

"The floater?" Pat questioned.

I didn't point out that she wasn't floating when I saw her. "Yes, that one," I answered.

"What about her?" Pat inquired. "Did you pull her out?"

"Yeah, I did," I replied. "She had a blue hotel key in her pocket along with one from the Tilly."

"One of those, huh?"

"It appears so."

"How old was she?"

"Young. Teenager."

"What's your question?" Pat wondered. "I don't deal with underage girls, you know that."

Whether I did know that or not was questionable. I doubted Pat ever worked with working girls that age, but he had a reputation for dating women who weren't quite old enough to drink.

"It's the blue card," I remarked.

"From the Royal Pelican?"

"That's my take."

"You still haven't asked a question, Gordon," Pat pointed out.

"Do you know anyone at the Azure Room?"

"Oh, do you want in?"

"Yeah, that would be nice," I replied. "Or at least someone who will talk to me there."

"I know a couple of guys over there," Pat explained. "I can get you in, as long as you promise to behave yourself."

"Have you been before?" I wondered.

"Sure. Not really my scene, though."

"Can I get some details, Pat?"

"Probably everything you think happens there does, but

it's not like that all the time. Imagine an upscale lounge. Lots of girls walking around the joint. I suspect most are working girls, either hired to make the place look prime or brought in to work the crowd."

"If the place is so exclusive, wouldn't people have to be invited?" I asked.

"Bingo bango," Pat confirmed. "No one gets in without an invite. Even calling in a favor is burning an invite."

Pat was reminding me that this was a big favor. He functioned like a lot of bartenders, including myself, as a provider of services. If a customer wanted some coke, he'd hit up the bartender. If he wanted a hooker, ask a bartender. Wanted an exclusive invite to the Azure Room, ask a bartender. Most of the time, the bartender only facilitated the connection. Pat didn't sell cocaine from behind his bar, but at least six people who came through the bar every night did. He had a figurative Rolodex of numbers for prostitutes and their agents (pimps were still a thing, but many independent women worked through calling agents and online scheduling).

Most customers who approached Pat about illicit activities paid for the connection. In my case, Pat was reminding me I would pay, too. Only it would likely be a favor tallied in an invisible ledger somewhere.

"Thanks, Pat," I said. "I'll owe you."

"Of course," he answered as if it was no big deal.

"You think someone there could have killed her?"

"Dude, you've seen those people. Cross the causeway to the island, and those folks are freaks of a different nature. All that money buys everything, and those bastards that can have anything find they want the things they can't have. It's a seriously fucked-up environment."

He wasn't wrong. People who never had to worry about

spending cash or what a thing cost lost sight of the value of the forbidden. Why should they deny themselves? After all, they had the means. Therefore, they deserved it.

It wasn't universal, of course. Nothing ever is. But entitlement was something that grew. The first instance, someone who stepped outside the lines often seemed like a one-time affair. But the second and third instances were suddenly easier. Before long, they did it because they thought they could. It worked with all vices when consequences seemed nonexistent.

"Why do you care so much, Chase?" Pat wondered after a beat.

"Pat, I don't like how someone threw that girl away. She was only a kid. No one even knows her real identity. Just her street name."

"What was it?"

"Huh?"

"Her street name," Pat clarified.

"Oh. Lyla."

"Want me to ask around about her?"

"Would you? I got the name from another girl named Diamond."

"Oh, shit," Pat replied. "She's like a little brunette. I think she's sixteen."

"You know her?"

"Kicked her out of the bar the other week," he said. "Too young to be in the place."

I noted he didn't seem to have qualms about her prostituting in his bar as long as she was old enough.

"Chase, you need to watch her, though," Pat warned.

"Why?"

"Pretty sure she's run by the *Les Loups Noirs.*"

"The Black Wolves?"

"Yeah. Bunch of crazy Haitians. I hear they are the go-to for certain predilections," he explained. "Probably makes them popular with some of our state politicians."

Pat only confirmed what I already knew. I'd seen them firsthand now.

"Pat, you ever deal with them?" I asked.

"No, man," he stated. "I don't want any part of those guys. Mostly, they aren't coming into a hipster bar, so I'm clear. I can't imagine they'd kill their own girl that way, though," he added.

"You don't think?"

"Don't get me wrong, Chase. They don't hold the girls in high regard, but they wouldn't leave a body someplace busy like the Tilly."

What he said made sense. It bothered me how she was dumped. There was probably a scientific method to determine where she went into the water, but I doubted I'd ever see that information. Intuition told me someone cut Lyla's throat and threw her from a boat during the night. It would have been late enough that no one would have noticed something like that. The current and boat traffic had a bigger hand in floating her into the basin at the Tilly Marina.

"Let me make a call, Gordon," Pat said. "Can I call you back?"

It was still well before the Manta Club opened, and I didn't want to wait for him to ring me back. "Pat, how about I call you back instead?"

"Right, I forget you're a Luddite and refuse to use a cell phone," he remarked. "Hit me up around two. I should be able to get you into the Azure Room tonight."

"Thanks," I told him before disconnecting. I stared at the

receiver for a few seconds. If I was going to the Azure Club tonight, I needed to trade my shift.

With the phone still in my palm, I dialed Hunter, the other bartender at the Manta Club. Much like the favors and deals I struck with Pat, Hunter and I had a similar relationship. He readily agreed to cover my shift, knowing that down the road, he'd come to me for the same thing.

10

Entering the Royal Pelican transported one back to the roaring '20s. The bellhops wore the traditional double-breasted uniform with eight ornate gold buttons on either side of the torso. I wondered how they worked in the South Florida heat in those thick wool suits. Even the pillbox hats adorning the three bellmen I saw looked uncomfortable. Missy strove to provide a similar atmosphere at the Tilly; however, the lengths that Clayton Connors or his management went to deliver the same immersive experience showed impressive detail.

It took me a minute to locate the security cameras. Despite that, I realized I'd missed a few. Careful design allowed them to blend into the Art Deco décor. In fact, there were no screens visible in the lobby. Of course, the front desk had computers to run their check-in system, but the monitors were below the top of the counter to remain out of sight of the guests.

The differences between the Tilly and the Royal Pelican seemed to be about color and light. Dark mahogany covered the lobby of the Tilly. The Pelican, though, used more pastel colors, reminding me that it sat right across from the beach.

When I called Pat back at two, he told me to ask for a bellhop named Daniel. It didn't take much to guess which one was Daniel. Two were older African-American gentlemen in their fifties. They both acted as if they'd been in the business for a number of years. The third was a young, dark-skinned Latino in his twenties. He struck me as the type that visited Pat's Bar after he got off work.

"Daniel?" I asked as I approached.

"You Chase?" he questioned.

"Yeah. Pat sent me."

He smiled. "He tell you what I need?"

Pat had, in fact, informed me of the cost. Much like anything else he facilitated, Pat only provided the connection.

A hundred-dollar bill secured access to the Azure Room. With a crisp Benjamin Franklin folded in my palm, I slipped the money to him. Daniel returned the gesture by sliding a blue key card into the place where the bill had been.

"He tell you what I was doing?" I asked.

Daniel shrugged, and I didn't know if that was a yes, no, or don't care.

"I've heard there are lots of girls available," I said under my breath.

"Pat told me you were a bartender over at the Tilly Inn?"

I nodded. "At the Manta Club. Come by sometime, and I'll buy you a drink."

"The ladies here aren't cheap," he whispered, as if warning me that I was in over my head.

It was my turn to shrug. "But I hear they are—how do I say this?—special."

Daniel nodded with a sly grin. If the Royal Pelican was

like most places, there was an unspoken rule about discretion. Hotels, even five-star ones, thrived on the prudence of their staff. When something as salacious as the Azure Room existed, those secrets spread through the employees like wildfire.

"You should enjoy yourself," Daniel assured me. "I need to get back to work."

I nodded. No point in getting the man in trouble.

Carina had limited storage space, and while most people had a collection of outfits for every function, I didn't. Most of what I wore were shorts, tank tops, and sandals. I had three shirts for my shifts at the Manta Club and two pairs of black pants. Now, I was wearing the only clothes I could consider fancy. Luckily, housekeeping had a small box of clothes that guests had left in the room. So, I'd found a rather stylish—at least from my point of view—Oscar de la Renta jacket. Since hell hadn't frozen over, I didn't bother with a tie.

While I was a permanent boat bum, I could put on airs when the need arose. I thought I could fit in with the upper echelon milling around the Royal Pelican. Most of the guests had come in from the pool or beach and changed into their evening attire. It wasn't quite the same as the Tilly, where most visitors weren't coming for the water.

The atrium in the lobby had windows around the domed ceiling to allow the abundant natural light to spill into the reception area. Before the sun set, the interior lights took over the illumination duties. Small groups gathered at small iron tables scattered about the area. The layout of the furniture seemed designed to be moved with some efficiency. Likely, the hotel offered the lobby as a rental space for receptions and parties.

The Azure Room was down in the northern wing. No

signs pointed me in the direction I needed to go. The only indication I was going the correct way was a small placard with a bright blue "AZ" on it. As I passed a second "AZ," I noticed the sign was bronze and hand-painted. It was another little touch that the Pelican did to transport its guests to another time.

The final marker was the blue door at the end of the hallway. It was the exact color of the key card. On the right of the door was a key card reader flashing a tiny red light. When I inserted the card, the red light flashed green, and a magnetic lock in the frame released with a *chunk-clunk*. For an instant, I found myself staring into the wardrobe like the Pevensie children. A bluish glow flowed out of the opening door. A trumpet called from within the bowels of this speakeasy.

I pushed through the opening. Inside this strange land, I discovered an ornate ballroom with no windows. Whatever natural light the lobby received, the Azure Room substituted for blue neon tubing curling along the friezes. In the center of the room was a dimly lit chandelier with at least a thousand crystal shards dangling into the basket. The support chain trailed from a large round medallion on the ceiling, and someone had added a blue LED light strip encircling the circumference of the decorative disk. The blue tint of the bulbs enhanced the ambiance, if one called the gentlemen's club atmosphere "ambiance." Beneath the blue crystalline glow, a circular bar with blue plush-covered stools surrounding the antique-looking drink rail also had a blue light strip under the countertop.

I stood still, taking in the scene around me. There were twelve people ambling through the room, four of them women moving around like lions stalking their prey. I walked to the bar, watching a redhead across the space lock her focus onto me. As I sat down, I clocked her in my periphery, making her approach.

A man in a white tuxedo shirt, vest, and black bow tie stirred a martini. He gave me a slow, appraising glance, following it with a nod of acknowledgment.

"Good evening, sir," he greeted me.

"Evening," I replied as Red slipped onto the seat next to me.

"Sammy, can I get another martini?" she asked the bartender in a singsong, whiny voice that made me think she was trying to emulate Betty Boop. Her attempt was more of a butchering than an imitation.

"Sure thing, honey," Sammy told Red. "How about you, sir?"

I gave him a nod. "I'll take an old fashioned. Is that Angel's Envy back there?"

"Indeed it is," he answered. "We have the Cask Strength and the 'Stairway to Heaven.'"

"I think the Stairway is overrated," I said.

Sammy shrugged. "Everyone has a right to be wrong," he quipped.

"Won't be my first time," I countered. "But I'll stick with the Cask Strength."

Sammy turned his back to me, reaching for the Angel's Envy on the second shelf from the top of the tiered liquor pyramid behind his bar.

"You don't like quality?" Red asked me.

I swiveled the plush stool supporting me to focus on the young girl. The blue glow of the Azure Room masked a lot of the details on her face, and I guessed it also assisted in adding a few years to the woman. As a responsible bartender, I'd have carded her in an instant. Nothing about her appeared to be legal, but that didn't mean it was true.

Plenty of people looked too young for a chunk of their twenties and even thirties.

"No, I value quality," I remarked. "But, in an old fashioned, it seems a waste to mix in a super high-end bourbon and then add fruit and sugar."

"Why not get it straight?" she inquired.

"Sometimes you feel like a nut, sometimes you don't."

Her grin broadened, and I realized my mistake.

"Do you feel like a nut?" she asked, blinking her eyes at me. I struggled to identify the color of her irises, with the blue aura around us hiding the real hue.

"I feel like a drink first," I countered.

"I'm Cleo," she greeted, extending a hand with manicured, press-on nails. While I was no expert, the fingernails seemed to be something she did on her own. At least she wasn't wearing those thick fake eyelashes that I'd seen on women working the bars. Few things turned me off as fast as fake eyelashes. Half the time, they were glued on crooked. I wondered how many women thought men cared about eyelashes, or perhaps it was just me who didn't like them. I might be the outlier in the entire male gender who found them more disturbing than anything else.

"I'm Chase," I introduced myself, taking her hand in my palm.

She had soft hands that were almost cold to the touch. Of course, she wore a green dress that hung from her shoulder, where a silver hasp seemed to be the only support the garment offered. The silky material spilled along her curves to her left ankle. A split in the skirt went from her right hip to the floor, revealing her leg from thigh to ankle. A simple anklet glittered in the blue glow.

"You like?" she asked, stretching her exposed leg out.

She was subtly yet intentionally offering me her best *Basic Instinct* move.

Behind the bar, I'd had my fair share of guests, both female and male, hit on me, though not usually in such a blatant fashion. Cleo hadn't mentioned anything, but she'd used one simple movement to entice me and judge my intentions.

"You don't like girls, huh?" she teased when I didn't get all googly-eyed with her.

"No, I love them," I retorted.

"Here you go," Sammy interrupted as he slid a glass across the bar. The amber liquor seemed darker than normal under the glow. "I'll get yours, Cleo."

"He forgot about me," she mock-whined to me.

"Oh, I doubt anyone forgot about you," I corrected.

"What brings you in here, Chase?" she inquired with a sly smile.

"I've heard this place is fun. It seems a little quiet, though."

"Tonight's a bit boring," she admitted. "Usually, Fridays are busy, but I like Thursdays. More guys traveling through are looking for some fun."

"I guess you are a regular, huh?"

"Somewhat," she replied. "Where are you from?"

"I live here," I told her.

"Oh?" The surprise in her voice was evident.

"Mostly out-of-towners, then?" I asked.

"Yeah, but we have some locals. Most are wealthy bastards. Not like you."

"Not like me?" I raised an eyebrow. "Should I be offended?"

"Not at all," she assured me. "Guys with money don't take care of themselves much."

"What makes you think I don't have money?"

She shrugged. "You worried about your high-end bourbon," she explained. "Most rich assholes want to flash their cash and don't care. They'll drink Cristol in a mimosa just so they can be seen flaunting it."

"Then why are you over here talking to me?" My head rotated around to a pair of men at a corner table. "They're wearing tailored suits."

"Yeah, but I was with the one on the right last night. He's not looking to repeat. Besides, Daria claimed them earlier in the back room."

"There's a back room?" I inquired, sipping the old fashioned. I was a little surprised they hadn't offered to smoke the cocktail. That seemed to be the rage these days, and as a bartender, I hated it. Smoked cocktails might be worse to make than the damned frozen daiquiris. And in my opinion, the fad was just that—a fad. A theatrical one, but still a pointless endeavor. Unless one enjoyed chewing on charcoal.

"Oh, yes," Cleo said. "I can take you back there."

Sammy reappeared for a brief second to pass a martini to Cleo before he seemed to fade into the background.

My gaze cut around the room. "Cleo, I thought this was just a fancy bar?"

Her smile never wavered. "Depends on you. Are you a cop or anything?"

"Just a bartender myself. Over at the Tilly Inn."

Her eyes blinked twice before she let them return to their fluttering. "What's a bartender doing here?"

"I've been meaning to check it out for some time," I told her while feigning a lascivious grin.

"You do want to see the back room, then?"

"What's it gonna cost me?"

"It's free to go back there," Cleo said, leaving out the part where we negotiated the price once we were out of the bar area.

I extended my hand. "Great, give me the tour."

With the same look a big-game hunter must have when he sees a lion in his sights, she took my hand and slid off the stool with her martini in her grip. Her other hand grasped mine and pulled me along. "Come along, baby."

11

—————

I wasn't sure what I expected from a back room in an already exclusive club, but what I encountered was beyond strange. Entry to this secluded section required going through a sliding door that I'd mistaken for a wall, complete with paintings to aid in masking the door's real purpose.

Cleo did nothing to trigger the door, so I assumed that Sammy or someone else controlled the entrance. She dragged me along by my hand toward the wall. Like magic, a three-foot section slid aside, revealing an even darker space than the bar we were already in.

As I followed Cleo through the opening, the wall sealed behind us. That seemed like quite a feature in and of itself. Whatever mechanics operated the portal uttered no noise. Another little detail that people didn't pay attention to. Even the automatic doors at the Tilly made a slight *swooshing* sound.

Inside the ultra-exclusive back room, I blinked as I took in my surroundings. Soft music surrounded me, and while I didn't recognize the artist or piece, it gave off strong Enya vibes. Beyond the music, the air itself carried lavender with other familiar yet unidentifiable scents—all designed to affect the mood.

This was a refuge from the world, set in its own universe. The blue-tinted light continued in here, but it was more subdued, casting more areas into shadowy darkness. It took a few seconds for my eyes to adjust even from the already darkened Azure Room. Anyone coming in from outside would struggle to see anything in this cavernous space.

The noises, however, were quite recognizable. Most were hushed and barely audible over the smooth female vocals piped in from the sound system. Heavy breathing and slight moans punctuated the soundtrack. As my pupils adjusted, a few shapes grew into silhouettes, which morphed into figures. Writhing figures. Couples engaged in their own carnal activities in the darker recesses of the back room.

"Over here," Cleo suggested, still pulling me along as if I was a lost puppy.

I would have liked to say that I was feigning the lost puppy image, but in truth, the spectacle surprised me. I was far from being a prude, and in my younger days in the Corps, I'd visited a few strip clubs. The difference here was stark. While most of the faces in the run-of-the-mill gentlemen's club carried at least a hint of despair, if not a vacant desolation, what I saw in this room pushed the boundaries. Perhaps it was the exclusivity of the space or the foregone conclusion of what was to happen there, but the parties involved seemed more at ease. I'd leave deducing the reasoning behind that to psychologists and sociologists, not some boat bum.

Cleo settled on a large plush sofa that resembled a Victorian fainting couch. It had what I thought was an additional curve that made no functional sense until I saw how the couple on a matching lounger were using it. For someone who marveled at the hydrodynamics of boat hulls, I had to confess that the engineer who developed that couch had applied a certain level of thought to it. Imagine being a designer who asked, "How best do people use this furniture?" and answered, "Carnally."

"Chase, you seem nervous," Cleo remarked.

It wasn't true, but she was trying to put me off. It was a subliminal technique used to unsettle even the most confident mark. A regular might feel unease at the suggestion that they seemed uneasy. Once established, Cleo could take charge, offering a level of comfort—for a price.

"Not at all," I countered. "Call it awe-inspired."

"What inspires you?" she asked, her fingertips reaching up and caressing my cheek.

"The entire thing," I admitted. "Quite a set-up."

"You like it? We can stay here as long as you like."

"Yeah, and what does that cost me?"

"Depends. For a thousand, it's anything you desire."

I almost stammered back, "A thousand?" but didn't. I'd expected a high number, but that threw me. It wasn't as much as I would have suspected.

"What about just to talk?" I asked.

"Why would you only want to talk?" Cleo implored as her fingers trailed down my neck and flicked my top button free with no effort. She'd manipulated the clothing far more deftly than I had ever accomplished with a bra strap. My only solace was reminding myself that she was looking at me. Almost every bra clasp I'd unhooked had been impossible to see from my position.

"I'm wondering about a girl," I told her.

"You have one right here," she stated.

"And a delightful one at that," I added. "But I met a girl when I was out, and she told me to meet her here."

Cleo furrowed her brow. "Who?"

"Lyla," I replied.

Cleo bristled at the mention of the dead girl's name. "I don't know her," she lied.

"Are you sure?" I asked. "That seemed to make you nervous."

She shook her head. "Look, if you aren't interested, I can walk you back out."

Cleo started to stand up, and I caught her by the wrist. "Wait, Cleo," I urged. "Stay."

The girl settled for a bit, but her face screamed out that she wanted to leave me now. My bet was that the only thing keeping her here was fear of causing a scene. The atmosphere of this sanctuary was paramount to its guests. No one would feel comfortable hearing a loud verbal exchange.

"I don't know her," Cleo repeated to me.

"You said that, but that's a lie, isn't it?"

"If you aren't interested, Chase, I need to go back out front."

"I'm the guy who fished her out of the water," I stated, locking eyes with hers.

She shook her head again.

"Cleo, someone threw her out to sea with her throat cut," I explained with a deadpan face. I wanted to see her reaction. My suspicion told me she was at least acquainted with the girl, and unless she was Lyla's murderer, the response she offered would be telling.

It was. She sucked in a gasp, blinking rapidly to prevent any waterworks from starting up.

"You knew her, didn't you?" I asked.

"Why are you here?" she demanded in a hushed tone.

"The police don't have her real name. Without that, she can't go back to whatever family she had."

"She didn't," Cleo muttered.

"Didn't have family?"

Cleo shook her head again, biting her lip.

"Where was she from?" I asked.

"Somewhere in Indiana. I don't know where."

"Did she work here regularly?"

A nod. "Some. Mostly she did out-call stuff."

"Like, she'd go to her client?"

Cleo nodded. "Most of the younger girls don't come in here. They don't want anyone getting caught."

"How old are you?" I asked, wondering what a younger girl looked like compared to this fresh-faced girl.

"I turned nineteen last month," she explained, and I tried not to let the shock show on my face.

"How old was Lyla?" I asked.

"Like fourteen, but she told everyone she was eighteen."

"Geez," I whistled under my breath. "Are you working for *Les Loups Noirs*?"

Her eyes widened more. "You said you weren't a cop."

"I'm not," I promised. "Just a bartender."

"You look more like a cop than a bartender. Where did you say you worked?"

"Across the way at the Tilly Inn. Ever been there?"

She nodded.

"I'm in the Manta Club there. Part-time."

Cleo leaned back and studied my build. While I wore long sleeves, the material didn't cover my muscles. While my biceps shrank in the last few years after I got out of the Corps, I still worked out. Most of the time, I did so in the fitness center at the Tilly, which limited my free weight training, but since I'd gotten out of the service, I discovered I wasn't as worried about that. I hated to admit that most of my PT came from a sense of competition with my fellow Marines. Often, Jay or Tristan were my main comparison.

"You look more like a cop," she repeated.

"Former military," I explained. "Some habits die hard."

"You promise?"

I nodded. "Cross my heart."

"I can't talk about it," she replied. Her face twisted, displaying her discomfort. "If you can't pay, I need to go."

"Cleo, do you think the Haitians killed her?"

For a split second, her chin quivered, and she almost shook her head. Instead, she blurted, "You have to leave."

Before I could beg her to stay for another minute, the girl bounced to her feet and dashed from the couch. She stopped in front of the wall and waited for a second before it slid ajar. Again, she did nothing to trigger the opening.

The doors remained open, and I wondered how long before I attracted attention as the solo male in the back room.

It took two minutes before two men wearing black suits entered in unison. Security, but not typical hotel security. These guys looked to be hired for their muscle. The hulking guards would be a deterrent to anyone looking to start trouble. They took a direct path toward me, and I pushed to my feet before they arrived.

"Sir, we need you to follow us," the man on the right stated. In the dark room, the pair could have been identical twins, as far as I could tell.

"I'm leaving," I assured them.

"Come with us, sir," the second one said. The tone came across as much more ominous than the first fellow.

"I'm leaving," I repeated, but both men flanked me on

either side. Two meaty hands grabbed my arm as they directed me toward the exit.

"Let's go," the first one ordered.

My mind calculated what was about to happen. I could offer plenty of resistance, but to what end? If these men happened to be two of the resort's bulkier security details, then there should be no need to fight it out with them. It was also possible they planned to just guide me from the property. I'd had Jacques at the Tilly perform similar tasks with unruly guests.

In fact, resisting might only make things worse.

However, I didn't like how they gripped my arms. It seemed more than just to escort me out of the building. Their grip squeezed tight. Perhaps they'd evaluated me and opted to show they had enough force to make me do what they wanted.

Shrugging, I let them lead me out. As we walked, I considered my options. These two stayed right next to me, which provided a pro and a con. If there had been only one, he would be in the striking zone. With a man on either side, I'd have to drop one before the other had time to react. That would be impossible.

On the pro side, though, the fact that they placed themselves in that position told me they were either overconfident—something I could use to my advantage in the near future—or harmless, only wanting to get me off the premises.

The sliding door whisked open without a sound, and the three of us marched through the opening. Sammy watched as the duo escorted me out, and I wondered if this burned any favors for Pat. I'd need to pay him back.

Cleo had found a new attachment at a table in the corner, but she trailed me with her eyes. Had she reported me to Sammy? Given how the bartender had followed me with his own eyes, I suspected he knew that I constituted a problem for the people in charge.

When Tweedledee and Tweedledum walked me through the exit of the Azure Room, I said, "Thanks, guys. I can get there from here."

Neither made so much as a grunt. They proceeded to march me toward a door marked as a stairwell.

"This isn't the way out," I pointed out.

"You're wanted downstairs," the one on my right told me.

We were on the first floor. It seemed odd that they'd put a basement in the resort after building up the land to avoid flooding. All the hairs on the back of my neck pricked up as the doors opened. Questions flooded my mind. Would I let them take me? What awaited me? Was there someone wanting to see me downstairs, or was something else waiting for me?

The elevator dinged as the doors opened to an empty car. Both men released my arm as Tweedledee on my right —or was that Tweedledum?—ushered me inside the lift. I complied, surprised, as the two brutes stepped back, allowing the door to close on its own.

Alone in the elevator, I glanced at the panel. No button for the basement existed, and no numbers lit up to indicate my destination.

Without so much as a groan, the elevator descended. On reflex, I stared at the ceiling, wondering where I was going.

12

______

When the doors slid open, I stared at a hallway decorated with thick carpet, two high-back antique chairs that no person ever sat in because they were impractical, and a dark, cherry-colored wood table with a gigantic vase filled with fresh flowers. Along the wood-paneled wall, someone hung a pair of massive oil canvases that reminded me of A.E. Backus, who was famous for his many paintings of Florida landscapes. As I looked at the paintings, I realized they might have been painted simultaneously, and if placed side by side, they might depict one expansive scene.

With some trepidation, I stepped into the hallway. As I entered, I noticed a second set of sliding doors designed to seal off the floor. The only visible parts of the thick metal doors were the edges. The doors probably slid into place in the event of a flood to prevent water from filling this area.

Beyond the cherry table were two wooden doors that matched the furniture and paneling on the wall. I stepped toward them, noticing the camera above the doors that seemed to focus on the only entrance: the elevator. Presumably, whoever had summoned me was watching me now.

I gave a slow turn, raising my arms as one did to show I was unarmed. It might not matter, but I wasn't sure yet what I was facing.

The double doors clicked and swung open automatically. From where I stood, I peered into the next room.

"Please, come in," a voice called from inside.

I approached the entry. At this point, if someone wished me harm, they had me in the right place to deal it out. I'd walked into the spider's web. Or, at least, I'd descended into it.

Through the doors was an office, complete with a side room that looked to be a living space. More paintings from the same artist adorned the office walls, and more fresh flowers filled vases around the room. Two sides of the room were completely covered with bookshelves.

Behind a huge wooden desk, also designed to match the doors and table outside, sat an older man with gray hair that was turning white in flecks.

"Welcome," the man offered, rising to his feet. "I'm Clayton Connors."

"The Clayton Connors?" I asked.

He chuckled. "You know, when I bought my first building, I never considered I'd end up being referred to as 'the Clayton Connors.'"

I shrugged. "You need more aspirations," I suggested as I slipped onto a sofa across from the massive desk. "I always assumed I'd be 'the Chase Gordon.'"

"Isn't that somewhat egotistical of you?" he questioned. "Your record is commendable, don't get me wrong. But you're not going anywhere fast, are you?"

I smiled. "I'm a sailor," I explained.

Connors furrowed his brow.

"Sailboats go nowhere fast," I detailed.

"Oh, cute," he remarked, probably not finding my response as cute as it was.

"See, I'm used to people telling me I'm cute."

"You seem to fill in the gaps in your own record," he observed. "No one mentioned 'smartass' in your service file."

"Weird. I was certain I had a commander who praised my wit regularly."

"I guess not enough to document it," he quipped.

"Clayton," I said. "Can I call you Clayton? Or Clay?"

He didn't answer. Instead, he held a bemused expression.

"I'm assuming you wanted to impress me with how quickly you accessed my file. It's not that difficult. Someone with the clout you possess should get it pretty fast."

Connors smiled at that simple word of praise.

"What impresses me, Clay, is how fast you skimmed it," I noted.

"I'm a quick study," Connors explained.

"Very quick," I conceded. "Especially if you got it in the last fifteen minutes."

Connors scowled.

I went on. "See, I've only been in your resort for about forty-five minutes. If I assumed you flagged me on the way in the door, which I consider unlikely but not impossible, then you would have flagged me upon entering the Azure Room. More likely, if you were tracking every guest coming and going. However, the converse is that I didn't have my own key card, so tracking my name would require more."

The bemused look had long vanished.

"Clay, that means you might have gotten my name from facial recognition software. That's plausible, given current technology. Casinos employ it regularly. And it is impressive if you've got a connection to the Pentagon's databases. However, it's more likely you pulled my name from a mug shot because, unfortunately, my spent youth hasn't kept me out of trouble."

"You admit to being a criminal?" Connors asked. His face betrayed him. This real estate mogul expected to leave me swooning by waving my personnel file at me.

"I admit to having been arrested and booked. Never charged and convicted. Something we might have in common."

"I've never been arrested," the billionaire declared.

"Give it time," I countered, adding. "You are the one who wanted to bring me in and wave your dick around like a majorette."

Connors's face reddened.

"Here's what I think," I continued. "You are just as interested in the body of a girl who frequented your secret club as I am. News broke, and your resources told you who discovered the body. Like any decent businessman, you did your due diligence and looked into me. After all, how much goodwill does a former lieutenant's service record require? That's as easy as getting a Big Gulp down the street. But, lo and behold, I show up on your doorstep. Only, you don't have secret facial recognition software connected to anything. Ol' Sammy at the bar didn't rat me out because he didn't know my name. Perhaps you snagged Daniel, who spoke to me in the lobby, yes?"

The man gritted his teeth and stared at me.

"When the girl came out and reported I was from the Tilly Inn, that triggered an alert. Your security detail was fast, but it still took a minute. Even the Joint Chiefs couldn't access and read my record in the time it took me to come down the elevator. That meant you already had it." I gave him a hard look. "So, let's ditch the pretense that you are some all-powerful deity with his hand in everything. You are a smug, shrewd businessman who overplayed his hand and underestimated his opponent."

Connors cocked his head. "Are we opponents, Mr. Gordon?"

"Depends," I admitted. "Did you kill Lyla?"

He smiled at me. It was supposed to be a genuine smile, and to some extent, it almost passed. But what it reminded me of was a warlord I confronted in Afghanistan. The man had been raping and butchering girls from the surrounding villages, particularly those he deemed guilty of offering aid to the United States. Our hunt for him drove him to the ground, and it took a small team, including Jay and Tristan, to breach his forces. I was the one who found him, hiding in an underground bunker that was similar, if far less elegant, than Connors's. The warlord held his last hostage, a nine-year-old girl who might have been his own daughter. The smug satisfaction across the man's countenance was enough for me to shoot him between the eyes.

Right now, I felt the same sensation. The lascivious grin on Connors's face begged me to wipe it off him. However, this wasn't the Afghan desert, and Connors wasn't a hunted warlord. He was an American billionaire with ties to most all factions of the US government. I couldn't kill him just because I suspected he killed Lyla. Although, with each passing second, my gut believed he was the culprit.

"Of course not," he finally answered. "What happened to that girl was tragic. Personally, I didn't know her. My understanding was that she gained access to the Azure Room once. As you yourself can see, such feats aren't impossible. We try to screen our guests, but sometimes dregs slip past."

"You aren't denying that she was here?"

"For what purpose?" he asked. "She was. We escorted her off the property. What else could we do?"

"Call the police?" I suggested.

"For a girl who wasn't causing issues?" Connors scoffed. "That would create mayhem with our guests. We tried to manage the situation discreetly."

"Dumping her in Lake Worth wasn't quite discreet enough," I advised.

"I had nothing to do with that," he argued.

"Probably not," I admitted. "Those two apes you had escort me out could handle that just fine."

"Mr. Gordon, you do have a mouth on you."

"If I were more of an asshole, I might point out how you could speak to your mother about my mouth, but I'm trying to remain a gentleman."

"Indeed," Connors replied, nonplussed. "I was hoping to discuss a business opportunity with you."

"Oh, you want me to run your prostitution ring?"

"Stop trying to be cute," he scolded, his tone sharpening.

"Sorry, it's bred into me," I retorted.

"I thought you might appreciate a job," he said after his ire melted a bit. "I'm looking for capable bartenders or even a good manager to work in the Azure Room. The pay is better than anything you'll find in the city for that position."

I nodded. "See, you should have led with that," I pointed out. "However, I'm not interested. The Tilly Inn pays me enough, and I don't need something like that to tie me down."

"Right. Because at your heart, you consider yourself a wanderer?" he scoffed. "How long before that grows old?"

"What? Waking up in paradise, with no one demanding I do anything? Swimming with dolphins? Fishing?" I countered. "Perhaps you forgot what it was like to not be tied to something like this." I waved my hand around his office.

"Why, when I have everything?"

I shrugged. "Then you can keep it. I'll stick with my slice of freedom."

"No one is truly free," Connors argued. "You'll regret this."

I folded my arms across my chest and stared at the man. "I already do," I assured him. "How on earth can I go on? After all, here I am, turning down employment from a guy I'm nearly positive killed a fourteen-year-old girl."

Connors opened his mouth to argue with me again, but I interrupted, "I'm sorry. *You* had a girl killed. Of course, you don't have the balls to cut a girl's throat, do you? Rape one, sure. Kill one? Well, that takes a different set of *cojones*."

"I think we're done," Connors declared.

"Wait, so you are rescinding the job offer?"

Connors ignored me and pressed a button on his phone as he put it next to his ear. "Mr. Gordon is leaving now."

I was already on my feet and walking out of the office.

"You can't get out," Connors called.

"I can get out of your office," I called back. "See, I already feel better not being in there with the world's richest douchebag."

Connors jumped to his feet. "How dare you!"

I stared at the man. He was shorter than I expected. The mogul glared at me.

"Don't worry," I told him as the elevator opened behind me. "There's no need to threaten me with how I'll rue the day or anything. Just remember this conversation."

Tweedledee and Tweedledum grabbed my shoulders and tugged me toward the door. Without causing any more issues, I allowed them to walk me into the elevator. As the doors shut, I smiled at Clayton Connors through the crack of the closing door.

The elevator glided up a level, depositing the three of us back on the first floor. I had yet to see how the two goons operated the lift. Much like the door in the Azure Room, someone might be controlling it from another location.

"I suppose you'll be walking me all the way out the front door?" I asked them.

Dee grunted.

"Could one of you call me a taxi?" I asked. "Otherwise, I'll be waiting forever for one to show."

Neither man answered as they herded me down a corridor to the lobby. We marched past the Art Deco furnishings and into the Palm Beach night air.

"Taxi?" I asked.

"You can start walking," Dum growled. "If you are still on our property in the next three minutes, we will have the police pick you up."

"No doubt," I remarked as I stepped away from the two men. I wondered which of these two might have killed Lyla. Or were they just hired security?

The portico where the Royal Pelican's valet stand was had terracotta paving stones covering the drive. My feet started across them toward the entrance from Ocean Drive. A black Cadillac Escalade pulled up beside me. The rear door opened to reveal the scowling visage of a black man with dark eyes.

"Get in," he insisted.

"No thanks," I replied.

He raised an American Eagle Colt 45 pistol toward me. The glint of light off the silver muzzle shone from the darkened interior of the Cadillac.

"Oh, you're offering me a lift," I remarked.

"Get in," he repeated.

13

The interior of the black Cadillac Escalade carried a stench of fried food, marijuana, and stale beer. All three aromas seemed to come off the three men in the vehicle. I slid into the back seat next to Scowler.

"Thanks for the ride, guys," I said as I got in.

The man in the front passenger's seat came out of the vehicle and closed the door for me. He was a thin guy in his forties with graying dreadlocks and a black sports coat over a matching black shirt. Someone might have pointed out that Johnny Cash had already taken that look, but he didn't strike me as the type to take criticism too well.

"*Kondwi,*" Scowler barked.

The driver, a younger black man in his thirties, shifted the Escalade into gear and accelerated away from the Royal Pelican.

"I'm just across the lake," I told the driver.

"Shut up!" Scowler demanded in a Caribbean accent.

"Okay, shutting up," I responded.

"What are you doing at the Royal Pelican?" he asked.

I stared at the man who was still holding the Colt. "Am I supposed to answer now?"

Scowler pulled back and punched me with his free left hand. Not being his dominant fist, the blow struck at an awkward angle and without the strength he could have put behind his right. That didn't negate the impact that drove my head into the window. Thankfully, the glass didn't break, but that didn't stop the punch from hurting.

"You ever watch the movie *Johnny Dangerously*?" I asked.

Scowler deepened the glower on his face. "What is this?"

"I'm going to let you do that once," I told him, raising my right index finger. "Once."

"What were you doing at the Pelican?" he demanded again.

"Why don't you start with what you are doing there?"

"Because I have dis," he replied, waggling the Colt.

I shrugged. "Fair enough," I conceded. "I was wondering why a young hooker whose throat was sliced from ear to ear had a key card for an exclusive club."

Scowler glared at me. "Why do you care?"

I leaned away from him, pressing my back against the door so that I could look at him. My knees pressed together, pointed at the driver.

"What's her name?" I asked, ignoring his inquiry.

The Haitian bunched his eyebrows into a cartoonish triangle, looking shocked at my audacity.

"She worked for you, didn't she?" I prodded. "Aren't you all part of the *Les Loups Noirs* group?"

His head shook. "You would do better to learn how to show respect."

"Respect?" I barked. "Here's how I see this going: you're planning to drive me somewhere secluded and ask me more questions. Now, I'm an asshole, and I won't give you the answers you want. That's not because I don't have them, but I don't care for how you ask them. Of course, that means that you have to kill me or look weak."

"I can do what I want," Scowler snapped.

Perhaps this wasn't just a lackey of the group. Maybe this was Mr. *Les Loups Noirs* himself.

"Sure you can," I replied. "You're the boss, aren't you?"

He didn't nod, but his chin dipped ever so slightly.

"Fine," I agreed. "Let's chat. But I'd like to go home tonight."

Scowler cocked his head. "We'll see what you offer."

I smiled. "There, I knew we could be friends," I assured him. "Here's the information I have." I lifted my hand to make a zero with my index and thumb. "*Nada*," I told him.

"Why are you looking into the Royal Pelican if you know nothing?" Scowler demanded.

"I know a girl was killed who had a key card to the Pelican. That's all I have. I suspect other things, though."

Scowler motioned with his barrel for me to continue.

"Her name is Lyla. At least that's what she called herself on the street, right?" I waited for a response but got none. "She's a prostitute run by a Haitian gang called *Les Loups Noirs*. That would be you guys. And she worked at the Azure Room from time to time. Now, here's where things get more speculative. I don't think you or your gang of pimps killed the girl. Not that you wouldn't, right? I'm sure there are bodies all over the place planted by your wolves."

I paused. Scowler said, "Go on."

"Whatever happened to her started in the Azure Room," I continued. "That's a hornet's nest by itself. However, you do business with Clayton Connors, don't you? And that makes how you handle it tricky. You can't shoot yourself in the foot and cut off the supply of rich perverts, can you? But at the same time, even a ruthless group of killers can't go head to head with a billionaire like Connors. He's the kind of guy that has enough leverage to keep you in your place."

"Nobody can control us," Scowler challenged.

"Oh, please," I moaned. "Don't feed me that alpha bullshit. Lots of people can control you. I imagine very few of you have actual citizenship in the US, so immigration can deport your ass if they find you. The cops can arrest you, but a billionaire who controls aspects of everything can certainly choke a wolf."

Scowler pursed his lips. "And you just met with Connors?" he wondered.

"I did, but you were already aware of that because he called you, didn't he?" I asked.

That made sense. There was no reason the Haitians would know to pick me up there if they hadn't been alerted. Unless they were staking out the resort, and the rich folks on the island called the cops at the first sign of thugs lurking about. The only logical conclusion was that they were on Connors's speed dial.

"Your silence suggests that I'm right," I said. "Now, what I don't know is how cooperative your relationship with Connors is. Does he control you? Or is he just a partner, offering a place to hawk your hookers?"

"Enough!" Scowler yelled.

I raised my hands in mock surrender. "Fine. Tell me what it is you want."

"Do you think Connors killed her?" Scowler demanded.

"Himself, no," I answered. "But I bet he had someone do it. Especially if it wasn't you."

"We didn't kill Lyla," Scowler stated.

"But she worked for you?"

He didn't answer. Instead, he asked, "Are you a cop?"

"No," I assured him. "However, I'm working with the cops." That was only a partial lie. I'd had a conversation with Detective Carlson, so I counted that. "The detective knows where I am. It won't be hard to find a witness who saw you kidnap me."

Scowler shook his head. "No, we are just offering you a ride."

"Great, then how about dropping me at the gas station across the lake?"

Scowler chuckled. "Don't worry, *Mesye* Gordon. We will drop you off."

The threat hung in the air as the driver took the Royal Park Bridge across the lake. At this time of night, the traffic was almost nonexistent.

I allowed my gaze to drift over the driver's shoulder for a second before I braced my arms against the passenger's seat in front of me. Scowler caught my reaction and turned to follow my stare.

My right hand grabbed the handle on the door, unlatching it as I pressed my weight against it. The rear door flew open, and I rolled out of the Escalade at forty miles an hour.

No matter how it was portrayed on film, there was no easy way to fall from a moving car. The best that one could hope for was a tight fetal position to protect the body from the impact and a grassy bank to cushion the landing. The Royal Street Bridge offered nothing that nice, and there wasn't enough time to curl up in a ball. Instead, I raised my arms up, bending my elbows to shield my head. A crushed skull or a snapped neck were the two most likely causes of death in a move like that.

As I fell, I twisted forward so that most of the impact would be on my right shoulder. A broken shoulder far outweighed a broken back or a shattered rib cage that might cause more internal damage.

None of that helped me feel any better, and I felt the joint in my shoulder dislocate when I struck the concrete. Once I hit the ground, I went into a roll, bouncing across the lane. Headlights raced up behind me as tires from the oncoming car screeched to a stop.

My head glanced back as the Escalade also squealed on its brakes. The black vehicle slid sideways, blocking two lanes of traffic. The passenger door flew open, and Dreadlocks barreled out of the Cadillac with a submachine gun in his hands. Scowler came around the rear of the SUV, raising his Colt and firing wildly at both me and the car.

I scrambled to my feet as Dreadlock released a burst of gunfire. The rounds peppered the street behind me as I sprinted toward the barricade. My right arm flopped at my side as I took a leap, catching the ball of my left foot on the guardrail blocking the pedestrian lane. With another striding jump, I skipped across the far railing before I launched off the causeway.

In a split instant, as bullets nipped at my heels, I prayed that the water below was deep enough. The fact was, I prayed that there was water below. With only the half-second it took me to drop the twenty-ish feet, I didn't have time to gauge my bearings. All I did was pivot so that both my feet hit the water first. Time seemed to slow to a crawl until my heels plunged into the water. Suddenly, I was submerged in darkness.

My eyes opened as I turned upward. Only a glow above suggested that was the surface, and I reoriented myself to swim toward the bridge.

Under normal circumstances, I could freedive for over three minutes. With some practice and added incentive, staying down for almost five minutes was conceivable, though by then, I would have a burning chest and a throbbing headache. That kind of endurance also required a couple of deep breaths to ensure the oxygen flooded my bloodstream—something I hadn't done before my desperate escape.

At just under two minutes, my lungs seemed to be on fire. My shoulder screamed in pain, sending tendrils of agony coursing through my nervous system. I propelled myself toward the surface, shedding my shoes as I did.

My head broke through the water to find myself under the Royal Street Bridge. As my feet kicked, I used my left arm to help tread water. With a dislocated shoulder, my right arm wasn't much good, and anything I did with it crippled me with pain. So, I left it to dangle beside me.

The chances of one of them following me down were zero. In fact, they wouldn't stick around too long. By now, someone had called the cops to report automatic gunfire on the bridge. All I could hear was water splashing against the pylons holding up the bridge. Rolling to my back, I kicked over to the nearest pylon, where I found a shallow, rocky shoal surrounding the concrete column.

I gritted my teeth as I threw my shoulder against the bridge support. It took six tries to get the glenohumeral joint reconnected. By the time I succeeded, I'd almost passed out from the pain. I turned, placed my back against the pylon, and slid down into a seated position, where I remained for half an hour before attempting to swim for shore.

14

———

The sky turned from a purple to a faint gray as dawn approached. I stared across the lake as I stumbled down the steps toward the marina. My bare feet ached from climbing over the rocks at the base of the Royal Park Bridge. Thankfully, I was only a few miles from the Tilly, but I couldn't get a cab to stop for me. Perhaps it was the barefoot, soaking-wet, vagrant look I'd adopted.

Exhaustion hung off my bones. I'd only had a couple of hours of sleep the night before, and my foray over to the Royal Pelican should have gotten me home long before five in the morning.

"What the hell happened to you, Chase?" Will Stovall asked as I stumbled past his slip. Will ran a charter company that took tourists out to hunt tarpon or, if they were lucky, a tuna or dolphinfish.

"Long night, Will," I replied. "Got stranded and had to hike back."

"What did you do?" he questioned. "Walk through a car wash?"

I chuckled. "No. I doubt I'd reek like fish if I'd done that."

Will feigned sniffing the air. "No shit, man. You might want a shower in case someone mistakes you for bait."

"Shower is on my agenda," I assured him. "Just not before I get a few hours of sleep. You heading out?"

"Yeah, got a couple of guys down from Atlanta who want to head out. They should be here any minute."

I waved goodbye. "I won't keep you."

"See ya, man," the burly fisherman said as I shuffled down the dock.

These had been my nicer clothes, but the roll on the bridge and dip into the water had ruined them. My shoes didn't float—or at least, I never saw them after I surfaced. I supposed that having to walk home barefoot was far better than being shot in a swamp somewhere.

As I climbed over the gunwale, I was already shedding my shirt. All jokes aside, I didn't think my clothes smelled great, either. My pants came off after my shirt, and I threw them into a pile on the floor of the cockpit. No point wearing them inside the cabin, as it took little to make the interior of *Carina* stuffy with the hint of mildew. Better to leave those garments outside to take to the trash later.

Below deck, I found a washcloth that I used to scrub my skin. My best friend, Jay Delp, would call that a "whore bath." And when I finished, I didn't feel a lot better.

I crawled up in the v-berth and pulled the covers up over my head. Before I drifted to sleep, I reached up and felt my M45, a near duplicate of the service weapon I carried in the Corps. The gun rested on the shelf that ran along the side of the bed. Comforted that it was within reach, I fell asleep.

The banging on my hull started ninety minutes later.

"What the actual fuck?" I moaned, reaching over for the M45 as I pulled myself out of the berth.

Bang-bang-bang!

I stumbled naked toward the companionway without grabbing the pair of shorts hanging on the hook next to the head. The double doors over my hatch swung open, and I rose on the steps, aiming the barrel of the forty-five-caliber ACP through the opening.

"Gordon, what the hell?" Carlson demanded. "Put that down."

"Do you have any idea what time it is?" I asked, lowering the weapon.

"You're naked!" he barked.

"I was sleeping. It's only 6:30 in the morning."

"How about you get dressed?"

"What do you want, Detective?" I inquired without moving.

"Besides not seeing your dick?" he countered. "I could arrest you for indecent exposure."

"I could shoot you for trespassing and climb into bed until the rest of the cops showed up."

"Get some pants on, Gordon. We need to talk."

"Fuck!" I groaned. "Come aboard."

Without waiting for him, I turned and went below.

"You better have something on," he called.

I dropped the M45 on the counter and found my shorts. As I stepped into them, Carlson came down the companionway stairs.

"This is cute," he remarked.

"Great, you made it for the boat tour," I growled. "If you come back at a more reasonable time, I'll take you for a sail. Right now, I'm running on almost no sleep."

"Were you on the Royal Park Bridge a few hours ago?"

"I was for a minute," I answered. "Then I was under it."

"There was a shooting on the bridge a few minutes after midnight."

I nodded. "It wasn't me shooting," I informed him.

"Reports said someone fell out of a truck before the people in the same vehicle opened fire on him."

"Yeah, that was me," I acknowledged.

"You didn't think to call the police and report something like that?" Carlson asked, folding his arms and leaning against my nav station.

"I need some coffee," I said. "You want some?"

He nodded, and I put a tea kettle on the eye before adding some water. "It'll take a minute," I said as I took my French press out of the cabinet and added three heaping spoonfuls of espresso.

"Wanna give me an answer?" Carlson asked.

"I had every intention of calling you," I told him. "After I woke up."

"What the hell happened? There are three people in the hospital."

"Haitians?" I wondered.

"No. They were fucking college kids. They were in the car behind the truck. They got shot."

"Damn," I whistled. "Are they serious?"

"One guy is. The other two will be fine," he answered. "Now, want to tell me who was shooting at you? Were they Haitians?"

I nodded and picked up a tangerine from a bowl in my galley. The only food I'd eaten had been last night before my run-in with Scowler and the boys.

"What happened?"

"This is going to go down better with coffee," I said as I peeled the fruit. When I flayed the citrus peel in a long piece, I dropped it on the counter and broke the segments into two pieces. "Want one?"

"No, I'm fine," Carlson replied as the kettle started to whistle.

I poured the hot water over the grounds in the press and added the lid. Ideally, the water should sit on the coffee for at least ten minutes to get strong enough. However, with only two and a half hours of sleep in the last forty-eight hours, I wasn't sure I had the wherewithal to wait a full ten minutes.

"I don't have any cream," I informed Carlson. "But I have some sugar."

"Do I look like a pussy to you?" he questioned, and I cast a glance his way. "You know what, Gordon?" he said. "Don't."

I pressed the plunger down on the press and poured each of us a cup. It wasn't as strong as I preferred it, but it would pass.

"Alright, you have your coffee," Carlson pointed out. "Now spill it."

"Clayton Connors had the girl killed," I told the detective as I swallowed the hot coffee.

"Clayton Connors?" he repeated.

"Yeah, I visited the Azure Room last night. That was a surreal treat."

"Did Connors try to kill you?"

I shook my head. "No, that was probably *Les Loups Noirs*."

"Some guys that tried to kidnap you the night before?"

"I'm hoping you still have the survivor in jail," I stated.

"Last I heard," he replied.

"These were obviously different guys, but, yeah, they're all associated," I said. "I think."

"You think?"

"They didn't admit to anything, really. Mostly, it was me speculating with Scowler."

"Scowler?"

"That was my little nickname for the guy who kidnapped me. Three of them picked me up on the street by the Royal Pelican."

"What does that have to do with Clayton Connors?"

"They showed up after I accused Connors of killing Lyla. Seemed like a coincidence, and I'm not a fan of those."

"You can't count on them," Carlson agreed.

"Exactly."

"What proof do you have that Connors killed the girl?"

"Not a bit," I admitted.

"What am I going to do with that?" he pressed.

I shrugged, took a sip of coffee, and ate the rest of my tangerine.

"Gordon, let's circle back to the shootout. What happened?"

"Like I said, Detective, they grabbed me at gunpoint. When I realized they intended to kill me, I bailed on the bridge."

"One witness saw you jump off the bridge," Carlson noted.

"Yeah, it was either that or get mowed down by a submachine gun."

"What if you hit a shoal? Or it was shallow? There are plenty of rocks under that bridge."

"My options were limited," I pointed out. "Somehow, hitting something under the bridge seemed better than taking a bullet."

"Damn," he said. "Missy said you were crazy."

"She has a type," I joked.

Carlson lifted an eyebrow. "Are you serious about Connors?"

"Dead serious," I assured him. "He dragged me down to his subterranean lair, where he tried to woo me with fear. He flashed my service record around in an attempt to intimidate me."

"Did it work?"

I smiled. "Do I look intimidated?"

"Are you ever fazed?"

"Oh, yeah," I answered without giving him details. "He said Lyla showed up, but they threw her out for being underage."

"Threw her out? They didn't call the cops?"

"That's what I asked, too," I said. "He stated it would upset the guests, and after all, she didn't do anything."

Carlson was quiet for a moment. "What's the Azure Room like?"

"It's strange," I recounted. "They have a back room that isn't easily accessible, but once you're back there, it seems whatever you want is available. The girl I talked to said for a grand, I could get whatever I wanted off the menu."

"What does that entail?"

"I saw couples having sex back there, so my guess is just about anything."

"Shit," Carlson muttered as he took a drink of coffee. "They let you in?"

"Yeah. It wasn't until I mentioned working at the Tilly that it got squirrelly. The girl I was talking with knew Lyla, but she didn't give me much else about her. She said Lyla didn't have a family, but she didn't know her real name."

"No way that the girl had no family," Carlson stated. "I'm searching the databases. She's probably not from around here, though. We have a slew of runaways hiding down here."

I nodded, recalling my own nephew who ended up down here after running away from home. Thankfully, he hadn't ended up like Lyla, though that had been a near possibility.

"The Haitian said they didn't kill her," I stated. "Take that how you will."

"Did you believe him?" Carlson asked.

I considered my answer. "I think to some extent. He didn't confess to anything, but it was the one thing he denied. And at that point, he planned to kill me. What incentive was there to lie about it?"

Carlson bobbed his head as if he understood. "Do you want to file a report?"

I shook my head. "Let the college kids do that," I replied. "I can corroborate if you want. But I don't think you'll get these guys that way, anyhow."

"You know, you could humor me," Carlson said. "The justice system does work."

"Does it?" I questioned. "I'm not sure Lyla would agree."

"We can't stop them all," Carlson conceded. "But we can put the criminals away."

"Good," I retorted while slurping my coffee. "Focus on Clayton Connors."

"Right," Carlson quipped. "Start me on Goliath himself."

"You said you put the criminals away," I reminded him.

"I do need evidence," Carlson reminded me. "Not just your opinion."

"When he tries to kill me again, I won't need evidence, either," I shot back.

Carlson sipped his coffee without commenting.

15

———

O nce Carlson left, I tried to catch a few more hours of sleep. The coffee started working on me, or perhaps it was just my brain that wouldn't shut off.

Today was Amanda's last day of her shift, but I expected she'd go home and crash for the night. We hadn't spoken now in over two days, and for the first time, I wondered if that was why people kept their phones on them. It would have been nice to share what was happening with her, even if it was only through a text message.

After staring at the ceiling in my v-berth until a few minutes past eight, I surrendered and got out of bed, deciding to take a shower before I found some breakfast since the tangerine didn't stick to my ribs for long. By nine, I no longer smelled like fish and rank seawater. The clothes I'd stripped off earlier were now deposited in the trashcan.

"What are you doing here?" Hunter asked when I stepped into the Manta Club. "You missed a busy shift last night. That real estate group came in yesterday, and those boys know how to drink." He flushed a little, adding, "Some hot chicks in that crowd, too."

"Oh? Sounds better than my evening," I remarked.

"For sure," Hunter grinned. "I only had to come downstairs, if you catch my drift."

I nodded and returned the smile the twenty-six-year-old gave me. Hunter, like Pat, had no qualms about bedding anyone who came through the Manta Club. I knew that he and Missy often paired up when I was gone. It was only my fragile male ego that wanted to pretend that Missy liked me better. However, it was also something neither Hunter nor I ever discussed with each other.

"Think I can get a tuna sandwich?" I asked him as I straddled the barstool.

"Rare, right?" he asked.

"Yep."

"Need a beer?"

"No. I'm running on no sleep at the moment, so just some coffee."

He pointed to the coffeemaker as if I didn't also work here. "Help yourself."

He wasn't being rude. There was an unspoken rule about visiting the bar one worked in. It was a lot like eating at your best friend's house. If there was no need to ring it up, you got it yourself.

The Manta Club opened at 10:30, and that initial hour was always a drought. On average, the first customer showed up around twenty minutes past eleven. Three more parties would show up in the next half hour. By noon, the lunch rush would be in full swing.

While the midday shift earned fewer tips than a weekend night, it offered the added value of only being six hours long—and the money wasn't bad if you could turn the tables. Another bonus was business lunches. Those guys expensing their customers never batted an eye at midday drinks and twenty-five to thirty-percent gratuities.

"Chase, I'm running to the kitchen," Hunter said, and I nodded in acknowledgment.

Standing up, I reached across the bar for the phone, a cordless type. When I settled back in my seat, I dialed my friend Rob Isip. Rob was a career officer in the Coast Guard who had found himself in a cherry position. His former commander had created a bureaucratic role beneath him, and Rob filled it. Most of his duties involved tracking vessel numbers, which took him less than two hours a day. Even if the job was pointless, it was an added responsibility under the latest commander, and an easy one at that. Nobody wanted to suggest cutting a budget line for fear that other lines and positions might disappear, too.

"Isip," he answered.

"Rob, it's Chase."

"Yo, Chase. How's it going?"

"Dandy. How's that sexy wife of yours?"

"Ha, she's still with me. I think that's only because she said you were unmarriable."

"Unmarriable?" I questioned. "Is that even a word?"

"Hell, it might be. What's happening with you?"

"You know Clayton Connors?"

"Who?"

"C'mon, Rob. He's a real estate mogul. Owns the half of Palm Beach that the other oligarch doesn't."

"Chase, how do you know that?" he wondered. "You don't watch TV."

"First, that's not true," I corrected him. "I have the entire DVD collection of *Mannix*."

"Damn, I'm not sure if I believe you or not," Rob

remarked. "I mean, had you said VHS, then I might have bought it."

"What can I say?"

"What about Clayton Connors?"

"I'm curious if he has a boat of some sort registered to him."

"If he's a mogul, it won't be under his name," Rob pointed out. "More likely, it's a tax deduction for a corporation."

I hadn't considered that. Of course, my taxes took almost fifteen minutes to prepare. I got a small W2 from the Tilly and my pension. No deductions and no investments. When I died, I hoped to have at least a week's worth of cash in my cruising kitty. No point in taking it all with me.

"Would you be able to search for that?" I asked.

"Maybe," he said. "Don't hold your breath, though."

"Great," I muttered.

"What's going on?"

"I think he killed a hooker."

"What?" Rob blurted. "What makes you suggest that?"

"Pure intuition," I stated.

"Geez," he mumbled. "I'll drop it because I'm not sure I want all the details."

"How about we grab a beer this week?" I suggested. "My treat."

"Should be your treat if I'm sticking my toe into some shit for you."

"How much trouble could it be?"

"Right. Some millionaire with hands in everyone's pocket won't care if I poke around."

"I think he's a billionaire," I corrected.

"Of course he is," Rob chuckled. "Let me see what I can come up with for you."

"Thanks."

"If you suss out his corporations, it might make it easier to try tracking those separately."

"I'll do a little digging," I agreed.

"Any chance the cops are looking into this?"

"I gave the detective on the case my thoughts, but there's no evidence."

Rob sighed. "They don't want to stick their neck into a hornet's nest without some proof, huh?"

"I can't blame them," I admitted. "Partly why I'm curious about it."

"Give me some time," he suggested. "I'll holler when I find something."

"Thanks," I told him as I hung up the phone.

Hunter returned with a plate as I dropped the cordless phone in its charging cradle. Before he set the sandwich in front of me, Missy came through the door.

"Let me guess?" she asked, settling on the stool next to me. "Breakfast?"

"I've lost track of what meal I'm on," I replied.

"You look like shit," she commented. "What the hell's up?"

"Miss, you sure can make a guy feel like he's king of the world."

"Don't blame me because you don't take care of yourself," she scolded.

An older woman appeared at the top of the stairs leading out to the lobby. I glanced up at the fifty-six-year-old woman, recognizing her as Mary Allison, Missy's executive assistant. Her face carried a frantic expression as she scanned the Manta Club.

"Missy!" she blurted, hurrying down the steps toward us.

"Health department is here," she announced when she reached us.

"Again?" Missy muttered. "They were just here. Is it Carlos?"

Mary Allison shook her head. "No, it's the supervisor. At least that's what he said."

Missy furrowed her eyebrows. "Carlos was here less than a week ago."

"Could be Carlos is gone, and now they are reviewing what he did," I suggested. "Or you got a new supervisor who is looking to put his fingerprints on everything."

Missy shrugged. "Where is he?" she asked Mary Allison.

"In your office."

"Why didn't you leave him in the lobby?"

"He barged in," Mary Allison defended. "I informed him you were in a meeting. He said for me to find you ASAP, or he'll write us up as noncompliant."

"What?" Missy barked. "That's some bullshit."

"Sounds like a bureaucrat trying to justify his existence," I told her. "We'd see officers act that way. Career people who only want to waggle their dicks in your face."

Mary Allison scrunched up her cheeks. She often scowled at foul language, and while I didn't care how she regarded it, I liked the woman. Missy never censored herself, but I figured why offend the older lady if I didn't have to.

"Sorry, MA," I told the assistant.

"It's fine, Chase," she assured me.

"MA, I'll go talk to him. Can you pass the word that he's here?"

She nodded as Hunter appeared at the bar. "Who's here?" he asked.

"Health department."

"Fuck!" he groaned, dragging the curse out into two syllables.

It didn't matter how spotless a workplace might be—nothing instilled fear in restaurant staff quite like inspectors. Even the aforementioned Carlos, who was more reasonable, always found some minor offense. The kitchen crew often joked that they were required to make stuff up if they found it spotless.

Hunter grabbed a towel and started working his way around the bar. It was a pointless endeavor, considering he had just opened and the bar should already be clean. I pushed my tuna sandwich to the side and jumped off my stool.

"I'll check your dates," I offered. Since we used lots of fruits and juices, the health department, not to mention good sanitary procedures, required us to date the containers we transferred fresh juice and fruit into. It was also the easiest thing to overlook during a busy rush. Inevitably, there was a single container that got placed in the fridge without a label.

"Thanks, Chase," Hunter said as Missy and MA scurried out of The Manta Club.

I knelt down in front of the cooler under the counter. As I pulled the containers out of the refrigerator, I scanned each one for a fresh date sticker.

"Excuse me," a female voice caught my attention.

I turned my head to see an African-American woman holding an iPad in her hand. She was in her thirties and scowling at me as if I'd just dropped a cockroach in her martini.

"Yes," I replied. "Can I help you?"

"Do you work here?"

I glanced around for Hunter, but he must have run into the kitchen. While I wasn't in my normal uniform, I still straightened up. It seemed easier to reply with an affirmative rather than explain that I was not working.

"Yeah, I do," I admitted.

"Diana Calhoun," she said, handing me a card. The little piece of paper stated she was an inspector for Florida Alcohol Beverages & Tobacco.

"You'll want the manager," I remarked, wondering who this lady was if the health inspector had Missy tied up.

"Where is he?" she asked.

"I think she's actually with the health inspector right now," I commented.

Her brow furrowed. "Weird."

"They do that sometimes," I pointed out.

"So do we," she responded. "This one's unusual, though."

"How so?" I asked, leaning on the bar to study the woman's face.

"Someone checked you guys last month," she explained. "Not me, but one of my colleagues."

"That's strange," I remarked.

She shrugged. "It happens, but you weren't on my list yesterday."

"They added us?" I questioned.

"Yeah, but that's not unusual. I get additions all the time. Although, most of the time, it's less... reputable places. Someone complains, and we come out to investigate."

"Oh, we got a complaint?"

"It doesn't say," she admitted. "I guess that makes it a little vague and weird."

Hunter came back into the bar and saw me chatting with Ms. Calhoun.

"Excuse me, Ms. Calhoun," I said before coming out from behind the bar to intercept Hunter.

"Alcoholic Beverages and Tobacco," I muttered under my breath as I passed him.

"What?" he blurted out. "Just when the health department showed up? That's strange."

I pursed my lips. "Could be a coincidence, but she said it's weird."

"I thought you always said you didn't believe in coincidences," Hunter pointed out.

Biting my lip, I answered, "I don't."

When I turned to find Missy, her husband stepped through the door. Michael Seine sneered when he saw me.

"Gordon, have you seen Missy?" he asked.

"She's with the health inspector," I answered.

"I need to talk to her," he declared. There was a nervous energy about the man. While he hated me and I wouldn't piss on him if he was on fire, this was a different interaction. He was giving me his typical disregard, but he'd normally have tacked on some childish barb.

"We have to find her," I said. "Is everything alright?"

"I don't know," he said. "We just got an incredible offer to sell the Tilly for two hundred million."

"What?" I stammered, turning to look back at Diana Calhoun.

"A lawyer for an unnamed agent called me to pitch the deal," Michael explained. "He's sending over paperwork."

"That's a lot of money," I remarked.

"No shit," Michael agreed.

"Would she sell?" I asked.

That must have been enough to squash his excitement because he barked, "You know, Gordon, that's none of your fucking business."

He spun on his heels and marched out of the bar, leaving me standing there.

16

———————

I sat in my cockpit, still thinking about the exchange I had with Michael Seine. Since Missy remained tied up with the health inspector, I found Lisha Sullivan, the front desk manager. Besides Mary Allison, she was the closest thing to Missy's second-in-command. She could handle the auditor.

Right now, I was enjoying the sunshine and considering a nap. With warm sunlight heating my skin, I drifted to sleep. I had to clean up and clock in by four, but until then, I should rest.

"What are you doing?" Scar asked from the dock.

I opened my eyes to stare up at the Cuban dressed in jeans and a western-style shirt that looked like he bought it before riding a bull at the rodeo.

"Esteban?" I questioned. "I was trying to nap."

"Don't you have things you need to do?"

"Yeah," I remarked. "Sleep."

"Get up. *Señor* Moreno asked for you to come see him."

"It's one o'clock," I told him. "I have to be at work by four."

Scar nodded. "I think you will want to chat with him," he suggested.

When someone like Julio Moreno summoned you, there were options. One could refuse him. That didn't always turn into the smartest move. People who did often regretted it.

I didn't have that concern. Deep in my heart, I was certain that Julio Moreno wished me no harm. Of course, I assumed he found my moral defiance endearing.

The other option was to go with an open mind. That could be just as unhealthy for a long life, but my confidence was unwavering. I had no issue hearing the man out, since I had no problem turning him down.

When someone like Julio Moreno sent someone like Esteban Velasquez, those options shrank. Although neither of us ever admitted it, Scar and I were friendly. I didn't think he came to drag me off to kill me, but Scar could surprise me.

"I'll drive you back," Scar assured me. "In time for you to mix one of those girly frozen cocktails."

"You should know I make manly frozen drinks, too."

"They have frozen beer?"

"They do," I remarked. "But those girly drinks have way more liquor in them than your shitty beer."

He shrugged. "Still not girly."

I shook my head in disbelief. "Can you let me change?"

He waved his hand, motioning me to get moving. I rolled off the bench and climbed through the open companionway.

"Don't step on my boat with those boots," I barked.

"You don't like ostrich?" Scar asked. "That's snobbery."

"I don't like scuffs on my deck," I corrected as I vanished through the companionway. "But I will say they are colorful."

"The girls like them," Scar noted.

"Just because they point and smile doesn't mean they like them," I scoffed from the cabin.

Two minutes later, I locked up *Carina* and followed Scar to his black Suburban parked in the marina parking area.

"Is there a cartel discount on Suburbans?" I asked.

"Don't be a smartass," Scar growled.

"Just saying. Those Haitian friends of yours drove one, too."

"They carry a lot of people," Scar remarked, as if the gangs were shopping for cars with the same forethought that soccer moms did with minivans.

The ride to Miami was an hour and a half, meaning whatever time I spent with Julio Moreno would be limited to a few minutes if I was going to make it back close to four. Still, I saw no reason to mention it to Scar again. He wasn't the sort of person to miss those details. If I reminded him, it would only annoy the hitter. While that could be entertaining sometimes, I didn't want him screwing up my timetable.

But we didn't drive to Padrino's, the Cuban diner in South Miami where Julio Moreno held court. Instead, Scar drove half a mile down Flagler until he stopped in front of Elisabetta's, an Italian restaurant with a patio overlooking the banks of Lake Worth.

"What?" I asked simply.

"He wanted pasta," Scar explained.

"I could have walked down here," I pointed out.

"Where's the drama in that?"

"You're kidding, right?"

For the second time in a few days, I saw a mischievous smile on Scar's face. I lifted an eyebrow in response.

"Are you coming?" I asked.

"No, too many carbs," he quipped.

"Seriously?"

"No," he replied flatly.

"We're going to talk about this," I promised, motioning between him and me.

"I'll be waiting," he explained as I got out of the Suburban.

Julio Moreno, the head of the largest cocaine cartel from Florida to Houston, sat at a small two-top table on the patio. The sexagenarian wore dark Ray-Ban aviators that reflected my face and a sports jacket. He'd colored his graying hair, bringing back a semblance of the black mop he once had.

I pulled the seat out opposite the Cuban drug lord.

"*Buenas tardes*, Chase," he greeted me.

"Julio, how are you?"

"Things are quite hectic," he remarked. "The economy has affected our supply."

"Really? I suppose people don't shove all their money up their noses when the market plummets."

Moreno chuckled. "Not at all. In fact, I'd say it's the opposite."

"I guess that makes sense," I considered. It didn't make sense to me, but I'd yet to figure out the average consumer. "What can I do for you?"

"There are whispers on the streets," Moreno began, pausing when a server arrived to ask me what I was drinking. After I ordered an iced tea, Moreno continued, "You have made some enemies."

"It's weird, isn't it?" I remarked. "After all, I'm a delight."

Julio Moreno smiled at me condescendingly. "Chase, you are more of an acquired taste."

I shrugged. "That's fair," I admitted. "What enemies are you talking about?"

"There's a price on your head."

My back straightened. "What?"

"Someone offered $100,000 on the street for your death. Of course, they need to prove it to the buyer. No one wants to pay if you died in a car accident."

"That makes sense," I said, wondering how I came to chat about a hit on my life with such casual ease. "Are you and Esteban planning to collect?"

"For a hundred grand?" Moreno scoffed. "That's offensive."

"Are you suggesting I'm worth more than that?"

Moreno smiled his sly grin. "I'd say that whoever collects will work harder than they expect."

"I'll take that as a compliment," I said.

Julio Moreno shrugged as he puckered his face. "Take it as you wish."

"Is that why you came here?"

"It wouldn't do for someone to gun you down near Padrino's," he stated. "I already have enough scrutiny on my activities. Adding in your murder so close to home would only complicate matters for me."

"Do you know who offered the hit?"

"Not sure. Although there's other hushed words about your conflict with *Les Loups Noirs*," he explained. "Lucien Baptiste is not one to overlook such actions."

"I feel like there is a 'but' in there," I said.

"But a hit doesn't fit him. He would want his people to handle the problem themselves."

The server appeared with my iced tea.

"Please, Chase, order some lunch," Moreno offered.

"Thank you," I told him, ordering the shrimp Caesar salad as he sipped a glass of sparkling water with a bright yellow slice of lemon hanging on the rim.

"You don't think it's the Haitians?" I clarified.

He shook his head. "*Es posible.* But I doubt it. They have added reasons for killing you. They might choose to take up the hit just to be the one to kill you."

I tapped my index finger on my cold glass. Facing a death threat wasn't something new. When my unit took out several high-priority targets, there was word that the Taliban issued specific orders to eliminate our squad. It wasn't something we ignored, but the consensus was that our Recon team could handle anything the Taliban army threw at us. After all, we were Marines, and if they wanted to take a run at us, it was their funeral—literally.

But back then, I had not only my unit but the combined forces of the United States military to back us up. Right now, I had no one. It was unlikely that Moreno would stick his neck out further than he had. Carlson would not be much help, either. He might put a uniformed officer on me for protection. That seemed more like a hindrance and an annoyance than being helpful.

I considered the possibilities, and my pensive look garnered Moreno's attention.

"Chase, do you know who did this?" he asked.

"If you're right and—what's the guy's name in charge of the Haitians?"

"Lucien Baptiste," Moreno answered. "Don't misunderstand me. Baptiste is a vile snake. He is not one to be trifled with."

"He worries you?" I asked.

Moreno offered a half-shrug. "He is dangerous and ambitious, but not very smart."

"I'm not sure what that means," I said.

"He's a thorn in my side, but time will remove him," Moreno explained.

"You seem confident," I noted.

"Baptiste has, so far, respected my trade. He deals in guns and women. The wolves are blanketing the area, and eventually something will put them in the spotlight. I imagine this dead girl you found might be just that."

"Is that why you sent Esteban to prod me into them?"

Julio Moreno paused with the same shit-eating grin he had on his face earlier. At that point, the server returned with my salad and a plate of penne for Julio. When she left, Julio replied, "You are quite effective."

"Julio, don't forget that I don't work for you."

"*Claro que sí*, you made that abundantly clear. That doesn't mean you don't work for your own agenda."

As I stabbed a thick Gulf shrimp, I remarked, "I bet you are badass at chess."

"I'll take that as a compliment," Moreno replied. "Now, you have an idea about who is behind this, don't you?"

One thing about being seen as useful by Julio Moreno was that even if I refused to work for him, my well-being still benefited the man and his business. As I considered that, I chewed up the shrimp.

After I swallowed, I asked, "Do you know who Clayton Connors is?"

Moreno's mirthful expression shifted to a quizzical one. "The billionaire?"

"That's right."

"You are saying Clayton Connors put a target on you?"

"I've only crossed paths with the Haitians and him. If you don't think it's the Haitians, that leaves him."

"Well, Chase, I don't know what to suggest," Moreno confessed. "Men like Connors have a different mindset."

I cocked my head to stare at Moreno. "You mean different than, say, a cartel leader?"

He flashed a smug expression. "Probably not that different," he allowed. "But definitely not like Lucien Baptiste."

"Seems pretty similar," I countered. "Connors is a criminal who believes he's untouchable. Most do."

Moreno shook his head. "You misunderstand. He *is* untouchable. I cannot say the same thing. It doesn't matter how much money I have. There is no way to use my influence on politicians without dirtying them. But Connors... he spreads favors around until no one will cross him. If he wants you to get a speeding ticket, I promise a cop will show up to write that citation."

"I don't own a car," I pointed out.

Moreno stared at me. "It's naivete to believe that matters. If I may be blunt, I can use force, but that doesn't have the same effect. I'm no fool. Threats never build loyalty the same way power does, and Clayton Connors has such power. He simply has to ask. Perhaps just a mere suggestion or comment from him might be enough to spur someone to act. Sometimes only to garner favoritism from him."

I listened as I chewed another shrimp.

"Chase, don't mistake that power," Julio warned. "He could buy this restaurant today if he felt like it."

Suddenly, the shrimp lost its flavor.

17

"What do you mean?" Missy asked as I wiped down the bottles. "You're saying that Clayton Connors sent the health department and the alcohol board in today?"

"I'd bet he's behind the offer you got," I said.

"I turned it down," she replied.

The smile that spread across my face was uncontrollable.

"What's the grin for?"

"I figured you wouldn't sell."

"Michael says it's foolish," she said.

"What can I say?" I replied. "I own almost nothing. If I had a hundred mil, I'd vanish over the sea."

She shook her head. "I don't buy that."

We held each other's eyes for a long time. I huffed a muffled chuckle through my nose. She might have been correct. There wasn't much keeping me at the dock now. I had a nice fat bank account from the little job I did for the CIA. Turned out they paid civilian consultants more than they paid Marine lieutenants.

I could disembark tomorrow morning and not return for a year or more with no trouble. Given that someone had put a price on my head, perhaps I should do just that. But besides the fact that I didn't like anyone forcing me to run, I didn't want to venture out to the islands yet.

Still, I argued, "I've left before."

"But here you are," Missy retorted. This time, she had a half-smile on her face. I hadn't seen that look in months. Since I got involved with Amanda, to be precise.

"You managed the health department?" I returned to the topic at hand.

"Oh, he wanted to write up everything. At one point, he complained about the type of soap we were using. Also, he tried to cite me for having bug zappers in the kitchen."

"You don't," I pointed out.

"Nope, just those bug lights, but this guy was so dumb—or maybe he wanted to stay focused on failing me—he claimed the bug lights we have in the back were in violation."

I furrowed my brow. "They aren't, are they?"

Missy scoffed. "Not at all. I had to point that out. At least the alcohol lady had some sense."

"It was Clayton Connors," I suggested.

"But why?" she asked. "Because you pissed him off? Why bother?"

"The man has more cash than we can imagine. He wanted to come after me."

"Does he expect to close down the hotel?"

"I bet he plans to entice you to sell and drop the price."

She shook her head. "I just don't get it. I still would end up with more money than I could ever spend. How does it hurt me?"

"It's not designed to hurt you, just to fuck with me."

"Seems stupid," she remarked. "I can always turn him down if he tries to lowball me. But he didn't."

"Why not do it?" I asked.

"Sell? My daddy would roll over in his grave."

"Please. You don't want to keep it because of your father."

She scowled at me.

"C'mon, Miss, you couldn't just hang around and lunch with the ladies on Thursdays," I told her. "You love this hotel."

She gave me a half-nod. "I do. I don't know what I'd do. Michael tells me I'm stupid."

"He should reconsider that," I said. "If you were home all the time, it might break your marriage up."

"Chase, don't."

"Sorry," I replied. "It wasn't intended as a jab. Just my opinion. The two of you don't like each other enough to spend all your time together."

She grunted, and I wasn't sure what that meant.

"Hey there," Detective Carlson announced as he entered the bar.

I watched Missy turn to face the policeman.

"That's why you're still here," I teased her.

She threw a wicked glare my way just before she turned to Carlson. "Hi there."

"Gordon," Carlson greeted me. "Did you get back to sleep?"

"No," I said. "I'm running on fumes."

"You don't look it," he commented.

"Don't give him a big head," Missy warned. "His is already large enough."

"Detective, can I get you a drink?" I asked. "It's Missy's treat."

Carlson gave Missy a curious gaze that included a joyful glint in his eye. The detective had grown smitten with Missy. Despite the obvious competition that Missy was engendering between us, I liked the detective. He impressed me as an honest cop intent on justice.

Nonetheless, it was easy to feel replaceable.

"Jake, let me go grab my phone from my office," Missy said.

"I'll have that drink while I'm waiting," he told her.

She smiled back, and a stabbing pang of jealousy struck me. It wasn't a sensation I enjoyed, but at the same time, I wasn't stopping the pair. It still didn't matter. Missy wasn't leaving Michael anytime soon. She had made that more than clear with me. While Amanda and I had no official commitment, at least I wasn't the second string in that relationship.

When Missy left, I gave the detective an appraising examination. "What do you want to drink, Jake?"

It was possible I put a heavy intonation on his name, and when Carlson faced me, I saw the wariness on his face.

"Do we have an issue, Gordon?"

"You know what? We really don't," I confessed. "Promise."

He nodded. "Can I get a vodka soda?"

"Sure," I agreed, stepping over to fix his drink. When I set it in front of him, I said, "Listen, I don't want to tell Missy this yet, but I heard a rumor that someone put a price on my head."

Carlson froze, the rocks glass a mere centimeter from his lips. He put the tumbler back on the bar. "What do you mean?"

"Word is that there's hit out on me," I explained.

"Why haven't you called me already?" he demanded.

"To do what?"

"Protection?"

"Protection? Like a rookie officer that would shadow me?"

"Not a rookie," he corrected. "But yeah."

I shook my head. "No thanks."

"Why are you telling me, then?"

"Today, Missy got hit by the health department and the alcohol board. At the same time."

The detective made a curious face and shook his head. "Doesn't that happen?"

"The woman from alcoholic beverages said it was probably a complaint," I told him. "And the health department was already here last week. Someone pointed them at us."

"Us?" he questioned. "You think Connors wants to take down the Tilly just to get to you?"

"It's a lot of coincidence. You see that? I get targeted, and Missy gets hit with these inspectors. Plus, she got an offer on the hotel. A big one."

"From Connors?"

"From an unnamed agent," I said.

"Not really proof of anything," he advised. "The health department and probably Alcoholic Beverages and Tobacco can inspect all they want. Especially if they have reason, like a tip. It doesn't mean it was Connors."

I nodded. "I realize that, but it could be. How many people have the power to get a bureaucratic agency moving like that?"

"Any politician," Carlson reminded me.

"But I didn't confront any of them last night."

"You also ran afoul of this Haitian gang. They are more likely who put the hit on you."

"My source doesn't believe it was them."

Carlson sipped his vodka soda before asking, "Is this source Julio Moreno?"

I didn't answer.

"You have notes in your file, Chase," he said. "The DEA marked you as a person of interest a few years ago."

"That's not a fair assessment," I told him.

He shrugged. "Look, I talked to Jay Delp. The chief and I got along pretty well. He vouched for you."

"I expect he would."

"Well, he suggested you had terrible judgment concerning Julio Moreno and his number-two... what's his name? Varquez?"

"Velasquez," I corrected.

"Right. I haven't crossed paths with him, but he also has a thick file."

"Carlson, I have crossed paths with both of them, and weirdly, they have some affinity for me. Moreno is the one who warned me about the hit."

"He'd know, I guess. There are countless bodies attributed to him or his people. Who knows how many Velasquez has under his belt?"

"You're preaching to the choir."

"Why would he warn you?" Carlson asked. "It sounds like he's protecting you."

"I think he believes I can be a problem for the Haitians. He has repeated that he doesn't like human traffickers."

"A drug lord with a conscience?" Carlson pondered.

"People are strange," I said.

"I'm ready," Missy announced as she came through the door.

"Good, I'm starving," Carlson said.

"Chase, we're going to the library," Missy told me, pointing at the raised portion of the dining room that sat in the corner. The little nook had several bookshelves with a hodgepodge of antique books. Someone long before me had coined the section "the library," and the name stuck. Most customers never saw the niche, and it made for a more intimate area when the bar filled up.

"I'll send Holly over," I promised.

"Oh, you aren't waiting on us?" Carlson asked, his voice a little snide.

I smiled in response. "No, I'm just a bartender. I doubt I'm smart enough to carry drinks on a tray."

"It does take a certain coordination," Carlson agreed.

I allowed him to walk away without poking him with another retort.

Over the next hour, we had several tables flow through The Manta Club, keeping Holly busy while I managed the four people sitting at the bar. Some nights, it was better to work the floor than bartend, but I hated dealing with all the running back and forth to the kitchen.

"Hey," a voice broke through my thoughts while I was stocking the beer fridge. When I turned, I smiled at Amanda, who leaned across the counter.

"What's a girl gotta do to get a drink around here?" she asked.

I straightened up and wagged my eyebrows at her with my best Groucho impression. "Well, I have some ideas, but most of them involve at least one of us naked."

Her grin lit up the room.

"I'm glad you're here," I told her.

"Good. I've had a long shift. We had a big accident last night, plus that shooting on the bridge. Did you hear about that?"

I bit my lip and nodded. "Yes, I did," I said simply. "What can I make you?"

"Surprise me," she whispered. "If it's good enough, I'll reward you later."

"You realize in the bar business, we like to get paid in the moment."

"I thought bars had tabs," she pointed out.

"Not here. But I can make exceptions."

I shook up a lemon drop martini with a sugar-coated rim and a frosted lemon, which was just a lemon covered in sugar and frozen. When I turned to hand her the drink, she took a sip and smiled.

"Oh, that's going to cost me," she quipped.

Three men stepped into the bar right then, and the sight of them made my hair up on end. Ignoring Amanda, I adjusted my stare on the tattooed black men. I recognized two of the three. They had been in the SUV with me last night—the driver and passenger. Their companion was a big man with more face tattoos than Post Malone.

All three focused on me, and I backed up a step.

"Amanda, I need you to leave out the back door," I muttered.

"What?" she asked, confused.

"You need to leave now," I said. My hand ran along the dish sink until I touched the handle of the bar knife I'd used to cut up the limes and lemons earlier. The big butcher knife was still waiting for me to wash it, but I gripped the handle.

"Chase, what's going on?" she asked again, still confused.

"Run!" I shouted as Post Malone pulled a chrome-plated Glock 17. Amanda followed my eyes to see the man with the gun raising it toward me. She let out a squeal as I hurled the knife.

The stainless-steel blade flew end over end at Post Malone, hitting him in the chest. Chef had sharpened it for me earlier, and the big brute's sternum didn't stop the thick steel. He'd barely gotten his gun up before the point skewered him. He froze with the Glock pointed up, staring at the butcher knife jutting out of his chest.

Post Malone blinked, lifted his eyes at me, and squeezed the trigger.

18

A bottle of Macallan 25 sitting atop the pyramid of liquor displayed behind the bar exploded only a foot from my head. Twenty-five-year-old Scotch and glass shrapnel sprayed me.

The gunshot ignited a chain reaction, with the few patrons around the restaurant diving for cover. Guests screamed, scampering to shield themselves. One table of men jumped from their seats and dashed for the door, only to reverse course when they saw *Les Loups Noirs* members blocking the exit.

Post Malone only had one shot in him, and he toppled forward, dropping his Glock as he fell. The handgun skittered across the floor.

In battle, there was always a shift in perspective. Time could come to a screeching halt. The body got pumped with an overload of adrenaline, which became crucial to the human's flight-or-fight response. Most of the patrons might have seen the gang member pull the gun, but their brains required a moment to register what they were seeing. Despite what the media told the public, violence wasn't so rampant that it touched everyone. Humans grew complacent, allowing their guards to drop. It could be why so many of these mass shootings surprised people. No one expected danger at a church or a nightclub, so they never prepared.

Thankfully, the Marine Corps had drilled preparation into me. Years of practicing situational awareness had stayed with me, triggering the amygdala, that little almond-shaped cluster in the brain that controls the surge of adrenaline.

From the moment I spotted the trio of *Loups* in the doorway, time slowed. Now, as glass and liquor spewed over me, I took in the scene. Amanda didn't run, but dropped on instinct. Only, she lay prone in front of the remaining Haitians. I sprinted the three steps across the service area to the bar. With a leap, I twisted in midair to roll my back over the top of the counter.

My mass plowed over the tops of the barstools as I rotated my feet toward the floor. The driver from last night saw his tattooed friend take my butcher knife to the chest, and like so many people in a high-stress situation, he needed to wrap his brain around what had just happened.

Their plan had been simple: walk in and shoot me. No one had expected their shooter to be dropped by a blade from twenty feet away. As the two remaining *Loups* realized what had transpired, they reached for their own weapons.

My feet and hands were already moving. As soon as my soles hit the marble tiles, I dashed toward the driver. I grabbed the backrest of the nearest barstool and hurled it in a wide arcing throw at the pair. It only struck the guy on the left, who had been the passenger last night, and it had only been a glancing blow. But it carried enough force to topple the gang member, sending him crashing to the floor.

The driver's hand came up with Smith & Wesson 1911. I

registered the pearl handle on the gun, which seemed an odd thing to realize a second before someone shot me.

Another gunshot rang out in the bar, and I watched the driver fall to his left, sprawling across the passenger, who scrambled to stand with his own nine millimeter in his hand.

From my side, Carlson fired again. His bullet hit the remaining Haitian in the chest. Before the gang member made it to his feet, he was dead and falling back to the floor.

A sharp and sulfurous stench filled the bar as the smoke hung in the air. I straightened up. My ears rang from the gunfire as time began to catch up. Amanda pulled herself up as Carlson, still holding his Glock extended in his grid, moved toward the bodies. His feet kicked the three guns away from the corpses. Missy cowered in the library, watching the aftermath.

Even following a gunfight, an unreality existed that disrupted the senses. I scanned the room. The guests who took cover began popping up from behind tables or the bar as the silence returned. From somewhere in the room, sobbing erupted.

"Are you alright?" I asked Amanda.

She nodded.

"Gordon, you good?" Carlson called.

"No holes," I declared before calling out, "Anyone hurt?"

Several people announced they were unharmed. Others, still in shock, either stared across the bar or wandered around aimlessly.

"Ladies and gentlemen, I'm Detective Carlson with the Palm County Sheriff," Carlson identified himself. "This situation is under control."

"What happened?" someone called.

"Was it a robbery?" another shouted.

"Stay calm," Carlson ordered. "We need everyone to remain calm. The situation is under control," he repeated.

Missy stepped out of the library and surveyed the bar. Several barstools lay scattered across the floor after I knocked them over. The bullet from Post Malone's gun had taken a divot out of the woodwork. Glass shards and the neck of the bottle were all that remained of the Macallan.

Holly, our cocktail server, peered in from the corridor leading to the lobby. She must have gone to the kitchen when the excitement began. Now she watched from the hallway. Some of the culinary staff came out to see what hubbub had erupted. No doubt, word spread fast that there had been an active shooter.

"What the hell was that, Gordon?" Carlson demanded.

"Two of those guys were from the bridge last night," I informed him.

"Shit, you said you had a hit on you," he moaned. "You weren't kidding?"

I shook my head. "I didn't know they'd come at me here."

"What do you mean, you had a hit on you?" Missy demanded.

"Chase, what's going on?" Amanda asked.

"Let's table this," Carlson suggested. "Until we handle this situation."

Two men in suits appeared at the entrance, having sprinted here. Carlson turned to them, his Glock still in his hand.

"Wait!" I called to the men, recognizing Jacques, the head of security at the Tilly.

"Ms. Seine, what's going on?" Jacques asked, surveying the bodies and the man with the gun drawn.

"Police," Carlson stated.

"Stand down, Jacques," I ordered, though it didn't matter much. Only Jacques carried a gun, and he didn't draw it.

Carlson holstered his service weapon and retracted his cell phone. "Missy, would you and your security corral the guests? We're going to need statements."

Missy nodded.

"Can I help?" Amanda asked her.

Missy appraised Amanda for a second before nodding. "Jacques, cordon off this area. We don't want the guests in the rest of the hotel to panic."

Jacques acknowledged her with a curt nod before telling the other security officer, a former Miami cop named Bradley, to get more officers to barricade the corridor to The Manta Club.

"These three were the ones who kidnapped you?" Carlson asked me.

"The big guy wasn't there," I explained. "That one was the driver." I pointed at the first man. "The other rode shotgun. But neither were in charge."

Carlson curled his lip. "What the hell did you get into?"

I shrugged.

"Think they were here because of last night or the hit?"

I shrugged again.

"What good are you?" he asked impatiently.

I considered reminding him how spot-on my knife-throwing skills were. However, it didn't seem like the time.

It took less than ten minutes for the first officer to show up. Soon, the Manta Club was full of cops. Missy, Holly, Amanda, and I sat at the bar, waiting as the police interrogated the guests and cleared them to leave.

"You want to tell me about this hit?" Missy said to me.

"I heard that someone put a bounty on my head," I told them.

"A bounty?" Amanda exclaimed. "What the hell?"

"Welcome to dating Chase Gordon," Missy remarked as she rolled her eyes.

"Who did this?" Amanda demanded.

"A lot's happened while you were at work," I told her.

"I'm listening," Amanda said.

Holly glanced between me and the other two women. She shook her head. "Good luck, Chase," she muttered.

"The girl we pulled from the water was a prostitute," I explained. "She was run by a Haitian gang. Those guys are part of the gang."

"They put a hit on you?" Amanda asked.

"I don't think so," I said. "I think it was Clayton Connors."

"The billionaire?"

I nodded. "That seems to be everyone's first question," I pointed out. "Billionaires can be murderers. In fact, I bet their temperament lends them to lean that way."

"Why, though?" Amanda inquired.

"Chase thinks Connors is running a sex ring through his resort," Missy explained.

"What? That's insane," Amanda said, shaking her head.

"Alright," Carlson announced. "We talked to all the guests and released them."

"This is a fucking nightmare," Missy complained.

"Sorry, Miss," I offered.

She shook her head. "Not like you knew it was going to happen—oh, wait! You did, didn't you?"

"This was brazen," Carlson admitted. "I wouldn't have expected this."

"So you knew about it, too?" Missy turned her ire on the detective.

"Only just," he said. "He mentioned it while you went to get your phone."

"What's next?" Missy asked wearily. "Can we reopen tomorrow?"

Carlson nodded. "You might need to clean the floors," he suggested.

"Dammit!" Missy cursed.

"Gordon, I think that protection detail is in order," Carlson told me.

"You can park someone in the hotel," I said. "They can't stay on *Carina* with me."

"You aren't going to your boat tonight," Amanda scolded.

"It'll be alright," I assured her.

"I gotta agree with her, Gordon," Carlson advised. "Find somewhere else to crash."

"You can come to my place," Amanda offered.

Missy turned away, so I didn't see the expression on her face. It didn't seem fair to discuss this in front of her, but it was out of my hands.

"I still need some things from *Carina*," I told Amanda.

"You have a gun, right?" Carlson asked.

I nodded.

"Might want to keep it on you," he suggested.

It was hard to argue with that as I watched the coroner move the first of the three bodies from The Manta Club's entry. I never brought my M45 to work because, like most of the people here, I'd always viewed the bar as a somewhat safe place. My mistake, considering this wasn't the first time violence had visited The Manta Club.

"We'll stay closed tomorrow," Missy announced. "I need to put out a statement. What am I calling this?"

"Can we say it was an attempted robbery?" I suggested.

"Or just an active shooter," Carlson added. "The media is

full of those, so most people's attention span won't last that long. Hell, you might even get some lookie-loos who want to check out the scene of the crime."

"See, Missy? The bright side," I said.

"Shut up," she snapped at me as she slid off her chair. "I'm going to put together a statement for the press. I can be vague."

"The department is already getting calls from the local news stations," Carlson told her.

"Great. My voicemail is probably full, too."

Missy started for the door, and Carlson followed her past the corpses.

"This is insane, Chase," Amanda told me.

"It certainly wasn't my intention to find myself in someone's crosshairs."

"Are you hurt? You're bleeding." She ran her finger over a nick on my temple.

"That was just a piece of glass scraping by," I informed her.

"My place," she offered again. "Okay?"

"You talked me into it. Let me go down to the boat first."

"Want me to tag along?"

I shook my head. It was one thing to be seen with me in the bar where there were plenty of people, most of whom were cops. But the marina was isolated, and someone could be waiting to ambush me. It would be better if I didn't put her in the line of fire.

"Hurry," she urged.

I winked at her as I headed out the back exit. "Five minutes," I promised as I pushed through the door to the patio overlooking the array of boats.

The night air was still compared to the atmosphere inside The Manta Club. A gentle wind blew my hair into my eyes, and I scanned the path down to the water. The way was clear and empty. At least, it seemed to be. I watched for over thirty seconds for any movement. Trained snipers could stay in the same position for hours, even days. But the average gang member didn't have that kind of patience. He'd squirm a little, shift his weight, or perhaps walk around to distract from the boredom.

By now, whoever had sent these guys to the bar would have learned they were dead. Or at least was wondering where they were. If they listened to the police scanners, they'd have heard the call for backup to The Tilly Inn. They'd know something was afoot.

Did they have time to put someone in place to finish the job?

I didn't think so. Despite that confidence, I remained alert all the way to *Carina* and back.

19

———

Amanda woke up before me. It had been the first real rest I'd gotten in three days, and we hadn't gone straight to sleep, either. She kissed my chest as she got out of bed, and I opened my eyes for a brief second to spy her naked form stalking out of the room.

The internal clockwork in my head told me it was after eight. From the comfort of the queen-sized bed, I heard Amanda rummaging around in her small galley kitchen. She lived inland a few miles in a one-bedroom apartment that overlooked one of a million manmade ponds. Developers came to Florida and thought every apartment complex needed its own useless lake. The smarter landscapes added a fountain in the middle to keep the water moving, which reduced the mosquito population. Although, it only helped this one water feature and not the collection of water in drainage ditches and canals. Plus, the fountain did nothing to prevent the alligators from making their home there.

Light streamed into her room from the balcony door, and I slid my feet to the floor. The television in the other room came on, and someone was promising "Traffic on the Fours." I stretched, staring out the French doors over the green pond.

"Chase," Amanda called.

"Yeah, I'm coming," I replied.

"You might want to check this out," she stated with an edge in her voice.

I walked into the living room to see her standing nude in the middle of the kitchen. Her eyes were focused on the television. My head followed her gaze as the reporter's voice caught up to my ears.

"This isn't the first time violence has struck The Tilly Inn. Just last week, a young woman's body was found in the hotel's marina. A few years back, over a million dollars of damage occurred at The Manta Club by what some called a gang attack."

"What the hell?" I remarked.

"The curious center of this violence seems focused on Chase Gordon, a former Marine who works as a bartender at The Manta Club. Based on the police report, Gordon was the one who discovered the body last week. He was also working at The Manta Club during the incident last night and the previous attack. Multiple other police reports, including deaths, have been documented at The Tilly Inn. In almost every case, Chase Gordon was involved."

I stepped back to lean against the bar between the kitchen and the living room. The TV, which had been showing stock footage of the outside of The Tilly Inn and the marina, flashed my picture on the screen. It was a few years old and pulled straight from my service jacket.

"Damn, Chase, you look hot in uniform," Amanda commented behind me.

I threw her a playful wink, but at the moment, my

stomach stayed busy knotting itself into a ball. If I'd considered getting a cell phone before, I was now grateful I hadn't done so. No doubt Missy was watching this on the television while her face brightened to a cherry red.

"Is that true?" Amanda asked. "About the attack a couple of years ago?"

"Yes, but they weren't after me. It was a hit squad, not a gang, and they targeted Michael Seine."

"Missy's husband?" Amanda wondered.

I nodded.

"You have a complicated life," she remarked.

On screen, the female reporter continued to talk. "While Gordon's service record is exemplary and complete with high honors, since getting out of the Marine Corps, he has been known to associate with alleged criminals. An anonymous source shared an image taken yesterday of Gordon having lunch with Julio Moreno, the suspected head of the biggest cocaine cartel in Florida."

A picture popped up on the screen of Moreno and me eating pasta on the patio of Elisabetta's.

"Fuck me," I muttered.

"Is that true?" Amanda asked.

"We aren't really associates, but yeah, I ate lunch with him yesterday. He's the one who warned me that there was a hit on me."

"This is bad, isn't it?"

I nodded. If Missy was pissed at me, that was tough enough. However, if I crossed Moreno, there would be far more to answer for. That was a price I didn't want to pay.

"What are you planning to do?" she asked. "Will this make you a target for someone?"

"I already am," I pointed out. "It can't get much worse than this. I better call Missy."

"She's going to be angry," Amanda warned.

"That might be the understatement of the year," I told her. "Can I borrow your phone?"

Amanda handed me her cell. I dialed Missy's number.

"Chase?" she answered.

"How'd you know it was me?"

"I'm watching this fucking bitch on TV right now. The first number I don't recognize that calls had to be you."

"Missy, this isn't really my fault."

"Oh, well, that comes as a relief when I have to lay off staff because our business tanks."

"This is Connors."

"Does that matter?" she asked. "It's not like they made shit up. Everything they reported is true. Now people will think that Moreno is running drugs through you in my hotel. Do you have any idea what this is going to do to my business?"

"No," I admitted. "I can fix this."

"You can't put the genie back in the bottle," she warned me. "This is just the first story. Now that it's broken, everyone will want a piece of it."

"I'm sorry, Miss," I apologized.

"Are you with the nurse?"

"Yes," I said without correcting her. It didn't seem like the appropriate time.

"Stay there," she warned. "I don't need you in or around the hotel right now. I expect the other stations and papers will hit me with reporters pretty soon."

"Have you talked to Carlson?"

"No, what's the point of that?"

I didn't have an answer.

"Okay, I'll stay away," I promised her.

"You need to consider getting on *Carina* and sailing

away," she suggested. "It might be best if you were gone for a long time."

"How long?"

"I don't know," she replied. "This won't go away."

"Yes, it will," I told her. "People forget about stuff like this. And most of your business isn't local, anyway."

"You don't think a story like this will go national?"

"I don't know," I confessed.

"No. Of course you don't. You're so out of touch, it's a fucking joke."

"Missy..."

"Chase, I have to go. My phone's already lighting up. I'm going to be fielding this bullshit all week now."

She hung up before I had the chance to say anything else.

"She's mad?" Amanda inquired.

"Seems like this might be a deeper hole than I initially thought," I said.

"You can't go back?"

"She just fired me," I admitted. "Or at least, temporarily."

"You're right," she told me. "About the media forgetting. This won't stay a story for long."

"But for the time being, I need to move my boat."

"Where would you go?"

"The kind of killers going after me for a hundred grand won't follow me to Mexico. Want to take a trip?"

"I still have work," she reminded me.

"Quit," I suggested. "You can always come back in six months. But it costs nothing to leave. Or at least, not much."

"I don't know, Chase."

Shrugging it off, I said, "It's fine. I don't run, anyway."

"What are you going to do?"

"Right now, my immediate concern is the Haitians. They have a beef with me, and it seems like it only gets bigger every time they make a run at me."

"How do you take on a gang?"

I smiled at her. "Head-on. Moreno told me the leader of the gang is Lucien Baptiste. I'll find him and address this issue at the source."

"Doesn't that seem reckless?" she asked. "No one knows you're here, right?"

"It won't take long to track that down," I explained. "You and I aren't keeping our relationship secret. It takes one person mentioning you, and people will start hunting you, too."

"What do you mean by 'hunting' me?"

I sighed. "Worst case: the Haitians come after you. If for no other reason than to draw me out. If I were in their shoes, I'd do that."

In my head, I added, *Or grab Missy.*

It wouldn't matter who they got. They'd come after those I cared for because there was no simple way to get to me otherwise. Even if I faced off with Baptiste, that didn't solve my Connors problem. I assumed he had something to do with the news report this morning. My connection to The Tilly wasn't secret, but those were dots that someone had to connect. Connors had targeted Missy and the hotel to attack me, so giving information to a reporter wasn't outside his scope.

"You're saying that I'm in danger, too?" she asked.

"Not necessarily," I assured her. "And I won't let it come to that."

"How do you find this Baptiste?"

My answer, normally, would have been Moreno. I doubted that Julio would blame me for the news report, but he might want to distance himself from me. I could try to call him, but the man had a twenty-four-hour DEA van parked down the street. His paranoia at being recorded was justified.

"I'm at a loss. When my buddy Jay was here, he could have directed me toward them based on any intel the police had. Carlson won't play that way."

Amanda's eyes lit up. "I might know a guy," she suggested.

"Really?"

"Yeah, he's on the gang task force in Miami. We hung out a bit last year."

"Hung out?" I echoed.

She reached over and pulled me against her naked breasts and kissed me. "We fucked, okay?"

I smiled. "I'm not judging," I promised her.

"Good, because I don't care about what you do with Missy."

"I assure you," I said, leaning in close to her lips, "there's nothing going on right now with Missy."

She pressed her lips against mine. "Yeah, right now."

I furrowed my brow, and she giggled. "You really have no idea how to take me, do you?" she commented.

My head shook. "Honestly, you are a bit confounding," I admitted.

"Good. Now, carry me back to bed."

"What about your friend?"

"He's not an early riser," she explained. "You have a few hours. I hope you can find a way to pass the time."

"I'm sure I can manage," I noted.

She reached forward with her hand to cradle my chin as she leaned close to kiss me. "I'll race you to the bedroom," she said, letting her hand trail down my chest and just past my waist.

My eyes widened with pleasure, and she spun around on her heel and walked away. My head tilted to watch her bare ass as she ventured into the bedroom.

"I'm going to beat you!" she announced, and I grinned before hurrying into the bedroom after her.

20

———

Garvin Wallace sat in a corner booth at the Waffle House. The six-foot-seven-inch black man sipped a cup of coffee that, while a normal-sized mug, was dwarfed by his meaty palms. He reclined in his seat with a paperback in one hand. The back and front cover bent backwards until they touched each other, and Garvin flipped to the next page with only his thumb.

"That's some dexterity," I whispered in Amanda's ear as we approached.

"You have no idea," she remarked with a smile. "Did you see how big his hands were?"

I had. While I wasn't one to compare myself to others, Garvin Wallace wasn't someone I wanted to face off against. Most men who bordered on body-building appeared much tougher than they were. There was no doubt they could bench a lot of weight or that a well-placed punch from them would knock a man silly. But that in itself didn't make a person tough.

Garvin, though, looked every bit as tough as I imagined. It might be the scars around his eyes that resulted from too many fists to the face. It might be the thickness of his biceps that stretched the fabric of the black t-shirt to its limits. But for me, it was the book. It barely mattered what he was reading, but when we slid into the booth across from him, I saw the title. *Zen and the Art of Motorcycle Maintenance.*

"That's a worn copy," I remarked.

"One of my favorites," he admitted. "I try to reread it once a year."

"Garv, this is Chase," Amanda introduced us.

"Pleasure to meet you, Chase," Garvin acknowledged. His face turned to Amanda. "Very nice to see you again, Mandy."

She blushed, and I suddenly got the sensation that I was a third wheel.

"No offense, Chase," he told me. "She's quite a girl. You guys been together long?"

"A few months," Amanda answered.

"Good," he replied. "Mandy said you're interested in *Les Loups Noirs.* What's the deal?"

"How much did she tell you?" I asked.

"That *Loup* Baptiste wants to kill you."

I shook my head in confusion. "What did you call him? Isn't the whole gang called the *Loups*?"

"They are, but named after Baptiste. He went by 'Loup' in Haiti. Carried the name here when he started the gang."

"He's the wolf?" I inquired.

"The man wants to be a myth," Garvin said. "He's as dangerous as they come. We have several missing-person cases we like him for."

"What about the girls?"

"Oh, I'm not even counting them. We can't track down all the stray kids in South Florida. It's like a fucking destination for all these runaways."

"They're all runaways?" I wondered. "The girl we found, Lyla... I was told she had no family."

Garvin shrugged. "She might not. Who's to say? Some kids run from some shitty situations. The parents are assholes and don't care what happens to them. Still, we get kids who ran away from healthy homes. It's quite a problem down here."

I nodded. "You can't touch Baptiste?"

"If we could, I'd have chained his ass up in a dungeon somewhere." I cocked an eyebrow, and Garvin chuckled. "You know what I mean," he said.

"Of course," I said.

"Right now, we have nothing to connect him to anything. As far as we can tell, the man might as well be the preacher at First Baptist."

"Did you bring a photo?" I asked.

Garvin reached below the table and retrieved a manila file folder. He slid it across to me, and when I opened the flap, I stared at the picture of Scowler, the man in the back of the Suburban the other night.

"That's him," I replied. "He kidnapped me the other day."

"You could press charges," Garvin suggested.

"Would it help?" I asked.

"You mentioned his guys attacked you at your work?"

I nodded.

"I saw the news report," he remarked. "Someone has painted you with a bullseye, haven't they?"

"It feels that way."

Garvin cocked his head. "That doesn't seem like Baptiste's style."

"No," I agreed. "It's a separate but connected issue."

"I did some digging on you when Amanda called."

"What did you find out?"

"A state attorney is looking at you right now. I'm not sure if he is working on charges or just trying to get a handle on you. Either way, watch your back."

"What kind of charges?" Amanda asked.

Garvin lifted his shoulders. "No idea. I got that from a little girl I see over in the AG's office."

"Great," I moaned.

"Seems like that might be a bigger issue," he pointed out.

"Depends," I countered. "If they throw me in jail and *Les Loups Noirs* wants to come after me, it would be a more dangerous place to be."

Garvin bobbed his head in agreement. "Listen, if it weren't for Amanda, we probably wouldn't be having this talk," he explained. "You're getting toxic. Whoever you poked with a stick is coming at you hard."

"I've noticed," I told him.

"Amanda's not always the best judge of character," Garvin commented.

"Hey!" she interjected.

"What about that asshole you dated before me?" he asked her.

"Mark," she said in a hushed tone.

"Bastard broke her finger," he informed me.

I glanced at Amanda, who dropped her gaze. When I turned back to Garvin, he told me, "He had to learn how to write with his left hand after I had a talk with him."

My right eyebrow popped up. "Is this your warning to me?"

"Do you need one?" he asked.

I shook my head. "If I ever hurt her like that, don't waste

your time breaking my hand," I suggested. "Come at me with more than that."

Garvin jutted out his bottom lip and bounced his chin on his chest. "Good to hear." He glanced at Amanda.

She replied, "Chase is a good guy, Garv. I promise."

"I recall hearing the same thing about Mark," he reminded her, saying the name "Mark" like it carried a bitter taste.

"Chase is the real deal," she assured him.

"Just 'cause you're seeing him don't mean you can't come visit an old friend," he noted with a suggestive tone.

I held my tongue, and Amanda gave me a sideways glance before she smiled at Garvin. "Right now, he's enough."

In that instant, I bit my lip, trying not to smile. It might not be the best optics to the big, tough street cop that I was smitten with his ex.

Garvin laughed. "Good. Chase here is about to bust open," he remarked.

Amanda leaned over and kissed my cheek. I broke out in the grin I was attempting to hold back.

"That's what I like to see," he joked. "You better watch this Baptiste, though. He's bad."

"Where do I find him?" I asked.

Garvin shook his head with a half-smile. "You were a Marine?" he inquired, nodding to the tattoo sticking out from under my sleeve.

"Good eye," I remarked.

"Eh, I was Army. You Marines always try to bulldoze a problem."

"That's 'cause we're normally coming to clean up after the Army," I quipped.

"Well, Baptiste has a small army," Garvin explained. "The influx of Haitian refugees over the last year has bolstered his numbers. We've seen a bump in arrests of alleged members of *Les Loups Noirs*. They are a tight-lipped bunch. Baptiste holds a heavy sway with these boys. Either it's fierce loyalty or fear. I doubt we've cracked a single member. Some bite their tongues and take the time like it's a weekend at the Hamptons."

"Ever been to Haiti?" I asked. "For some of them, it might be."

Garvin shrugged. "True. How do you fight that? These kids come in and can't find work—most have no green cards. Lo and behold, here comes Baptiste, offering them money and standing. Hard to say no to easy cash."

"Yeah, but at some point, you have to decide that what you do matters," I said.

"Ah, Amanda, you got an idealist," Garvin joked. "It's that unbroken sense of honor and stupidity prevalent in young Marines. Most never grow out of it."

"We can't all become jaded," I replied. "Someone has to do something."

Garvin turned up his nose. "Most don't, and they get along just fine."

I shrugged.

Amanda chimed in. "Personally, I'll take him," she remarked with a glint in her eye that brought a grin to my face.

Garvin watched my reaction and offered me a knowing stare. After a second, he said, "Hey, it's your funeral." Then he gave Amanda an intense smile. "When he's dead, perhaps we can hook up."

"Let me die first," I interjected.

"You seem intent on doing so," Garvin replied. "Just getting in line."

Amanda laughed playfully, but I sensed it was faked for Garvin's benefit. At least, I hoped that was the case.

"We don't know exactly where their base is," Garvin stated. "They float around. I think the last guy we thought was a wolf walked two days ago. One of our squad tailed him west toward the old Swampland."

"Swampland?" I questioned.

Amanda spoke up. "It was an amusement park back in the '80s. Wasn't it Hurricane Andrew that flooded it?"

Garvin nodded. "Yeah, they were over-leveraged and under-insured. The company never reopened."

"You think they're out there?" I asked.

Garvin shrugged. "My guess is someone is. Swampland is in Broward County. Doubt the Broward Sheriff does much with no trespassing complaints. People been going in and out of there for decades now."

"The owners don't care?" I asked.

"It's probably a single line in some corporate portfolio. Until some flunky comes along and wants to do something with it, no one will pay any attention to it." Garvin sipped his coffee with a smirk. "We can put surveillance on the property, but it's a huge tract. They could be anywhere in there, and that's assuming they are there. Could be a false lead. In which case, I got nothing for you."

"No bars they like to frequent?"

"We haven't found them," Garvin said. "I think this group stays tight with the community. If they want food or drink, they have it brought in. They run the girls, too."

"Do you have any idea which girls?"

"They cover the spectrum. Midwest white girls, local girls, and, of course, illegals. Most are underage or young. We aren't sure if they age out or what, but it seems some just disappear. They might ship them elsewhere, we don't know.

And we have a lady in vice that tracks them like they're on her fantasy team."

I cocked an eyebrow. "If you know they're there and minors, why leave them there?"

"What do we do? Haul them in? They never give us their real names, and if they don't match someone on the missing person's report, we put them in the system. Juvie facilities aren't the most secure. We save the ones that are for the violent criminals, not hookers. They take days, if not hours, to walk out. Doesn't matter if it's a foster home or group home. Most end up running away again."

"Some of those homes are just as bad," Amanda pointed out. "We've answered a few calls to those. It's not pretty."

"That's true. Our girl, Becky, goes out and talks to them. She's been able to track where a lot came from. If she runs across a girl who people say came from Wichita, then we know where to look."

"That seems risky," I said. "You can't be sure she'll stay safe while you look."

Garvin nodded. "True, but if they spook and run off, no one knows where they are. We've actually tracked down more families in the last year since Becky started this program. The woman is dedicated."

I smiled.

"What, Marine?" Garvin snapped.

"You have a soft side," I remarked. "It's cute."

"Oh, fuck you, asshole," he growled. "Where'd you find this guy?" he asked Amanda.

"She stitched me up after someone stuck me with a knife," I cut in.

"Can't blame them," Garvin said. "Amanda, you better keep your gear ready. He's not coming back after a fight with the Wolves without a few bites and scratches."

21

———

"You should have stayed home," I told Amanda.

"Are you kidding?" she said. "This is exciting."

"Well, I want you to stay in the car," I informed her.

She smiled. "Oh, I'm not suicidal," she replied. "Someone needs to call the cops when you don't come back out."

"You need to give me at least an hour. Probably ninety minutes."

"What's your plan?"

We waited in the front seat of her Toyota. Amanda sat behind the steering wheel, and we both stared across the parking lot at the dilapidated gates of Swampland. The giant sign had lost a couple of letters, leaving us with "Swa pl nd. A Gatorific Time."

Rising above the barricade, several rollercoasters loomed. The years had borne down on them, and even from a quarter mile away, I saw the flaking paint and rust resulting from decades of neglect. The parking area had been left barren for so long that a few volunteer trees sprang up in the fissures in the asphalt. Little saplings that fought through the tar and rock had crumbled the blacktop with their burgeoning roots. Weeds bordered the lot where manicured grass and landscaped flowers once decorated the land.

"It doesn't look like anyone's here," Amanda remarked.

"I don't expect them to park in the employee parking," I said.

"You should have gotten a phone or something."

"It'll be okay. I'll be in and out."

I had a simple plan. We'd scouted the amusement park, and now that the sun was setting, I wanted to use the night to mask my entry. This was going to be a reconnaissance mission. There was a solid chance that the only people hiding in there were a few homeless who had found their way into the grounds.

Recon or not, I checked my weapon, removing the M45 and ensuring my magazine was loaded. I chambered a round and holstered the gun on my hip. While I maintained a concealed carry permit, Florida had changed the law to allow anyone to carry. It didn't change much. The same people who armed themselves before still carried. Now, the people who had been breaking the law could display their guns with no fear of repercussions.

"If someone drives by, you get out of here," I warned Amanda. "If you aren't here, I'll take cover until dawn. Just come back by."

"What if they kill you first?" she asked. "I thought I was to call the cops."

"I doubt anyone will bother you, but be ready to bolt. Don't get trapped here."

"Roger," she agreed.

I leaned over and kissed Amanda before I stepped out of the Corolla.

"Be careful, Chase," she warned.

"Ten-four," I acknowledged, slamming the door.

When the developers built Swampland, they must have scored the land cheap because the theme park was far west into the rural sections of the county that bordered on the literal swampland. With no one tending to the lights and, more likely, no one paying the power bill, darkness shrouded the park. Moonlight illuminated the white paint of the tallest coaster. From the parking lot, it was hard to distinguish that the shape was a roller coaster. Had I not already seen it in daylight, I'd have struggled to identify it.

The trees tearing through the asphalt provided cover as I crossed the expansive empty lot. In an ideal world, I'd make this incursion around three in the morning. That was the hour when most people dropped their guard. Any roving patrols would be bored at that point, making them lax in their duties. Everyone else was asleep or had partied long enough to be incapacitated.

But since we weren't sure that Baptiste or any of his men were even here or that they were using Swampland as a permanent base, I might only discover an empty space with everyone home in bed. I didn't intend to engage with anyone, so as long as I stayed out of sight, I could map the park and track the Wolves.

The barricade, erected after the business closed, did little to prevent entry. Years earlier, someone snipped the chain link, allowing me to squeeze through it, rattling the galvanized fencing.

Reconnaissance required one to enter and leave without being noticed, all while taking in all the information needed.

I'd done my fair share, and if I was alone, my preferred tactic was a spiral that started on the outskirts. Each pass shrank the perimeter until I found what I was searching for.

When they designed this park, pedestrian traffic funneled into a line that wound through stanchions to the front gate. The uprights still stood sentry, although the lines between each post were long gone. I touched one pole, and it wriggled in its slot. The poles were intended for employees to pull them up and rearrange them as needed. It shocked me that nobody had stolen the poles.

In fact, I found it odd that no one had scavenged the park for scrap metal. Given that this was Florida, where I'd once seen a man unbolt the guardrail from the interstate to sell it for a few bucks, the fact Swampland was still intact seemed unusual.

I watched the front gate. It was the easiest entry point to the park. There were other entrances, but most had been employees only, and I'd be testing each one to see if they were unlocked. Besides, the issue with barred entries during a recon mission was problematic. One should never open a door unless he's certain what's behind it. Any one of these doors might take me inside, but they could put me anywhere.

After two minutes, I'd seen no one moving around, and I risked the dash for the turnstile. As I sprinted toward the entrance, I vaulted the gate without slowing down. As soon as my feet hit the concrete, I scurried to the nearest wall, where the shadows absorbed me. Then I waited.

A lot of warfare involved either waiting or not waiting. It sounded stupid to say it like that, but it proved to be the polar opposite. When in the middle of a gun battle, there was no pausing. It's high-pressure, full-on action. The reverse occurred when nothing happened. During that time, everything slowed down, and one's actions became more deliberate.

Once pressed against the ticket booth, I took a deep breath and scanned the courtyard. Open space was the enemy in a covert incursion. Someone running across an open field presented an easier target than the same man moving through a forest of trees. Whatever I needed to do, I wanted to take a beat before I decided my path.

Something chittered in the night, and my head snapped around. An animal somewhere had taken up residence in the overgrown area. Even in the dark, the cheesy décor from the '90s stood out. It reminded me of a similar amusement park we went to in Branson. I forgot the name of that one, but it featured some cartoon mascot from long before my time.

Swampland appeared to be laid out similar to other theme parks. The front had remnants of souvenir shops and food stands in a circular formation around the entrance, which acted as a funnel for the guests coming through the gate. At the center of the curve, the street narrowed into a lane with structures on both sides.

After a few seconds, my brain deciphered what I was seeing. Facades covered the buildings, with stores and eateries on the ground level. But the faces of the buildings had fake cypress trunks designed to mimic a swamp. A happy alligator wearing a straw hat and smoking a corncob pipe leaned against a log. The tip of his nose had been knocked off, leaving a flat end poking out. His white eyes glowed in the dark, and from across the galleria, it seemed as if the alligator was staring at me.

Nothing else moved in the area, and I skulked along the wall around the circular street. Had Swampland been open, I would have picked up one of the paper maps they kept at the front. Hindsight suggested I should have looked up an old map online. There was bound to have been someone who had saved an ancient copy.

Without a guide, I needed to survey the entire park to find the best location for *Les Loups Noirs* to hole up. The theme park was once a secured fortress, and it would have needed guards set up along the faux tree buildings. Anyone coming in would, in all likelihood, come through the front gate, and a single guard with a rifle could halt their progression.

It seemed no one had thought that way, though. If Baptiste and his *Loups* were here, they weren't in these buildings. That offered them a certain level of protection, too. The best method to stay hidden in a place this big was to burrow deep in the hole and wait.

I wagered on a different tactic. *Les Loups Noirs* weren't hiding; they were staking a claim. Since they had no one on guard duty, they either didn't feel like they needed it, or they weren't here. The latter seemed more likely. I'd seen no signs of them so far. Not even fresh trash, and the few Wolves I'd encountered didn't strike me as the type to be too concerned with littering.

Once I reached the end of the street, I came to an inter-section. The road resembled an old dirt road. Instead of actual dirt or gravel, brown rubber covered the pavement. It reminded me of the material installed on playgrounds to let the kids bounce when they tumbled off the monkey bars.

At the crossroads stood a sign fabricated to look like two hand-painted placards nailed to a pole. One sign pointed left, saying, "Ma Jessup's Fuming Flume." The other sign directed visitors to the right and stated, "Calvin's Crocodile Ranch."

I sighed at the cheesy signage before turning right

toward the Crocodile Ranch. My reasoning was nonexistent, but I wondered if the supposed ranch might have more buildings than what I assumed would be a log ride.

Something screeched in the distance, and I froze. The instinctual side of my brain didn't register the noise, and after my logical side factored it in, I realized I'd only heard an owl crying across the night.

As I crept along the pretend dirt path to Calvin's Crocodile Ranch, I marveled at how well-preserved the facilities remained. They carried the wear and tear of thirty years in the South Florida climate, but truth be told, they'd fared better than some buildings I'd seen built in the same time-frame. Perhaps its inland location allowed the park to avoid the worst damage from the heavy storms and salt air, but that didn't always offer adequate protection. The ultraviolet rays from the sun often did as much damage as the water and salt. Somehow, this park appeared to only require some weed control and fresh paint.

Of course, my assessment came while I was in the pitch dark of the shadows. I knew full well one couldn't just slap some paint on a building and start up an amusement park. All the rides would need complete refits and retrofits to bring them up to date. It would be a costly endeavor just to turn everything back on. Not to mention, Swampland had its own branding everywhere, including the many images of characters, like the smoking gator at the front. Whoever purchased it would have to revamp everything. At some point, tearing down the park might cost more than buying an empty lot of land to build on.

That was likely the problem with this property now. Anyone who bought it had to deal with the existing structures. At some point in the future, the earth would swallow this place up, but that would be a few more decades down the road. If the county ever wanted to find a user for the site, it might have to fund the razing of the buildings.

I heard the crack of wood behind me, and my head whipped around, scanning the sidewalk at my back. Shadows clung to the side of the building, and if someone were creeping up on me, those pockets of darkness were perfect cover. Just as I used them now.

Nothing moved. I held my position with my hand resting on the butt of the M45. In my mind, I replayed the sound.

Crack.

Or was it a *creak*?

I wasn't sure. It might have been something my movement knocked loose. Or it could have been a single footstep on the wooden path that acted as a sidewalk.

My eyes adjusted as best as possible, and I saw nothing in the dark. Was I overreacting? Resolute, I turned to continue along the walkway. My ears strained to hear the slightest motion as I moved with light steps.

Creak. Thud-thud-thud.

Then the window beside me shattered as a figure barreled through the glass.

22

The instant the window shattered, I jerked away, shielding my face. The last thing I wanted was glass in my eyes. That was a surefire way to lose any advantage I had.

As if I even had an advantage. Two arms wrapped around me in a combination of a bear hug and a full-body tackle. At the sound of the second creak, my legs braced. When the figure plowed into me, I rotated my hip to carry the weight with me. It was too big an impact to keep me on my feet, but by twisting with it, I carried my attacker around before I came off the ground.

My sore shoulder—the one I'd dislocated jumping from the car the other night—slammed into the rubber road. Luckily, my shift when he tackled me kept my assailant from landing on top of me. Instead, the pair of us spilled onto the street.

I ignored the twinge of pain as I rolled away from the shape. In the pale moonlight, I saw droplets of black sprayed along the rubber. With no time to check if it was me or him bleeding, I jumped up to my feet, reaching back for my M45.

My hand came up empty. My holster had nothing in it.

I'd been resting my grip on the butt, with the strap that buttoned behind the hammer left free. When I fell, the gun must have fallen out of its sleeve.

Across from me, my attacker shoved off the ground. He turned to leer at me. The whites of his eyes glared at me, and blood covered his face. I stepped back, planting my left foot at my back in case he lunged at me.

He snarled at me. In the dark, I saw only the yellow teeth and fury-white eyes. The air filled with the familiar coppery aroma of blood.

The man struck out at me with a wide haymaker swing. I dodged with a slight shift back. Infuriated, he charged at me again, and I caught his right wrist as he threw another punch. With a quick jerk, I pulled him off-balance toward me. Before he could recover, my elbow drove into his face with a resounding crunch.

The man recoiled with a howl that sounded like a wounded dog. In fact, he growled at me, retreating away from me into the street. Out of the shadows, I caught a better glimpse of his features. He was a white guy, not Haitian. His clothes were dirty and torn. Now, blood stained them.

"Dude, you're bleeding out," I warned him.

"Stay away from me," he howled, backing up.

"I'm not trying to hurt you," I tried to assure him.

He shook his head and turned to run off into the dark. Had anyone else heard his screams? I didn't need to stick around to find out.

My guess was he was one of the many forgotten people who wandered down to South Florida. Often in a drug-induced daze or in a mental fog, these lost souls settled in the gaps of the region, like this old theme park. One day, someone would find his body, and the best I could hope was that he found peace at that moment.

For now, I hurried from the broken window. If anyone had responded to the cries and sounds of broken glass, I needed to take cover. Without someone charging at me, enraged at my presence, I found my gun. It had dropped out of the holster when I rolled away from my crazed attacker.

I cross the rubber street, where a placard read "Swamp Sally's Mercantile." Most of the lettering had faded on this sign. Beneath the marker, I pushed my good shoulder into a door, breaking the jamb and my rule about knowing what was on the other side of a locked door.

Luck stayed with me, and inside, I found an old kitchen. Swamp Sally didn't have a general store, but she had a food stand that sold Gator Bites and hot dogs. The M45 remained in my grip as I cleared the building. It was a small space, and it took me only a few seconds to determine I was alone in it.

Then I waited, watching out the front window.

Only a couple of minutes passed before two figures strolled down the wooden walkway across the street. The pair didn't hide themselves, waving the flashlights on their phones around. I couldn't make out the features on either, but they were both black.

Once knelt down and peered at the shards of glass and blood. He looked at his partner and said something that the second man nodded at. The pair entered the building across the street through the broken window. Both shone their lights around as they inspected the space. One picked up a blanket and showed it to the other.

The two men climbed back out of the window and

looked up and down the faux dirt lane. One pointed at the ground, and I guessed it was the blood trail the homeless guy had left. I hoped they didn't follow him.

They seemed to discuss it before turning to head the way they came. When they were out of sight, I exited Swamp Sally's Mercantile and followed them.

I lingered about fifty yards behind them, keeping them in view. These two had the stealth features of a tuba. They kept their flashlights glowing as they walked, and their conversation, while audible, was indecipherable to me.

The pair meandered down the rubber road. I caught a whiff of marijuana in the air as the pair shared a toke. They passed under a sign declaring they just arrived at Calvin's Crocodile Ranch. Warning signs told visitors not to pet the errant crocs along the street. Statues of cartoon-like reptiles peeked out from the corners and under long dead bushes.

Light spilled into the night when they entered a door on a faux shack. I scanned around for more lights, but the park remained pitch dark. Somehow, they had power in that building.

I lingered in a nook across the street, watching the entrance. After several minutes with no movement, I made my way along the walkway. If I crossed the street here, I would put myself out in the open. Better to move down the lane and cross over in the shadows.

When I was fifty yards from the door, I gave the makeshift avenue through the crocodile ranch another look. It was still empty, and I ducked low before running across the street. Back in the darkness, I crept along the walkway.

A door opened twenty feet from me, and I froze, slinking back against the shadows. It wasn't the same door the other two had entered. This one was barely visible from the exterior. The park's designers had created the entry to look like another fake tree, obscuring it.

A lanky kid stepped out and lit a cigarette. When the tree door slammed shut, he plunged us again into darkness. Only the pinpoint orange glow from his cigarette showed in the shadow where he lurked.

The young gang member was so close that I could inhale a lungful of secondhand smoke. It wouldn't take his eyes much time to adjust to the dark enough to distinguish my silhouette. In fact, he faced me, and I wondered if he was trying to make sense of the shape in front of him.

As if to confirm my suspicion, the kid took a long drag on his cigarette and stepped in my direction. He came out of the shadow of the building as he walked down the walkway. So far, it was only curiosity that had provoked him. That itch one had to scratch when something made little sense.

I remained motionless, but it would only take another step or two for my features to become obvious to him. The M45 in my grip felt hot in my palm, ready to fire if the need arose. That was a last resort. A gunshot would only bring the members lurking indoors out. There were at least two others I'd seen go inside, but my bet was that there were more than that.

I had a quandary. This was to be a fact-finding mission. If the crew hiding here learned of my investigation, they might vacate their hideout, leaving me with no idea how to find Baptiste if he fled to another nest. Already, the homeless guy who'd encountered me could blow up my plan, but I counted on him staying out of sight of *Les Loups Noirs*, too.

Now, I had no choice. My covert mission was two steps from becoming an overt one. The only thing left to do was improvise.

So I did.

With only a slight movement, I turned the M45 in my grip. I sprang out, thrusting my right hand with the gun in it toward the glowing ember. The side of the handgun hit the tiny red ash cherry with enough force to knock the smoker back.

Smoky hadn't been prepared for the blow, and the impact struck him in the mouth, reeling him off his feet. I followed through with my left hand, formed into a tight fist. Smoky's head had snapped back from the first strike, and my second punch targeted his throat. The new angle of his neck presented the underside of his chin instead of the man's Adam's apple.

"Argh," he howled. "My tongue." It sounded like "Ny pung."

My right arm cocked back, bringing the M45 up by my head before I swiped it butt-first into his temple. The blow felled the Haitian, and he slumped over like a giant oak after a chainsaw sliced through the trunk. Smoky sprawled across the rubber street, and I thought he might be glad they didn't have a concrete road here to catch his face.

The entire ambush had taken less than three seconds, and Smoky wasn't moving. I knelt down, checking his pulse. He was unconscious, but still with me. A blow to the temple was often precarious and could cause massive brain trauma or even death. I didn't want to kill the guy, but I needed him out of commission.

After holstering my M45, I grabbed Smoky by the arm and hoisted him on my shoulder with the fireman carry. With the Wolf draped over me, I hurried toward the exit without lurking in the shadows.

I ran across the empty parking lot with an extra hundred and eighty pounds on my back. Amanda's car sat where I left her, and when I reached it, she saw me coming.

"What are you doing?" she demanded, eyes wide.

"Kidnapping," I explained. "Open the trunk."

"Who is that?"

"Not sure yet, but I plan to find out," I explained as she leaned back into the vehicle to get her keys.

"Isn't this a crime?" she asked.

"Well, I already assaulted the guy," I admitted. "No point in not committing to the full felon package."

"Just what I wanted in a man."

I dropped Smoky into the trunk with a thud. Amanda bent over and checked his pulse.

"I did that," I informed her as I patted down the man, retrieving a small snub-nosed Smith & Wesson 38 and a cell phone.

"You didn't search him first?" she asked.

"No time," I confessed. "I didn't want to be caught with him."

I slammed the trunk closed and dropped the phone under the rear tire. Once we drove off, it would be useless.

"Where are we taking him?"

"Someplace we can chat in private," I said. "Ol' Smoky here is gonna tell us everything we need to know about Lucien Baptiste."

23

———

"I don't want you anywhere near this guy," I told Amanda. "Stay out of his sight."

She puckered her lips into a pout. "You have him tied up," she pointed out.

"But I don't plan to kill him," I advised. "So, at some point, I have to let him go. If he knows your face, you might be at risk."

"Would he come back?"

I didn't think so, but thinking something didn't make it true. The kid was only twenty-one and scared shitless. That tended to happen when you were dragged off unconscious and kept disoriented. That was Interrogation 101. Don't give the subject time to develop clear thoughts.

Right now, Smoky sat in a chair in a ramshackle hovel off a dirt road in west Broward County. This area was all part of the wildlife refuge bordering the Everglades. It had taken an hour to find the perfect spot. I'd planned to just drag him out to the wilderness to ask him what I wanted to know, but Amanda found a trail that led to a tin shack.

My goal was to give him a sufficient scare to loosen his

lips. Smoky was too young to understand my tactics, and I could manage that. Besides, I'd seen the fear in his eyes when I pulled him from the trunk at gunpoint.

But that didn't mean he wouldn't get back with his pack and find some bravery. If he came after me, that was one thing. However, I couldn't protect Amanda all the time, so it was best to leave her out of it.

"Just stay out here," I pleaded.

With a resigned expression, she nodded.

I returned to the shack to see Smoky staring at me. His sclera was wide and bright with fear.

"Who are you?" he asked.

"I'm talking," I informed him.

He shook his head. "What do you want?"

"How many men were at Swampland?" I questioned.

Smoky didn't blink. "Are you a cop?"

"How many cops have you seen dragging suspects out to the Everglades to interrogate them?" I questioned.

He shook his head again.

"Exactly," I explained. "Let me ask you again: How many men are at Swampland?"

His eyes rolled up as he counted in his head. "Seven," he responded.

"Is Baptiste there?" I asked.

The kid's brow wrinkled, and he didn't answer.

"Is Baptiste there?" I repeated.

"Who?"

"Lucien Baptiste. He's your leader or alpha, or whatever you want to call him."

"Loup?"

It was my turn to give him a blank gaze. "What does that mean?"

"Loup. You're talking about him?"

It dawned on me. "Oh, he goes by Loup?"

"Yeah, that's what everyone calls him."

"He named the gang after himself?" I asked.

Smoky shook his head, confused.

"Where do I find Loup?"

"I don't know," he replied. "He just comes by sometimes."

"What happens there?"

"Where?" the kid stammered.

"At Swampland," I clarified. "What are you and your pals doing there?"

His chin vibrated with tiny shakes. I'd seen that look before. I'd asked something that would make him break some trust established by the gang. Cult psychology depended on that fear that any betrayal might as well be a complete violation of trust. Baptiste expected his crew to die before breaking their loyalty. That expectation came with a threat. *Tell anyone, and we'll kill you.*

It was a solid method for containing a secret. The technique improved when coupled with real-life examples, like finding someone who'd broken that trust and killing them for the rest to see.

The problem with loyalty like that was that it wasn't real. In the Corps, loyalty meant sacrifice. In *Les Loups Noirs*, it came at a price. I didn't need fear to test my faithfulness to my fellow Marines or my country. That was true loyalty.

What Lucien Baptiste engendered was nothing but fear. It was a strong motivator, but there wass no sturdy base to it. I only needed to create a bigger fear to topple it.

Smoky held fast to his belief that if he told me the details, then someone would kill him for it. I drew the M45 from my hip and leveled it at his right eye. From his perspective, he saw the gaping hole in the barrel hovering a few inches in front of his eye while his left could focus up the barrel to my stern countenance.

"You're thinking that if you betray Baptiste, he'll kill you, correct?" I asked.

He gave a microscopic nod, not moving his chin more than a millimeter.

"That's fair," I admitted. "He probably will. Of course, as I've already pointed out, I'm not a cop. So, nothing I do here has to be legal. That includes killing you."

"But..."

I shook my head. "Don't waste my time. Your friends are still hanging out at the theme park, so I can put a bullet in your head and go back to find someone with more incentive to live."

"I don't want to die," he mumbled.

"Then answer my questions," I said.

"They'll kill me, though," he whined.

"It's a quandary," I admitted. "My suggestion is that you worry about the immediate threat. I'll only kill you if I don't get what I want. Once you provide that, I'll cut you loose. The smart thing at that point is to run and hide."

"Are you going to kill Loup?"

I shrugged. "Depends on him."

"He won't give in," Smoky said.

"If I kill him, that probably saves your ass, don't you think?"

Smoky blinked. Several times in a row. He was processing my words.

"On the other hand," I continued, "if you don't tell me, I'll put a hole in your head and find someone who will."

I added a smile that spread across my face. Smoky swallowed hard.

"Do I need to repeat my question?"

"Heroin," he answered. "We move heroin through there."

I cocked my head. "Really?" I asked. "How does it work?"

Smoky shook his head. "I'm not in charge, so I don't have the details. We get a shipment in, and we divide it up. A couple of Loup's guys come pick it up."

"How often?"

"Every couple of days," he replied.

"When did you get the last delivery?"

"Yesterday."

"Meaning they'll get it up soon?"

Smoky nodded.

"When?"

"They never call. We just have to finish it before they get there."

"How long till you finish with this batch?"

"Tonight," he said. "We were almost done."

"Do they come right away?"

He shook his head. "Depends. Usually the next day."

"Where do they take it?"

"The street, I guess," he told me. "No one tells me anything else."

The M45 lowered in my grip, and Smoky released a breath of relief. "I don't want to die," he confessed.

"Can't blame ya," I replied. "Here's the deal. I'm going out, and while I think you realize what will probably happen to you if you return to Swampland, let me clarify it. I'll make sure everyone knows you rolled over on them, even if it's the last thing I do. Understand?"

He nodded, though with increasing fury.

"Once you don't return, your friends will go on high alert. If you show back up, you either have to confess that you ratted them out or wait until I strike and they figure it out on their own. Either way, it's a death sentence."

"I won't talk," he promised. "They wouldn't know I was gone. Doubt they noticed or cared."

"Still, you'll be staying here," I said. "If luck is on your side, I'll come and cut you loose later. How many of your friends are there tonight?"

"You can't leave me like this!" he cried. "What if I need to pee?"

"No one is stopping you," I pointed out as I stood up. "I'll bring you some water when I come back. But I'm going to need an answer."

"There were six of us."

"Only five left?"

He nodded.

"Good," I said, turning to leave.

"No, wait," he begged. "Let me go, please. I'll just run. I won't go back to them."

Staring at him, I shook my head. "Can't take that chance," I explained. "But I almost believe you."

"I will. I swear it."

I walked out of the shack, letting the tin door slam shut with a reverberating clang.

"Don't leave me!" he shouted from inside the dark shed.

When I got in the car, Amanda asked, "What did you learn?"

"Not much," I admitted. "But enough. They're bringing in heroin there."

"You gonna call the cops?" she asked.

"I doubt they'll do much," I said. "I can't exactly explain how I got the information, and that won't be enough to send them in."

"What are you going to do?"

"If Smoky isn't high enough on the food chain, then I go out and find a bigger lion."

24

No matter what one was doing after three in the morning, there was a stillness that hung in the open. If I'd thought Swampland appeared quiet at nine when I made my first incursion, it was a surreal, still life at a quarter till four. In less than a couple of hours, the first twinges of daylight would creep across the sky. Early risers would get ready for work. Coffee pots, triggered by a timer, would begin brewing fuel for those early birds.

In the wild, actual wolves were diurnal, expending most of their energy during the wee hours of the morning and after dusk. However, I wagered the crew from *Les Loups Noirs* didn't function that way. They partied late and slept in. Of course, that presumed the remaining members never sounded the alarm when Smoky went missing. It depended on how closely monitored the gang was.

Smoky said they'd finished repackaging the heroin, so I imagined they had reached a period of downtime between finishing their previous job and receiving the next shipment. It seemed unlikely that Baptiste instilled a level of discipline that kept the foot soldiers on alert. No, like too many, once the job ended, they broke out the weed and possibly some of the heroin for their own party. Given the pair I trailed last night were puffing joints while investigating the broken window left by the homeless man who attacked me, I bet they sank deeper into that party mode.

I made my way back through the faux dirt roads to Calvin's Crocodile Ranch. While my instincts told me there was no watch in place, I wanted to be sure. After three passes up and down the street in front of the door where Smoky came out, I knew if they had guards, they were so good that I never saw them. But based on what I'd seen from Smoky and the two toking patrols, that wasn't likely.

The door masquerading as a tree had no visual handle on the outside, leading me to assume it could only be opened from the inside. It struck me that it would make a better entry point, but I didn't like wasting time trying to figure out how to open it without a sound.

That left me with the obvious entrance marked by the "Swamp Rats Only" sign. I tested the handle, finding it unlocked. If I were in charge of this group, the lax security would trouble me. They thought they were secluded enough, or they felt they were untouchable. Either way, they hadn't performed the simplest of security measures—locking the door.

Music drifted out of the opening, and I turned away from the light as I pulled the door ajar. All I heard was rap music rattling through the thin walls. The door closed, and I took in the hallway until my eyes adjusted. Exposed studs faced into the corridor, with OSB plywood on the other side of the wall.

I removed my M45, keeping it low as I inched through the maze. The thumping bass from the rap song carried through the path from deeper in the building. I moved forward until I reached the first corner.

There were two ways to secure a building. With a squad of Marines, the task was fast, based on force and surprise. Alone, nothing moved that quick. I had no one covering my six, so I had to do that myself. My ears were my first line of defense. If I could hear the enemy before seeing them, I had a better window to react. Of course, bumping bass and loud music disoriented that sense, but I relied on it still.

At the corner, I paused, straining to listen for anything beneath the melody. The brain can decipher sounds that fall out of a pattern. The rap music became the pattern I listened to. If someone talked in the room, the cadence, rhythm, and tone would be out of sync with the music. At least in an ideal world. That was still reliant on the lack of operational security the Wolves displayed.

Strings of Edison lights, probably purchased at some big box store, trailed along the top of the wall. While they illuminated the corridor, they left shady gaps on the floor. They weren't dark shadows but dark spaces between the spotlight illumination. Overall, they made little difference, but I could use the ones at the corner to judge if anyone walked toward the bend in the hallway. If someone crossed paths with a bulb's beam, I'd see a fluctuation of some sort.

When nothing showed, I trusted there was no one around the edge. I followed the passage to a double door propped open by a five-gallon bucket of Corona beer cans. There had to be something heavier under the aluminum cans to keep the door from pushing the bucket away and closing.

Through the open doors, I saw three couches. Four sleeping soldiers stretched out on them, with a pair taking up one couch. All seemed deeply asleep, and the music came from a fifty-inch television hanging on the wall. The lights and the TV attached to two separate portable power banks. I'd seen similar battery packs around the marina. They'd become popular. Most could charge with solar or when plugged into an electrical outlet. Both were some of the bigger-wattage units that cost a pretty penny.

I moved through the room on the balls of my feet. I lift the M45 a bit, readying it to aim and fire if one of the Wolves woke up. Although, the two water bongs suggested they were zoned out, and they still had a small clear bag filled with weed next to two cheap gas station lighters. Everything these guys needed for a party.

Smoky said there were five of them, and I only saw four in here. There wasn't anywhere for the fifth to be sleeping, either. Not in this room.

A single door on the far wall was closed. It could be another room or an exit, although there was no exit sign over it. I wasn't certain what the building code down here would be, so I didn't want to base my actions off that.

I angled my head to keep both the door on the far wall and the sleeping soldiers in my sight. No one stirred. They had that partied-till-they-dropped-into-slumber look going on. That was good. Hopefully, if they woke up, the effects of the drugs would leave them in a stupor for a few seconds.

I counted three guns in view: two Glock 19s and a Smith & Wesson 45. One of the Glocks was within reach of a gang member stretched out on the far sofa. He'd removed it from his waist before passing out. I surmised the same of the guy who had set the Smith & Wesson on the floor. The third Glock jutted out of one man's waistband as he sprawled out in a slumped, seated position on the couch. It was a fair bet the fourth man had a gun that wasn't visible.

Their inebriation would benefit me, but it didn't protect

me. I once encountered an Army Ranger in Iraq whose aim improved the drunker he became. Besides, even stray bullets kill. If any of these four jolted awake, they'd most likely be shooting nothing but stray bullets.

Still, until I knew where the fifth man was, I didn't want to start a fight. Far better to know all the players and their positions before engaging in battle.

I turned the doorknob until I felt the latch click. There was a slight resistance in the hinges as I pushed the door open, and if the music hadn't been blaring, I thought there might have been a squeak as it opened. Darkness shrouded the area beyond the door, and I lifted the M45 as I entered the room. The light from the common area shone through the opening, offering me a glimpse into the room. Two mattresses sat on the floor against a far wall. Sprawled on one was a black man in boxer shorts that didn't hide anything he was packing. At least I couldn't see a weapon.

The light cast across his body, and he stirred. I started to pull the door closed before it woke him, then I saw a table in the corner stacked with what looked like bricks wrapped in white butcher paper.

"Kisa? Kiyes ou ye?"

My head snapped toward the figure, who pushed up on an elbow. The split second it took the man to say whatever he'd just mumbled and register that I wasn't one of his comrades took too long. By the time it clicked for him, he lunged across the side of his mattress. Before the Glock appeared, I squeezed off a shot that hit him in the center of his chest.

With four men behind me, I didn't wait to watch him slump over. I had no doubt I'd killed him, and if I didn't react, those stray bullets might catch me. The M45 retracted to allow me to spin on my right heel around without striking the door frame.

The man with the Glock in his front waistband jerked up from his reclined position. His eyes found me, and as realization dawned, he reached down his front for the pistol grip that poked out just below his navel. His hand just caressed the black finish when I fired.

The M45 bucked in my hands, but my aim remained steady. The explosion of gunpowder boomed through the room, and the slug struck the wolf in the face. My extended arm rotated right as a man stretched out prone on the far couch rolled off the furniture to grab the Smith & Wesson he'd left on the floor. He didn't make it farther than the floor when my next round hit him in the back of the head, spewing bits of brain, blood, and bone across the couch.

The other man lying on the sofa nearest to me copied his friend's movements. He was luckier, and the back of the sofa shielded him from me. It took less than a second, but that brief interlude hung in the air like a hot air balloon. The fraction of time rushed forward as he bounded up with his Glock in his grip. He pulled the trigger, but his muddled brain was off-target.

Mine wasn't. My shot hit him in the throat, and I followed it with a second round that blew through his nose. He flopped back before he crashed to the floor, dead.

The fourth man still sat frozen on the couch. He was the only one whose weapon I hadn't seen when I entered. Either he'd fallen asleep unarmed, or he'd just witnessed his three friends with guns die despite their weapons.

His pupils looked like pinpoints, and he held a dazed confusion in his eyes. He blinked twice before raising his hands above his head. I stared at the man for a full five seconds, trying to decide what to do with him.

Finally, I asked, "Is there anyone else here?"

He blinked twice more before shaking his head from side to side.

"What's your name?"

"M-M-Manno," he stuttered.

"How long have you been one of them?"

"Uh, a few months," he confessed.

"For your health, I'd suggest leaving this organization."

"But you can't leave," he muttered.

"I'm going to be honest with you," I explained. "I can kill you or let you go. If I choose to cut you loose, you better get as far from South Florida as possible."

He blinked twice again. Then he nodded.

"Where is Lucien Baptiste?" I asked.

"Loup?" he questioned.

"Yes."

"I don't know," he admitted, his voice shaking.

"Who would you call to report what happened, Manno?"

He glanced past me at the opened door where the guy in his boxers had been sleeping.

"Him?" I inquired.

He nodded.

"He will not help you, so who's next on your list?"

"Andre, I guess. But I don't have his number."

"That's problematic," I noted. "I should have shot you and kept Ding-A-Ling in there alive."

He shook his head, fearful that I'd changed my mind about letting him go.

"How would you tell him?" I asked. "If you can't call him."

"I guess wait for him to come get the stuff," he said after a pause.

My cheeks widened into a grin. "I'm going to let you live, but you need to deliver a message to your leader."

Manno blinked again. "What's the message?"

I stepped toward him and bent over to pick up one of the lighters sitting next to the bongs. My thumb snapped at the wheel, igniting the flame.

"Tell him he's out of business," I remarked in my most menacing tone. It came out with just the right level of cliché for the moment.

25

———————

Amanda's phone buzzed, and I felt her reach out from beneath the sheet to find the device vibrating across her nightstand.

"Hello," she murmured into the receiver. "Hold on." Her hand swatted at my back. "Chase, it's for you," she groaned.

I pushed myself into a seated position. Light streamed in from Amanda's window, and my internal clock told me we'd been sleeping for about four hours, making it just before noon.

"What?" I asked into the phone.

"You sound like you're asleep," Carlson suggested.

"I was trying to be, but you have this uncanny desire to disrupt me every morning."

"It's lunchtime," he pointed out.

"That's subjective," I advised. "What do you need, Detective?"

"I'm curious now if there's a reason you're still asleep."

"Besides being tired? No."

"So you weren't out and about in the middle of the night?" Carlson asked. "Because there was a fire at an old abandoned park this morning. Firefighters found four corpses and about three hundred grand's worth of burnt-up heroin."

"Hope they had ventilators on," I commented.

"The interesting thing is that the bodies belonged to *Les Loups Noirs*."

"The bodies did?"

"Don't be a smartass. The victims, okay?"

"So *Les Loups Noirs* started a fire?"

"Since the guys we found were all dead before the fire started, it seems unlikely."

"Oh?"

"You aren't surprised?" he asked.

"About what, Detective? Are you implying I might have something to do with it?"

"There was a witness," he stated.

"Detective, let's get real," I said, sitting up in Amanda's queen-sized bed. "Are you asking me if I was there?"

"Were you?"

"I was in bed."

"Exactly when did you go to bed?"

"I don't know. Around eleven."

"But you're still asleep after twelve hours?"

"Who said I slept that entire time? In fact, I'd say there was very little sleeping."

Amanda let out a muffled giggle into her pillow.

"Hmm," Carlson mused. "Our witness might suggest otherwise."

"No, they didn't," I corrected him. "Otherwise, you'd be here in person. Who was this eyewitness?"

"Homeless guy we found living in the park," Carlson stated. "Guy said someone tried to fight him earlier in the evening. Fellow got cut up pretty bad. Looked like he went through a window. He relayed that there's been a lot of activity there lately. The Haitians must have set up shop."

"But it burned down?" I asked.

"You aren't curious where the park is?" Carlson inquired.

"I'm patiently waiting for you to tell me," I explained.

"Fuck you, Gordon," Carlson barked, but I could hear a twinge of mirth in his voice. "They'll fish the bullets out of those boys. Wonder what we'll find?"

It wouldn't match my gun, I knew. At least not the gun I had on *Carina*. The one I'd used last night was wrapped in a towel and sealed in a Ziploc bag before I buried it next to a bridge near Swampland. I owned a couple of guns, including three different M45s that I'd picked up along the way.

"You'll have to let me know," I said nonchalantly. "I'm happy to bring my gun down for you to test against, assuming you get a warrant."

"I figured you'd be helpful like that," Carlson quipped.

"Always at your service."

"I assume *Les Loups Noirs* will be on the hunt for revenge. I don't think I'd want them thinking I was involved."

"Yeah, that might be problematic," I admitted.

"Gordon, these guys already took a hefty swing at you," he reminded me. "What happens when they try harder?"

"Hopefully, the local law enforcement can protect me," I replied.

"Does that mean you want a detail on you?"

I glanced over at Amanda. It didn't matter to me, but I was putting her in danger. "You could put someone on Amanda and Missy," I suggested.

Amanda sat up, turning to glare at me. It was hard to

take that expression seriously when she let the sheet fall away from her body and exposed her naked form.

"I don't want any protection," she scolded me.

"Fine," I rasped back. "Just Missy. Put an officer at the Tilly."

"Not at Amanda's place, too?"

"No," I answered. "I don't need anyone there. Somehow, I doubt Baptiste has the brains to track her down if she's not with me."

I didn't actually believe that, but Amanda had made it clear she didn't want protection. The one question I hadn't raised was why Carlson, a Palm County detective, was contacting me about a fire and multiple homicides in the next county over. Of course, had I asked that question, I'd signal I knew more than I let on. And what fun would this tango of words be with the detective?

"I doubt Missy will like having cops in the hotel," Carlson pointed out.

"No, she'll hate it," I agreed. "She's already angry with me, so tell her I insisted."

"Or I just don't tell her," he considered. "It doesn't have to be a uniformed officer."

"I love the way your brain works, Carlson," I said with a grin.

"Did you always work on the idea that it's better to ask for forgiveness than permission?" he wondered.

"Actually, no. I did what I was told in the Corps. Now, I don't have to."

"I'm struggling to believe that," Carlson said. "I'd like to connect today. You seem to turn over things I can't touch."

"I didn't burn down the building," I lied.

"Whatever. There's at least a quarter of a million dollars of heroin that's not hitting the streets. That's a win."

I didn't respond. The drugs were a big problem, but it didn't stop anything. All I did last night was poke a small hole in Baptiste's pocket. He'd lose some money, and it would piss him off. However, he'd bring more heroin in and set up a new distribution center before the week ended. At best, I'd caused a slight hiccup in the pipeline, but that was nothing to get excited about.

My worry was where Baptiste kept the girls. I didn't like the drugs, but it was the runaways he preyed on that ground against my nerves. Across the globe, people did awful things to other people. The average person might see a girl like Lyla or Diamond and assume they'd brought this life upon themselves when, in reality, they were just kids sucked into a maw that had spun out of their control. In some cases, the family situation the girls had escaped might have seemed worse than the life of slavery they lived in now.

"Baptiste is far worse than heroin," I pointed out. "He's connected to Clayton Connors and funneling those girls through that elitist's sex club."

"I'm working on that," Carlson assured me.

"To what end, though?" I asked. "Connors will not let you get close. If you keep digging, he'll come after you."

"I guess the chips fall where they fall."

Many people might make bold statements like that, but Detective Carlson seemed sincere. He reminded me a great deal of Jay as far as how he approached the law. He wanted to bring down Baptiste and Connors despite what the latter might do to his career. If Connors would go so far as to attack Missy and the Tilly Inn to get to me, then reaching out to the sheriff or a county commissioner to rid himself of a pesky detective would be a piece of cake.

I had the luxury of snubbing my nose up at the system. Carlson didn't. He seemed like a hard-working cog in the machine, and he had no control over who operated the entire thing.

"Meet me at that burger shack at the end of Flagler," Carlson said.

That was all the details I needed. The burger shack in question had no real name. It was nothing more than a tin building with a makeshift food trailer attached. The original burger joint had been called Tom's or Tim's, or maybe Todd's. The consensus wasn't sure, as it had been gone since a storm blew it away. Now, a new guy had shown up and started pushing good greasy burgers. The menu could not be more simple. Burgers. Fries. One could get cheese on it or double up on the patties, but the condiments remained the same: mustard, grilled onions, ketchup. The owner had even added a metal sign with John Belushi in his smock and apron with the words "Cheeburger, cheeburger."

"How about two?" I asked. "That will give me a couple of hours."

"Fine, I have some work to do," Carlson said before hanging up.

"Are you in trouble?" Amanda asked.

"Not at all," I said.

"I found that thrilling last night," she told me. "I mean, I've always realized what an adrenaline junkie I was, but damn, that was awesome."

She leaned over me and kissed me as she pressed her naked body against mine.

"I think I enjoyed this a lot more," I stated when she pulled away from me.

"That's the right answer," she said as she ducked beneath the covers, allowing her hair to drag along my torso.

My head arched back as a smile crept across my face.

26

"Let's say that hypothetically, I was in complete agreement with what happened last night," Carlson said as he plopped onto the wooden bench of the weathered picnic table. "Why would someone torch all that heroin?"

My hamburger steamed in front of me. That was quite a feat in South Florida, where everything seemed scorched by the sun. Even from my seat under the metal carport that the burger shack owners had added to provide shade for their outdoor diners, I watched the streams of heat rolling off the asphalt and distorting the air.

"It could have been a message," I suggested.

"Do you think Baptiste is going to take that message lying down?" he asked.

"If I were the one delivering it, I would hope it disoriented him. Left him reeling."

"I imagine it did," Carlson said, picking up his burger and chomping into it. Grease ran out the bottom of it in a small stream, pooling on the butcher paper that lined the red plastic basket. "He'll come charging back, though."

"That will be his mistake," I assured the detective. "He's been unchallenged so far. Even the cartel hasn't crossed him despite being obvious competition."

"Was it the cartel that burned the amusement park?"

"Could be," I agreed with a half-smile.

"Want to ask your buddy Moreno?"

"Sure. Would he shoot straight with me?"

"Can't say," Carlson said. "I don't know the guy."

"I doubt it matters who was responsible," I said.

"Yeah, tell that to the detectives investigating it," Carlson countered.

"I mean, dead gang members are better than dead teenage girls."

Carlson bobbed his head in agreement. "I get it, but some of those gang members are stuck in a situation not dissimilar to the prostitutes. This might be the only path they see to escape their situation."

I pursed my lips. It wasn't untrue. In fact, it was something weighing on my mind. Sure, those Wolves last night had guns and appeared to be working of their own free will. But then, when I met Diamond, she seemed to be doing the same. It shifted the idea of human slavery. Some of those boys from last night might have joined up with *Les Loups Noirs* when they were teenagers with little to no options. Yeah, they appeared to have more freedom because they had more responsibilities, but what choices did they really have?

The answer for me came just as simply. I'd faced off in war against ten-year-old kids armed with Kalashnikovs. It was an awful day when my squad killed four of them in a single gunfight. Had there been a better way, I would have taken it. Not one man in my unit cheered at the end of that day. The only thing we shared that night was despair.

And those kids' deaths hadn't been our fault. We hadn't armed them. In fact, we'd begged them to put down their weapons, to no avail. Did they believe the way their Taliban leaders did, or were they also victims of circumstance? The question persisted, and nothing I could do would solve that philosophical riddle.

Those kids in Afghanistan would have shot any one of us, just like the Wolves at Swampland. Of course, in both cases, my presence was the impetus to the gun battle. I would argue that the kidnapping and attempt on my life had started this.

"You're starting a war," Carlson noted.

"I'm not starting anything," I corrected him. "But if you want to speed this along, figure out who killed that girl."

"That's a dead end," he admitted. "All I have is a bunch of hearsay from you that I can do literally nothing with."

I nodded, already suspecting that was the case. "It was Connors. You need to speak to him."

"I plan to," he told me. "We're stymied by his lawyer right now."

"Start smaller," I suggested. "The bartender at The Azure Room, or another employee. Someone who will talk."

"Oh, I wish I'd considered that," Carlson moaned in a sarcastic whine. "I should totally do something like that. Oh, wait... we did that. Even the busboy has a thousand-dollar-an-hour lawyer on retainer."

"Guess Connors gets away with it," I commented. "Find someone who's benefited from The Azure Room."

"Oh, like another billionaire with a fetish for teen girls?"

"Might be a politician," I suggested. "There are a few in office now."

"Not sure I can flip one of those," Carlson sighed.

"A lawyer won't block me," I told him.

"You know that I cannot condone you harassing Clayton Connors."

"But if I did, I'd give you a chance to arrest him for killing me," I offered.

"That's not a lot of help here," Carlson refuted.

I bit down on the hamburger, feeling the grease and juice run down my fingers. Currently, I faced two fronts, and I wasn't sure how connected they were. Connors had Lyla killed, and judging from her body, it wasn't a crime of passion—although, who can judge anything nowadays? But it had struck me as someone tidying up. She was garbage that needed to be disposed of.

"The question I keep coming back to is why?"

Carlson swallowed his last bite. As he chewed, he asked, "What do you mean?"

"Why kill Lyla?" I clarified. "Connors has to come up against a lot of people. What did Lyla see that sentenced her to death?"

"Did she see something?"

"What else?"

"She fucked the wrong person?"

I shrugged. "But it's the same problem. This wasn't a psychotic murder. It was a cleaning. A sloppy one, too."

"If Connors had someone do it," Carlson said, "he'd have been pissed they handled it so poorly."

"Maybe the intention was to carry her out to sea, and something went wrong."

"Like, they tried to cut her throat, but she survived long enough to jump off the boat?"

I shrugged. "It's possible. If you don't cut deep enough, death isn't instant. She'd end up bleeding out, but how long would that take?"

Carlson tilted his head. "This is a good theory. No way to prove it, though."

I shook my head. "No. But it helps understand what happened. I thought dumping her in the lake was sloppy. They could have gone an hour out to sea and tied an anchor to her. No one would have found her."

"Ninety percent of the cases I solve are because of people either being stupid or fucking up. The rest are chalked up to luck."

"Don't be so hard on yourself," I admonished him. "I bet at least one percent are solved based on your deductive reasoning."

Carlson wrinkled his forehead and squinted at me. "I don't know you well enough to tell if you're full of shit or not."

"Good. Let's keep it that way."

With his burger devoured, Carlson folded his hands in front of his face. The index fingers on both hands formed a steeple he pressed against his nose. His eyes glazed over as he settled into some mental process he kept to himself. I finished my burger, leaving him to his silent contemplation.

After several minutes, he spoke. "Gordon, I don't see how we get to Connors. The *Loups Noirs*, yeah, we can catch them eventually."

"Perhaps," I considered. "But they seem to be operating under your nose."

He shook his head. "Gangs are tough. They get a constant fresh intake of kids, most of whom never break a serious law. Until they do. By then, it's almost always too late. They cross the line, and it's done. But the guys in vice and gangs struggle to make arrests. Add to it that nobody talks, it makes the task so much harder."

"It's a hydra," I pointed out. "Cut off one head, and two more grow back."

"Exactly," Carlson agreed. "Leaves us in a pickle."

I shook my head. "Not me," I replied.

His head bobbed thoughtfully. "No, I guess not you. Just don't let me have to investigate your murder."

"You'll have plenty of suspects," I said consolingly.

"Great," he muttered.

27

I needed a change of clothes and to pick up another sidearm. Amanda said she'd wash what I wore last night to get rid of the smoky odor. The middle of the day seemed like a safer time to pop into the marina and grab some extra things, so I borrowed Amanda's Toyota so I could head back out after visiting *Carina* and release Smoky from the hunting shack. While I didn't expect him to give me any trouble, I planned to be ready for it.

My head stayed on a swivel as I left *Carina*. Before getting off, I locked the cabin up tight and loosened the dock lines enough that *Carina* drifted a few feet away from the dock. She remained secured, but now anyone who wanted to get on or off her had to pull the lines to drag the hull closer to the dock. It wasn't foolproof, but it created an inconvenience. I was often surprised by how often people skipped the inconvenient things.

One thing the Tilly provided was storage lockers for some of the liveaboard tenants willing to pay a few dollars more to access a small closet near Randy's office. I'd negotiated the space with Randy and Missy as part of my free rent.

It became, among other things, my weapons cache. Over the years, I'd picked up guns and weapons that I just didn't have room for on *Carina*. Besides, whenever I sailed to any other country, they frowned on bringing weapons over the borders.

I always had one or two handguns, usually an M45 like the one I'd carried the other night. In my locker, I kept plenty of ammunition, along with an array of rifles that saw little use. I didn't hunt, and unless I planned some target practice, they didn't get dragged out.

All I wanted from my weapons closet was extra ammo. I snagged two boxes of .45 hollow points and threw them into my backpack, which also had my extra clothes. As I turned to leave, I grabbed a switchblade knife and placed it in the back pocket of my shorts. It wasn't much, but it could do some damage in a pinch.

There seemed little point in visiting the Tilly. After the run-in at the Manta Club and subsequent argument with Missy, I didn't think I needed to show my face. I skirted the building on the sidewalk that led to the parking lot.

I spotted a Mercedes idling across the street. The vehicle itself fit in on Flagler with the business crowd; however, it sat on the curb in front of a juice store that had gone out of business. That in itself wasn't curious, but the location offered a hundred-and-eighty-degree view of the street and front of the Tilly Inn. It was the parking spot I would want for long-term surveillance. Then there was the fact that the car sat idling and a single individual was in the driver's seat.

The hairs on the back of my neck straightened. Without turning to stare, I got into the Toyota, throwing my bag onto the passenger seat. As I buckled in, I removed the M45 from my waistband and slid it into the space between the driver's seat and the center console. When I pulled out onto Flagler, I drove south, passing the Mercedes.

A quick glance assured me the driver wasn't Haitian. He was a white guy in his forties, and he had the seasoned look I'd seen on many former military operatives. Even the swift sideways flash I caught suggested to me he wasn't a cop. As if the Mercedes didn't give that away.

After I made it halfway down the block, he pulled out into traffic. He'd tried to wait until a wave of vehicles got between us to make a U-turn to follow me. Unfortunately for him, I remained focused on him when the group of cars behind me passed him.

Satisfied that it wasn't one of Baptiste's *Loups*, I reviewed the gamut of who might be following me. The Mercedes suggested it wasn't one of Carlson's guys. They might use a luxury sedan for a drug bust or some undercover operation, but employing one for casual surveillance was unlikely.

I still had the matter of that target Clayton Connors had painted on my back. Someone gunning to collect a hundred grand might be waiting for his opportunity. I reached down and touched the butt of my M45, feeling a sense of relief.

If I had a way to contact Carlson, I would drive this fellow right into the police's outstretched arms. That wasn't an option, and once more, I questioned my decision to not have a cell phone.

One thing I would not do was let him play this out on his timing. Besides, I didn't want any innocent victims to get caught in the crossfire. It seemed if I had to go make sure Smoky went free, it would be at an isolated place to handle whoever was stalking me.

I turned west and started out of the city. The guy in the Mercedes was good. He trailed far enough behind that had I not known he was there, I wouldn't have seen him. In fact, multiple times, he seemed to vanish. While I considered slowing down to allow him time to catch up, that might tip my hand. I decided either he was good enough to keep up or not.

He showed up every time, though. That made him very good. Still, given that he was half a mile back, I strained to let him keep up with me without looking like I was trying to let him keep up.

When I reached the dirt road we took last night to the hunting shack, I figured he'd drop back even more. As the route became more rural, it would be far more difficult for him to remain unnoticed. I imagined he was questioning his vehicle choice now. At the heart of West Palm Beach, a Mercedes blended into the scenery on Flagler. At least, that was the intent. In the swampy stretches of West Broward County, a high-end sedan didn't fit. This was off-road country, even if we stayed on the old hunting road.

In my rearview mirror, I saw only clouds of dust trailing behind me, as if I had initiated the smokescreen feature on my spy Toyota. It meant I couldn't see through the dust for my tracker. That also ensured that he only saw the cloud, and when I saw the trail leading off the road, I took it. Calling it a trail was generous, though, because the Toyota squeezed through the trees wide enough to fit an ATV, but anything wider than the Corolla would scrape the sides of the doors.

I was out of the car as soon as I came to a stop. It took the Mercedes five minutes to catch up. He'd hung back on the road, giving me time to widen the gap between us. That prevented me from spotting him on the back roads, but more importantly, it gave the dust cloud ample opportunity to settle some.

Hunkered down in the ditch beneath a thicket, I

watched him roll past at only ten to fifteen miles per hour. The Mercedes passed the turnoff I'd made and traveled about a hundred yards before it stopped. The car idled on the side of the road for two minutes. Technically, it idled for two minutes and thirty-seven seconds, but that didn't matter. Then his reverse lights came on, and he started backing up.

Though the majority of the dust had settled, the air became clearer after the trail. Kudos to him for noticing the change. Or maybe he had a GPS tracker on the Mercedes. I doubted that was the case, or he'd have kept an even greater distance between us.

The Mercedes stopped at the head of the ATV trail, and I watched the man get out of the vehicle. He stared at the path and glanced back at his car, weighing his options. Did he want to drive his rather expensive car down a narrow dirt path?

Dressed all in black, he looked like a hitman. Most likely, he bought the black t-shirts online with his black fatigues. Probably the same place he ordered his ammo. I estimated him to be in his early forties. The short haircut, combined with blond dye, masked the graying hairs. Or they would if he'd maintained his coloring regime.

He removed a Ruger 22 pistol with a silencer. I watched him unscrew the suppressor. That was smart. If we'd been in the city, the small-caliber pistol had been designed for an up-close kill, and the suppressor did more to protect the assassin than it hindered in accuracy. After all, how accurate did one need to be at three or four feet away?

But out here in the woods, he had no guarantee he'd get that close. The Ruger was pretty decent, but if he took a shot at any distance, he'd want every advantage available. The suppressor would only impair his precision.

He holstered the Ruger on his waist and removed a

semi-automatic rifle I thought was a Knight's Armament SR-25. The rifle gave him far more reach and better aim. Now he only needed to find me first.

The SR-25 was accurate, more so if mounted on a tripod. He had large optics attached to the rail, and judging from the size of the scope, he didn't need to get very close to me at all. I found his choice of weapon disconcerting, but at least I knew where he was.

He flipped the SR-25 over and caught it with his right hand on the grip. With the gun in a two-hand carry across his chest, the assassin strode into the woods. Before he disappeared into the trees and out of my sight, I bounced up on my feet, moving in a crouched position.

I moved my feet slowly, making sure to land each step on the outside of my foot and rolling my sole down flat. Most people traipsed through the woods, thinking they weren't making any sounds when the crunch of leaves and twigs underfoot carried through the trees. The fox walk I was doing curtailed some of that noise. It wasn't something one could do in a hurry, but taking each step mitigated a lot of sound.

I wasn't too concerned with the hitman getting a lead on me. He would be moving cautiously, too. If I'd been him, I'd pause every ten to twenty feet to scan the woods for any movement. When I saw him do just that, I resisted the urge to smile.

Instead, I straightened up and aimed my M45 toward the killer, who leaned against a dead cypress tree with the SR-25 raised and his eye pressed against the scope. The Toyota Corolla sat two hundred yards down the trail, and he focused on the vehicle as I stared down at the sights.

I steadied my breath. There was no reason to rush this, and I trusted my marksmanship. The only thing preventing me from squeezing the trigger was the little voice in my head that wondered if I should keep him alive to question him.

After at least three seconds of consideration, I chose not to spare him. After all, he wouldn't do the same for me, would he? And what questions did he have answers to that I didn't already know? Clayton Connors had farmed the hit out, though I thought it unlikely that this man even knew that. He'd gotten the job through a third party and would deliver the results through the same contact. There was no way I would connect him directly to Connors. The mogul was too smart for such a mistake.

Once I cleared that moment of indecision, I sucked in a breath and held it just before I pulled the trigger.

Then he moved. In a sudden flourish, he swept around a hundred-and-eighty degrees toward me.

I fired half a second before he did.

28

———————

We both missed.

When he moved, his entire body shifted about six inches to the left. Since he hadn't had time to aim, his shot hit the tree next to me. The .308 bullet blew chunks of dried bark out like shrapnel. I fired again as I broke into a run.

We had twenty-five yards between the two of us, and in that chunk of woods, there had to be close to a hundred trees of various sizes. A few old cypresses and oaks provided a wide enough trunk for protection, but I kept moving.

I moved the M45 to my left hand. It felt awkward to fire from my nondominant hand, but at this point, accuracy seemed less important than preventing him from taking the time to get a clear shot. It would only be a second or two before he realized I was way off-target, but during that brief turn, he'd take cover and not fire on me.

Or so I hoped.

The SR-25 sounded like a cannon in the dead quiet of the swamp. The resounding boom stopped my heart, and that little voice that earlier questioned me about leaving this assassin alive now shouted for me to keep running. Everyone knows a moving target proved harder to hit, but not impossible.

When the three-inch diameter sapling to my left exploded, severing the tip from the bottom, I knew I was facing a top-notch sniper. Had that tree not been there, the bullet would have hit me.

Another crack echoed through the forest. I dove through a bramble of thorns and scrambled across the mucky earth. In ten seconds, I belly-crawled thirty feet as the barbs on the plant sliced at my arms and face.

When I stopped, I rolled onto my back and held the barrel of the gun, ready for anyone who approached. The trees made no sound, remaining silent after the eruption of battle. The lingering ringing of the gunshots appeared to be the only sound.

We played a waiting game now. Mr. Mercedes had time to take cover, and with the scope on the SR-25, he only needed to wait for me to raise my head. This wouldn't be an unfamiliar situation for him if he were as accomplished as he seemed. Snipers had the perseverance of Job and might hunker down for days. It was a skill that my buddy Jay often pointed out I lacked. I disagreed with him. I thought I had an increased level of patience compared to the average person.

My other option was to slink out of here on my stomach. If Mr. Mercedes had equipped his rifle with thermal optics, he would have no trouble finding my heat signature. As long as I stayed as low as possible, my heat signature might be unrecognizable.

The canopy overhead didn't help matters. If I'd taken refuge in a dry gulch in the open, the ground temperature might hide my heat signature. Not completely, though—I would be like a well-camouflaged animal. As long as I remained motionless, my heat signature should blend in with that of the surrounding earth. However, in the shade of this swamp, my red blob would stand out as soon as I raised myself up.

He might not have a thermal scope.

The voice didn't come from the logical center of my brain. I wouldn't have called it my emotional self; I envisioned my two sides more like the angel and devil that sat on Bugs Bunny's shoulders. Only mine didn't portray good and evil, but logical and instinctual. They balanced each other out, with the angelic logical side cautioning my risk-taking demon side. Sometimes it took listening to both sides of that yin-yang argument.

The odds seemed up in the air. If Mr. Mercedes was a professional or just well-trained, I had to assume he had the best possible weapon. But he might also be confident in his abilities. I suspected he thought this would be an easy hit with a nice payday. However, I didn't keep up with the going rate for assassinations. Part of me hoped I'd garner a high fee, although my logical angel pointed out that such a wish was counterintuitive to my survival.

So I waited. He waited. And ten minutes ticked by. The birds, blessed with short-term memories, apparently thought the loud sounds from earlier must have all left and began to resume their calls.

The brush shrouded me but also prevented me from seeing past it. My only defense was my ears, and I strained to listen for the slightest crunch of a twig or leaf. My arm remained raised the entire time. I didn't plan to allow Mr. Mercedes to walk up to me without being prepared to shoot him.

Ten minutes lasted an eternity. Most people couldn't stay

alert that long. They could muster a two-minute plank before they get antsy and give up. I didn't. Instead, I focused on my senses.

The birds and bugs chirped. I inhaled the scent of dirt and foliage. Some floral notes filled the air, although I couldn't identify what they might be. Somewhere, a trickle caught my ear. It sounded like a very light stream of water bubbling close to me.

Slowly, I rotated my head around. I saw nothing in my sight, but my vantage point was from the ground. When I turned back, I found myself still alone. Mr. Mercedes hadn't come closer. Or at least not where I spotted him.

The next ten minutes passed slower than the first, but now my ears focused on that trickle. In my mind, I envisioned a stream, although it might have been a puddle. On the edge of the Everglades, water was abundant. If I found a deep enough flow, it might provide an escape route downriver.

Of course, this is South Florida. Anything deeper than six inches of water was guaranteed to contain something. Still, that prospect sounded better than being shot. I thought so, anyway. I'd been shot before but never bitten by a gator. The latter sounded worse. However, my odds with an alligator would be higher than with a sniper.

Most people didn't realize how rarely an alligator attacked, much less killed, an adult. There were some big enough to do so, but most would just as soon leave a person be. The sniper, on the other hand, was only looking for a split-second appearance in his scope.

Nothing happened, and I realized I needed to move from my location. Of course, it was what Mr. Mercedes was waiting for. I assumed he'd pinpointed the general area where I'd taken cover. He had the better position, and I found myself trapped.

That left me with either waiting until he gave up and came for me or changing my position. Neither option was great, but I liked the idea of not hanging around. That reasoning was what Jay told me was my weakness. It made sense. I preferred to be on the offensive, and whatever I needed to get on the attack, I would do.

I broke my vigilance long enough to track the source of the water. If my estimation was correct, the gurgling came from about sixty feet to the north of me. At a full-speed crawl, which wasn't quick, I could make it in twenty to thirty seconds. That was a lifetime—literally—when in the scope of an assassin. He only needed half a second with me in his crosshairs to end me.

Before I launched into my belly run, I wondered how long before someone found Amanda's car out here. At least a couple of days, I suspected. All traces of my killer would be gone by then. Hell, those alligators that wouldn't attack me alive would have no qualms about dragging me off after I expired.

That prospect sounded terrible. I found it strange how my brain had created a hierarchy of ways to die, but it was the postmortem treatment of my corpse that disturbed me.

Just don't let him kill you. That sage bit of advice came from the devilish, risk-taking voice.

In a burst of speed, I slithered forward. In five seconds, I covered ten feet when all hell broke loose.

Hell came out in the form of a gigantic swamp rabbit. It must have hunkered down itself during the gunfight. The furry creature had more patience than me, staying motionless until I crawled up on it. A blur of fur shot off like a cannon away from me. My brain barely registered what it had been when Mr. Mercedes fired.

I didn't know what he saw, but I suspected it was the sudden flurry of movement. He might have been tracking my movements by watching the motion of the brush and vines I was climbing through. When the rabbit broke cover, he tracked the movement and opened fire.

I rolled over with my M45 raised. The mangled body a few feet from me was all that remained of the creature. Mr. Mercedes had hit his target, and I guessed he did so without getting it lined up in the scope.

Could he see it now, though? That made the next few seconds and even minutes vital. If he realized he'd only killed a rabbit and not me, he would go back to waiting. Now that I'd seen how talented the man was, I didn't like the idea of offering him another chance at me.

Again, we waited. Ten minutes. I remained motionless, with my M45 at the ready. The muscles in my right arm burned as I held the pistol aloft. Twenty minutes passed, and I still maintained my position.

Twenty-eight minutes ticked by before I heard the twig snap. It was barely audible, but I could tell it was close. I swallowed and waited. Mr. Mercedes stepped closer. I couldn't hear him, but the low, buzzing din of insects tapered off.

Another crunch of a leaf underfoot sounded. It was almost on top of me. The devil's voice shouted, *Now!* I sat up, saw the shape in the trees, and fired three shots.

Mr. Mercedes was only fifteen feet away, but he'd stalked toward the fallen rabbit. His head swiveled as I sprang up, but before he could turn to aim, my three rounds hit him. The first round didn't kill him, but it tore through his neck in a spew of gore. The other two struck him in the torso, knocking him to the ground.

I let out a breath as I held out the smoking handgun. When I stood up, I saw the man clutching at his throat. Blood puddled in the swamp dirt. He had seconds before he bled out, and in those last bits of life, he stared at me with a dumbfounded expression.

"You shot a rabbit," I told him.

He said nothing back.

29

Before I left Mr. Mercedes in the swamp, I rifled through his pockets, removing his cell phone, almost five thousand in cash, car keys, and his wallet that contained only a driver's license. One that looked legit, but I would bet money was an elaborate fake with the name "Jacob Williams." He had no other identifying marks.

Out of sheer curiosity, I traipsed through the trees to locate the trickle I'd heard earlier. Sure enough, a small stream of water cut through the woods. By small, I meant an inch-wide line of water that dribbled between the brush and into a pool about eight feet across. The pool was covered in intertwined vines and sprigs sprouting along its banks. I was relieved I hadn't had to crawl through that to find whatever made its home in that oversized puddle.

However, it was the perfect spot for Mr. Mercedes. I dragged him over, pushing him through the branches and vines. He splashed face-first into the water, and I pulled the brush closed around him. It might take some time before someone discovered him.

The cell phone was probably a burner, and when I

opened it, I discovered only one number in the call history. More confirmation it was a prepaid one. Disposable or not, I had no intention of carrying it around for long. Mr. Mercedes struck me as the type to protect his privacy, and it was unlikely anyone was tracking this phone. But on the off-chance they were, I pocketed it.

I shouldered the SR-25 and carried everything back to Amanda's car. Once I stowed it, I got in the driver's seat and backed out of the woods on the same trail until I was back on the gravel road.

Amanda had pulled through for me, and I found a box of latex gloves in her glove compartment. In fact, that might be the first time I'd ever seen gloves in a glove compartment. After I donned a pair, I walked to the Mercedes and drove it toward the highway. I parked it on the side of the two-lane with the keys in the ignition. Before I abandoned it, I wiped the car down.

A twenty-minute hike took me back to Amanda's Toyota, and I went on to release Smoky from the hunting shack.

"I thought you left me here to die," he groaned.

"Sorry, something held me up," I told him as I cut him free.

"Looks like you've been rolling in the mud," he observed.

"Here, I brought you a water," I offered, handing him a bottle. "You have a long hike ahead of you."

"You're just leaving me out here?" he asked, groaning again.

"Can I assume you plan to head out of Florida?" I said. "Right now, I suspect that your esteemed leader isn't happy with you. After all, you are the only survivor after someone torched all his heroin. I wouldn't want to cross paths with him if I were you."

"Yes, I'm leaving," the Haitian swore.

"Good. If you're lucky, you can find a car and drive far from here."

"But I have family."

"What is Baptiste going to do to your family if he thinks you betrayed him?"

Smoky didn't answer.

I gave him a smile. "I hope I never see you again," I remarked as I left him alone in the shack.

Two minutes later, I was heading back toward civilization. My arms were sore, and the hundreds of little scratches across my face and arms made it look like I'd lost a catfight. Plus, mud and leaves were stuck to me.

Five miles down the highway, I broke the law and tossed the wallet with Jacob Williams's driver's license out the window. I frowned on littering, but being caught with the identification of a man I just shot seemed worse. I decided to go out this week and pick up some roadside trash to make up for my discretion. Especially since I repeated the action with the burner phone as I crossed the stormwater treatment canal. I sent it flying from the car into the drainage ditch. Again, I felt guilty, but if someone were tracking it, they would lose it here.

"Where the hell have you been?" Amanda demanded as I came through her front door. She stared at my mud-caked clothes and scratched-up face. "What the hell happened to you?"

"Someone tried to kill me," I stated. "You mind if I use your shower?"

"If you expect to get close to me, you better wash up," she replied.

I started stripping my clothes off, depositing the M45 and my wallet on the counter.

"Chase, you got cuts all over you," she remarked. "What did that?"

"Thorns, mostly," I explained.

Amanda trailed behind me as I entered the bathroom. With two fingers, she lifted my muddied clothes and asked, "What happened?"

I turned the shower on and waited for the water to warm up before stepping inside.

"Picked up a tail at the Tilly," I told her. "I had to go back out and cut our friend free, so I tried to trick him. It didn't work out like I planned."

"You're still alive," she pointed out.

"Yes. It worked out even worse than my assassin planned."

"And the guy in the shed?"

"He was okay when I left him. Hopefully taking my hint to book his ass out of town."

"Chase, this is getting a bit much," she declared, holding my dirty clothes. "I'm going to throw these in the laundry."

"I agree. It's time I have a heart-to-heart with Clayton Connors."

"What about the gang?"

"At this point, I'm not sure who should take priority," I admitted as I lathered soap on myself. "*Les Loups Noirs* seemed like it was more pressing, but the guy today almost did me in."

"He wasn't Haitian?"

"No, but we didn't have time to chat," I told her as I rinsed the suds off my skin. "I don't think I should stay here, though."

"You can't go back to *Carina*," she warned. "You just said this killer was waiting for you there."

"I know, but Connors is smart. He pulled my military

file. That takes clout. He arranged for both the health department and Alcoholic Beverages and Tobacco to do a surprise inspection. More clout. There's no doubt he can figure out that we're dating."

"I'm fine," she insisted. "I've been taking care of myself long enough."

A sigh escaped my mouth, and Amanda twisted her face.

"Chase, I'm going to assume you don't think I can't protect myself."

Knowing a booby trap when I saw one, I shook my head. "Not at all," I replied. "You should just be careful."

"If I was careful, I wouldn't be dating you," she retorted. "Now, dry off."

She watched me turn the water off before walking out of the bathroom. As she passed the counter, she grabbed my clean clothes and carried them out.

"I'm going to need those," I called as I pulled a fresh towel off the rack.

"Not for what you're about to do!" she shouted back from the other room.

A smile spread across my face. "Hey, does this mean we're officially dating?"

"Don't ruin it," she warned me as a knock sounded on the front door.

I listened to her footsteps, wrapping the towel around my waist as she walked across the apartment to answer the door.

"Who is it?" I asked, walking out of the bathroom.

"No one," she answered. "Probably a kid running down the terrace."

I stopped in my tracks. It was the middle of the school day, and Amanda's complex was an adult-only apartment building. My skin prickled, and I turned toward the bathroom, where my M45 rested on the counter.

"Don't move," a deep voice said before I retreated back into the bathroom.

When I spun around, I saw a large brute of a man. If he had been painted green, I might have mistaken him for a young Lou Ferrigno. Lou had a partner about half his size with greased black hair. The runt wore a gray sports coat over a black t-shirt. He had a SIG Sauer nine millimeter pointed at Amanda.

Lou folded his massive biceps across his chest. He hadn't bothered with anything but the black t-shirt, and he'd chosen a size that was a little too small for him. The result was his pecs popped out. The effect was intimidating. Or, at least, that was the intent.

"Why don't you get dressed so we don't have to see your dick?" Lou suggested.

"I can show you mine if you show me yours," I replied. "I've always been told steroids make it shrink. Do you find that to be true?"

"This can go a couple of ways," Lou explained. "You can cause me trouble, and I'll crush your head. Then my pal Davey can fuck your little princess to death. Or you can shut your mouth, get dressed, and come with us."

"Where you'll kill us somewhere quieter?" I asked.

Lou shook his head. "I'm only delivering you to the boss."

"Would that be Clayton Connors?"

"Get dressed now!" he ordered in a threatening tone.

"You mind if I pee first?" I asked.

Lou smiled. "Just pee where you stand."

"C'mon, I'm not an animal," I argued, turning toward the bathroom.

"If you take a step toward that door, Davey will shoot her in the head."

I gave Davey a hard stare. His beady eyes didn't blink, and his intent matched Lou's words.

"Fine, I'll hold it," I conceded. "I'll go along peacefully. Just let her go."

"Sorry, boss said bring her along," Lou explained.

I grabbed the pile of clothes Amanda had stolen from the bathroom. There was something in the front pocket, but I resisted the urge to remove it. Instead, I slipped my legs in and pulled them up around my waist. With the shorts on, I recognized the object. Amanda must have moved the switchblade from my muddied clothes to my shorts.

Unlike Lou, I bought my shirts bigger, and this one hung down over my pants, covering any sign of the knife. Mud covered my sneakers, and I reached for them.

"Find something else," Lou ordered.

"What?" I asked, holding the mud-caked sneakers.

"You aren't wearing those in my car," he demanded.

"It's all I have," I argued.

"Find something else," he repeated in an unwavering tone.

"I think my flip-flops are in the bathroom," I told him.

Lou smiled and waved me toward the door. But before I reached it, he clamped his hand down on my right shoulder. "Why don't you wait right here?" he suggested. "Davey, if he moves even his head, shoot the bitch."

Davey nodded, pressing the barrel of his SIG against Amanda's temple. I didn't move.

Lou stepped into the bathroom and chuckled. When he came out, he had tucked my M45 into the front of his waistband. He held a pair of black flip-flops in his right hand.

"Was this what you were looking for?" he asked, tossing me the sandals.

I slipped my feet into them with a shrug. "Can't fault a guy for trying," I said.

"You might live to regret that," Lou quipped with an eerie smirk on his face.

"Let's hope so," I countered.

"We're going to the car. Davey will shoot your girl before he does anything else. Do you understand?"

I nodded.

Lou's half-smile lingered. "Are you sure? Because you've developed a reputation. Whatever you do better be faster than Davey's finger."

I stared at Davey, who held Amanda tight. His expressionless face scared me more than Lou's impressive size.

"Don't worry," I assured the pair. "I'll cooperate."

I expected to be shoved into the back seat with Lou. Instead, as we approached the hunter-green Jaguar XF, Lou directed me to the driver's seat.

"I'm not exactly the best driver," I pointed out.

"Well, you better not scratch it," Lou reminded me as he slid into the passenger's side. Amanda and Davey got into the rear, Davey still holding the SIG pressed against Amanda's side. At least it wasn't her temple.

"Now drive," he ordered.

"Where to?" I asked. "I might need a GPS. Driving isn't my thing."

"You can manage this," Lou assured me. "Take us to the Tilly Marina."

I glanced at the brute seated beside me. If they planned to kill us, why bring us somewhere public? It made more sense to drive us out west of town to dump our bodies around Lake Okeechobee or in the number of drainage pools out that way.

My eyes checked the mirror. Amanda gazed back at me. She didn't look scared. It was more an expression of resolution. She blinked at me in rapid succession. My brain took me longer than it should have to realize she was timing her blinks.

Morse code.

"D-O-N-T/W-O-R-R-Y," she told me with her eyes.

I blinked out, "K."

She blinked another message, repeating it three times so I could catch all the letters.

"K-I-L-L/T-H-E-M."

This time, I gave an almost imperceptible nod. I'd already planned to do just that, but until I could take out Davey first, I had to wait.

When we pulled into the lot, Lou said, "We're going to walk casually to your boat. Understood?"

I nodded.

"Good, 'cause Davey will be about fifty feet behind us. If you get rowdy, he shoots her."

"I understand," I confirmed.

"That's a smart lad," Lou replied with a hint of encouragement. It was a far more casual tone than I expected. He thought he had this under control, and that made him relax. How calm was he really, though?

Lou had some sense, at least. He'd figured out a method to make me cooperate, but surely he wasn't foolish enough to assume it would work forever. Of course, how long did he need to keep me in check? And why were we going back to *Carina*? I had a guess. The best way to get rid of a guy with a boat was to let the sea take him. On average, two to three people go missing while out fishing or boating. Long-term solo cruisers might be higher. I'd seen at least one alert a month where someone missed their arrival window. Some were held up by weather and other factors, while many never showed up at all.

It was only a few years ago that a sailing vessel appeared in the South Pacific with the long-dead corpse of its captain still in the cabin. The sailboat had been drifting since the captain's family had declared him missing eight years earlier.

I complied, getting out of the car. As we walked down the steps toward the marina, I asked, "What's the move? You taking us out and sinking the boat?"

"Just walk and don't talk," Lou ordered.

"Yo, Chase!" Tanner Gleeson called from the cockpit of his thirty-six-foot Bertram.

"Tanner," I said curtly.

"I snagged a huge tuna this morning," he boasted. "You and your friend want some? I can't eat it all."

"Yeah," I said. "Hit me up later, though. Okay?"

"Will do," Tanner agreed, returning to washing off the aft deck where he'd butchered the large fish.

"Good job," Lou praised. "You played it smart."

"I don't have much choice, do I?"

Lou chuckled. "No, you don't."

"Look, just allow Amanda to go," I urged. "I'll play along. There's no reason to hurt her."

"My orders are to bring her with you," Lou stated. "It seems no one trusts you to behave."

The switchblade rubbed my leg through my pocket. I calculated how quickly I could pull the knife and jab it into Lou's jugular. It would require me to incapacitate Lou, grab my M45 in his waistband, and then kill Davey, who was trailing at a distance behind me. And I needed to do all that before Davey pulled the trigger and shot Amanda.

There might as well be zero chance of pulling all that off. The first part was a piece of cake. I knew I could surprise Lou. That would be required. If the beast saw the attack coming, he would fight back. A scuffle evened the odds for him, but would plummet for Amanda.

For the moment, I was stuck.

"Get aboard," Lou told me.

"Could you take your shoes off?" I asked.

"Fuck, no," he snarled.

"You'll scuff the finish," I pointed out.

"Do you think it will matter?" he barked. "Now, do what I tell you."

I gave a gesture of resignation. Since I'd loosened the dock lines, there was a big gap between the gunwale and the pier finger. I pressed my foot down on the line attached to the cleat and pressed down. My weight dragged the sailboat closer, and I stepped toward the cockpit. When my left foot touched the gunwale, I pushed off with my right foot. The motion looked like a simple step, but at the same time, I shoved the boat away from the pier.

"Cute," Lou commented. "Now pull the boat back over here."

I hadn't come up with a plan, but I hoped he'd try to repeat my action. Since I'd been living on *Carina* for a while, my move with the dock line was second nature. If Lou tried to follow me the same way, he ran the risk of missing and landing in the water. But alas, he proved smarter than I thought. That was important to note, though.

I pulled the side of the boat closer to the dock, and Lou stepped aboard.

"Get below," he told me.

If he followed me into the cabin, we'd be out of Davey's sight. Lou must have been reading my mind because he stated, "If I don't come up in two minutes and signal Davey, he will shoot your girl. Long before you can reach him. If he sees you pop up, it's the same thing."

Deflated, I nodded.

"Didn't want you to come up with any ideas," Lou remarked.

I unlocked the cabin and climbed below. Lou was right behind me, no doubt determined to ensure I didn't have any time to pull anything tricky.

"Hands behind your back," he ordered. "And don't turn around."

When I obeyed his command, I felt him encircle my wrists with a zip tie. A thick one, too.

"Stay still," he demanded as he put another around my hands, pulling both tight enough to hinder the circulation.

"Now, sit down and don't move," he said as he climbed the companionway steps and signaled for Davey to bring Amanda. Once she was below deck with me, Lou secured her wrists as well before pushing her down on the settee.

"Why don't you two rest here for a bit?" Lou said. "Davey's going to keep an eye on you." He turned to Davey. "If either of them moves, shoot him, then her."

Amanda sat on the other side of the cabin from me. She settled on the more comfortable salon while I leaned back across from her on the quarter berth.

"What are you planning to do with us?" Amanda asked as Lou climbed the companionway steps.

"If you do like we say, it will work out," he offered before stepping into the cockpit.

I didn't notice him grabbing the ignition keys I'd left in a small magnetic bowl on the navigation table. But he must have done it while I faced the other way, because the diesel rumbled to life.

"They're going to take us out and kill us," Amanda declared. "Aren't they, Chase?"

I nodded without saying anything out loud. However,

my eyes blinked one letter in Morse code: P. She studied me as I repeated the code.

"Can I use the bathroom?" she asked the men.

Davey shook his head.

"Look, please, I won't cause any trouble," she pleaded. Her pitch raised, giving a heightened desperation in her voice.

"What's the problem?" Lou asked, sticking his head through the companionway just over Davey, who took a perch on the stairs to observe us.

"I need to pee," Amanda complained.

"Do like I told your boyfriend," Lou said. "Pee, then."

"Wait," I interjected. "Give her a little dignity, man."

Lou glanced at me, then at Amanda. "Fine, she can pee. Davey put the barrel in her mouth. If she—or he—does anything, pull the trigger."

"Can you undo my hands?" Amanda asked.

"No!" Lou barked. His eyes turned to me. "This will end badly if you try anything."

"My experience suggests that it's going to end badly no matter what," I remarked.

"Remember what I told you at the apartment? I can kill you now, and Davey and I will enjoy a long time with the bitch. Or, it's fast and simple. Which do you prefer? It would be easier to not have blood all over the cabin, but I can deal with that."

I nodded in understanding.

"Take her," Lou ordered Davey.

The big man watched me as his partner stood up and grabbed Amanda by the right arm. He pulled her to her feet and shoved her aft toward the head. Lou watched until Davey pushed the barrel of his SIG into Amanda's mouth. She winced as it went into her mouth.

"Mah ants," she mumbled.

Davey stared at her.

"She needs her pants down," I said.

Davey glared at me. He used his free hand to unbutton her shorts, a pair of jean cut-offs that hit Daisy Duke vibes. Amanda jerked away from his fingers, which seemed to linger longer than they should, and wriggled her hips until the shorts dropped to the floor.

My eyes cut up to see Lou hurry forward on the deck to untie the dock lines. I arched my back, letting the switchblade slide up. As the end of it began to prairie-dog its little head out from my pocket, I saw Lou coming past the porthole as he moved aft to the other lines.

I sat down fast, allowing my body and the settee cushion to shove the knife out of my pants. I lifted my butt and shifted six inches to my left, settling on the blade just as Lou climbed back into the cockpit.

"Get her to her seat," Lou ordered.

Davey complied, yanking Amanda off the toilet without the decency of pulling her pants up. She waddled like a penguin toward the salon, where Davey shoved her down.

"Could you help me with my shorts?" she asked.

Davey stared at her before walking away.

"Fuck you, asshole," she barked, rolling onto her back on the floor of the cabin and lifting her feet in the air. Her denim cut-offs slid above her knees, and she arched her back several times, combined with some jiggling to get the shorts most of the way over her ass.

A smirk played on Davey's lips as he took in her acrobatics. While his attention remained on her, I shifted forward until my fingers found the switchblade's handle and worked it into my palm. I leaned back as Amanda rocked into a seated position again.

"Nice job," I remarked.

"Hope you enjoyed it," she said. "This is looking like the last time you'll see my ass."

"There are the worst things to see before one dies," I commented.

Davey just shook his head, and I couldn't tell if he found the exchange humorous or not.

"Do you talk at all, Davey?" I asked.

His attention turned toward me, and he raised the SIG. With the barrel pointed at my forehead, he grimaced.

"Someone cut your tongue out?" Amanda asked. "I've seen what that looks like. It ain't pretty."

Davey focused on her and lowered the weapon. He settled back on his perch on the top companionway step.

"You got them, Davey?" Lou asked over his shoulder.

The mute raised his hand with the thumbs-up signal.

"We're pulling out," Lou said with a smile through the opening. "*Bon voyage*, boys and girls."

31

Lou must have had some boating experience. He maneuvered my sailboat out of the dock and headed north toward the Lake Worth Inlet. From where I sat, I watched him behind the helm. The man might be taking us out to our deaths, but he seemed to be enjoying the journey.

"Were you the one that dumped Lyla?" I asked.

Lou glanced into the cabin without saying a word.

"You seem to know how to operate a boat," I commented. "I'm guessing you drove the boat, and Davey here did the deed. Am I right?"

Davey sneered at me, but there was a look in his eye that told me I was correct.

Carina only motored at about five knots, and it would take us an hour to get out of the lake and into the Atlantic.

"You should raise the main," I suggested. "At least before you hit the ocean. Someone might find it weird that you're only motoring."

Lou ignored me. Amanda, though, watched me. I cut my eyes to Davey, hoping she'd distract him.

"Hey, Davey, could you please come fasten my jeans?" she asked.

Davey didn't move.

A horn blasted as a trawler passed us from behind. Davey jerked his head to peer out the hatch at the fishing boat. I hit the button on the switchblade, and the spring-loaded blade snapped out. At least I had the good sense to aim the sharp end away from me.

The rip sounded louder than the spring action, and I cringed, knowing I'd just stabbed my upholstery. I rotated the handle to slice through one of the zip ties. It popped loose, allowing some circulation to return to my hands.

Davey's attention turned back to us. He eyed Amanda with a leering gaze I didn't like. Amanda seemed to notice it, too, and I noticed a twitch in her eye. She remained collected except for that tell.

The problem I now faced was when to act. The second zip tie still bound my wrists, and I needed another distraction to break it. Once I freed my hands, I had to take out Davey first. He had the orders to kill us if we caused trouble, and that made him priority number one.

From where I sat to the companionway stairs where Davey stood was six feet. And the galley counter was between us. He wasn't holding the SIG on us the whole time, but he was close to ready. My chances of getting to him before he shot me were better than my odds of taking him on the dock, but not much. I could throw the knife like I did to the *Loup* at the Manta Club the other night, but we were on a moving boat that pitched and yawed. Even if my aim was dead-on, the switchblade made for a terrible throwing knife. The thin blade would, in all likelihood, break on impact. It was too big a risk, and the best I'd accomplish would be tossing away my only weapon.

"Where are we going?" I asked.

"Doesn't matter," Lou called down.

"I'm guessing you are heading out to the Gulf Stream, right? Far enough from land to be out of sight."

Neither man answered, although at this point, if Davey uttered even a breath, it would shock me.

"What are they going to do?" Amanda asked.

"If it were me, I'd throw us overboard," I considered. "Probably with a bullet to the head. Maybe just with an anchor tied to our feet. Drop us in the middle of the Stream where it gets deep. Might take an hour for us to sink to the bottom."

"Fuck, Chase," she muttered as Davey huffed a silent chuckle.

She glared at the greasy little man. He returned her gaze with lecherous eyes, and his visage turned my stomach. He had no intention of a quick death for her. Not that I trusted the guys taking me out to the middle of the ocean, but realizing that my instinct was correct didn't sit any better with me.

"Dammit," Lou cursed as the sound of a power boat ripped past *Carina*.

The subsequent pitch to port caught Davey by surprise. He tumbled off the step as my Tartan 40 rocked violently in the trough of the powerboat's wake. A plate I'd left on my counter rocketed through the air, smashing against the sole.

In fact, everything loose flew across the cabin like dice in Yahtzee. Since Lou had secured nothing before leaving the dock, anything not tied down scattered across the inside of the boat. I had the best balance, having sensed what was about to happen. Amanda spilled toward me, tumbling to the floor as Davey almost rolled onto the deck in the galley.

I tried to spring up, but Davey came off the ground

like a monkey. He held onto his SIG, and the barrel leveled at me. The evil grin he offered dared me to charge him.

My shoulders sagged as I dropped back into my seat. His ego was satiated by my relenting. As I reclined on the quarter berth, the other zip tie was now in my fingers. I pushed the bits of plastic between the cushions.

Amanda struggled to sit up and scooted across the sole until she could use the nav station to push herself to her feet. Davey reached up and grabbed the handhold next to the companionway with his left hand while his right kept the SIG aimed in our general direction.

"Everyone alright, Davey?" Lou asked. "Fucking assholes all over the place up here."

Davey let go of the bar to give him a thumbs-up signal.

Now that I was free, I needed to get closer to Davey before I acted. Even in these tight quarters, there was no way to cover the ground between us and kill him before he fired that SIG. Unless he put on an incredible act, the little man wouldn't miss at this range.

If I judged the two of them correctly, Lou would bring Amanda and me up on deck. I figured they would wait until we were out of sight from land, or at least far enough from any gawkers. If I was lucky, they'd put a bullet in my head before dumping me in the ocean. Or, if they were sadistic enough like I'd told Amanda, they might weigh me down and let the last two minutes of my life pass as I watched the surface recede in desperation. I doubted they would just throw me over, though. My chances in the open water were bad, but they were better than being on a fast drop to the sea floor.

I wondered which would kill me first: drowning or the increased water pressure. Whatever happened to me, once I was off, Davey had plans for Amanda. I knew those plans included nothing as nice as a bullet to the head.

As long as they took us up on deck. At least then we had more options.

Over the next few hours, my eyes flicked from Amanda to Davey. The four of us traveled in utter silence. Davey didn't speak, and Lou must have been used to that behavior because he didn't try to change it. The pair had a casual familiarity about them.

Amanda shifted in the salon, and I watched her. While she kept her composure, I could see the stress affecting her. Beads of sweat formed on her forehead. Of course, the cabin was stuffy. Normally, I'd open a hatch or two just to keep the air flowing through the space. Otherwise, the sun turned it into an oven. At least Davey was resting in the companionway with the doors ajar. It didn't help bring sea breeze in, but it allowed some of the hot air to escape.

Some—not all. And Davey was getting plenty of fresh air where he perched.

But it was more than that. I saw Amanda swallow seventeen times in two minutes. Her eyes glassed over at times, and I imagined she was absorbed in her thoughts and worries. In that moment, an immense wave of guilt hit me. She was facing death because of me.

I hadn't felt this way before. Men had followed me into battle, and some had never followed me home. That resulted in a kind of survivor's guilt that every warrior had, but this was different. It filled me with a dread of responsibility.

I had to make it right. And I wanted to reassure her it would be okay.

Then another realization hit me. This was more than a self-imposed responsibility.

"Bring up the girl," Lou barked.

Davey narrowed his eyes at Amanda before motioning with the SIG for her to accompany him. Amanda glanced in my direction as Davey turned the barrel of his weapon toward me, pursing his lips into a smug smirk. The greasy gunman stepped to the side, allowing Amanda to ascend the steps.

"Davey, you come on up," Lou said. "Mr. Gordon can follow. If he tries anything, the girl dies."

Davey backed up the stairs while keeping his SIG directed at me. After Davey climbed into the cockpit, I heard Lou order him to hold Amanda. Since the little shithead didn't speak, I couldn't hear his response, but I assumed he did as he was told.

"Gordon, come on up," Lou called. "Don't try anything, or I shoot you. Then Davey can have some time with your girlfriend."

The switchblade handle fit in the palm of my right hand, and I covered that hand with my left. With my hands behind my back as if they were still bound, I struggled to get up the stairs without tripping up and grabbing the handles by the steps. The feat challenged me as I balanced with the pitching of *Carina* in the Atlantic.

As I emerged, I caught a glimpse aft. The Florida coastline was barely visible on the horizon, so I guessed we were twelve to fifteen miles out. Lou hadn't listened to me and raised the sails. I imagined he wasn't a sailor, but he could handle a powerboat. He'd set the autopilot, and I heard the computer-controlled gears turning the helm.

I was almost out of the companionway when Amanda jerked away from Davey. The action occurred in my peripheral vision, and when my head turned toward her, I saw Amanda and Davey flip over the lifeline into the sea.

Shock hit Lou along with me. He'd remained focused on me, and whatever happened between Amanda and Davey had been on the edge of his view, too. Before the pair splashed into the water, I flew forward, bringing both arms around.

As my right hand came around, I thumbed the switch, popping the blade out. Lou, now with all his attention on me, drew the M45 he still had in his front waistband. He cleared the barrel as I stabbed him with the knife. The blade caught him in the right forearm. When it punched through his flesh and tissue, Lou released the gun and jerked back. The knife wrenched from my grip as he stumbled back from the helm.

This was my cockpit, and if there was one thing I could do well, it was maneuver through it, as I often had to leave the wheel to man a line or fix something in a hurry. My feet came off the deck, barely touching the starboard settee as I hit him with my left fist in the face.

Lou grasped for the hilt of the blade embedded in his forearm, and I hit him with a snap punch with my right fist. My knuckles caught him in the throat. The bodybuilder gasped as he tried to swallow a breath of air.

By now, my body slammed against him, wrapping my arms around him. We hit the stainless steel railing around the cockpit. For a split second, I worried our collective weight might be more than the railing, the hull, or the bolts holding it down could endure.

Lou slung an elbow up, catching me under the chin. The man wasn't fast, but he made up for that deficiency with power. My jaw cracked up, slamming my teeth together and stunning me long enough for him to break my grip.

I plopped down hard, face-first, onto the port settee. Thankfully, the impact was lessened because of the cushions. My left foot shot out and slammed into his patella. The kick didn't bend his leg back like I'd hoped, but it sent him reeling down on that knee.

Lou howled in pain and reached for my ankle as I tried to kick again. Blood dripped off his arm as he caught my ankle and jerked me aft. As he pulled me back, I slammed down on the bench, knocking the wind out of me.

In a fit of desperation, I grabbed the helm, jerking the wheel to port. *Carina*'s rudder turned, and the entire boat came about ninety degrees. Lou, who struggled to drag me off the stern, wasn't ready for the sudden change in direction. When her bow plowed into a wave, *Carina* yawed forward before see-sawing up and down through the water. Inertia lifted both of us off the seat for a split second, and I thrust my right foot out. My sole struck gold, hitting him in the crotch.

Despite the blow sending him back, Lou yanked me with him. His grip on my left ankle remained there like a vise. I kicked again with my right foot, shoving him back again as I tried to regain my own footing.

Lou managed to catch himself from falling off the stern. In the second it took him to grab the railing, I rolled forward, putting my feet beneath me. Springing toward him, I drove my shoulder into Lou's gut. The impact picked him up off the deck.

His meaty hands grabbed my shirt as he tumbled over the handrail, and he dragged me up and carried me with him over the rail. My left hand wrapped around the stanchion, where it attached to the gunwale. Lou held on to my waist now as I clung to the back of *Carina* with only one hand.

I got my right fingers up to reach for the upper rail as Lou struggled to scale me at the same time. He didn't have three hundred pounds trying to pull him off the boat. If I didn't shake him, he'd scramble over me while I managed to just hang on.

I reached past the next railing to the coiled line hanging off the top rail. When my right hand grabbed the end, I let go of the stanchion and twisted in an about-face. Water swallowed the two of us, and I took the three seconds before the rope went taut to wind the line around my hand. Lou clawed at my torso, desperately struggling to get over me to the departing boat.

My timing was off, and at four and half seconds, the line finished uncoiling, the slack vanished, and *Carina* began dragging us like bait on a hook. The autopilot was now attempting to correct the sudden change in heading, and the bow turned back east. As she returned to her original course, *Carina* slowed, and my lifeline slackened.

I grabbed the hilt of the switchblade and jerked it free. Lou let out a gurgled yelp before I drove the tip into his eye. His grip released as he fell off me.

In the brief respite and slack, I inhaled a lungful of air a second before *Carina* returned to her heading and started dragging me along. The line I clung to was a hundred feet long, and when I was alone at sea, I kept it fastened to me if I went forward in case I ever fell overboard. It was something I'd never used for survival. Normally, I just used it to stay connected to the boat if I wanted to take a quick dip.

Now I was forced to pull myself up to the stern and board the vessel while she was underway. Luckily, I'd done similar things in the past. All of those experiences had been with powerboats running from ten to twenty knots. *Carina* was only clipping along at four knots. Maybe less with each wave she bashed into.

When I reached the stern, I grabbed the swim ladder,

heaved myself up into the cockpit, and flopped onto the bloody seats.

32

I disengaged the autopilot, flipping a lever that separated the gears keeping the helm on course. Now the computer could relay the need to change it to the gear, but without the gears being attached, nothing had changed. Behind the controls, I turned hard to port, judging the oncoming wave so that rather than bashing through it, the hull rode it. There was still some significant pitching, but it was far more controlled than what we had endured earlier.

My brain started rewinding. How long ago had it been since Amanda went overboard? Five minutes. Give or take.

I checked the SOG gauge. We were now moving at five knots. With the about-face, I figured we'd lost forty seconds or so. That meant we had gone only a quarter of a mile. Probably just at an eighth. The problem was we hadn't maintained a straight course. The chartplotter showed our route, though, and I tried to follow it back.

With one eye on the panel to keep us on an identical reverse course and one eye scanning the water for Amanda,

I worried I'd miss her. I was assuming she was still on the surface. Hell, I prayed she was still on the surface.

We were in the strongest current in this part of the ocean, too. She shouldn't have drifted a great distance in that short time, but in these three- to five-foot seas, a body could hide in the trough of the waves, especially if she moved a few hundred feet off our track. I scanned around the vessel, searching as far as I could see. The seas would carry her north, so as long as I stayed close to our previous track, I focused my attention off the starboard with consistent checks to port in case I missed her.

What color shirt did Amanda have on? It took me a second to remember it was a yellow tank top with the Palm County Fire Department logo on it. Yellow was good in this situation. It stood out in the water. Though, some of the local divers referred to it as "yum yum yellow," so they avoided the color when diving with sharks. Apparently, the bright color attracted them. I figured it was because yellow fish were easy to spot and quite delicious, but I didn't have a shark's mentality.

I thought about that as I retraced our route, searching for Amanda. Something bobbed off the starboard bow as a wave lifted it up. My hand jerked the throttle into reverse, slowing *Carina's* inertia. It wasn't Amanda, but a body floating face-down.

Davey's body.

I circled the body by locking the rudder all the way to starboard. While the engine was now in neutral, nothing remained still on the ocean. My boat hook hung under the bimini, and I yanked it down and extended it. The plastic handle stretched to twelve feet, and I reached down as I passed Davey. The hook caught his shirt, and I dragged him to the swim ladder.

When I climbed down to check the body, I found him very dead. A jagged shard of something jutted out of his neck. After I pulled it free, I recognized the design on it. It was part of the plate that shattered in the cabin earlier. Amanda must have picked up a piece when she was on the floor. Neither I nor Davey had noticed it.

I gave Davey a quick search. He had a wallet and cell phone in his pocket. I didn't see his SIG, assuming it must be at the bottom of the ocean now. His cell phone was still working, so I scanned his face to unlock the device before I pushed him away from the stern and returned to the cockpit.

While *Carina* made a circle, I jumped below deck to grab my binoculars. If Davey was here, Amanda should be close by. I pieced together what had happened. Amanda had taken advantage of the pair's closer scrutiny of me to use the plate shard to cut her zip ties the same way I'd used the switchblade. It might have taken her more time to slice through the plastic, but neither Davey nor Lou had paid her as much attention as they did me.

Once on deck, she waited until the right moment to strike. I guessed she stabbed Davey in the jugular. After all, she was a paramedic and not the least bit squeamish. He must have dragged her over with him. I hadn't heard a gunshot, but if it had been underwater, the water might have muffled the sound.

Still, I hoped that she was treading water nearby.

I climbed up on top of the cabin with the binoculars and scanned the ocean surrounding the vessel. Nothing.

I repeated the search, making a complete three-sixty rotation. No sign of her. The water was choppy enough that *Carina* pitched around. I needed to get higher.

My eyes turned up to the mast. I had pegs that acted like

steps to ascend the mast. I'd had to climb it only once while at sea, and I'd rigged a line and a bosun's chair to save me should I fall. That day, I didn't need either, but right now there wasn't enough time to rig the safety setup.

Instead, I grabbed the jackline I'd used to haul myself back to *Carina* after I killed Lou. With a quick knot, I attached it to my waist. With the binoculars hanging from the strap around my neck, I scaled the mast. The anchor light sat atop the stick at a little over fifty-eight feet from the waterline. At the halfway point, I hooked my arm through one of the pegs and lifted the binoculars to my eyes. With careful movements, I started at the front of the boat and worked my way around the clock. After the third rotation, I was about to climb higher, although I felt that was futile. I should have been able to see her by now if she was still out there.

Then a flash of yellow crossed through the viewfinder. I swung back, and it was gone. As the boat bobbed up and down, the mast made wide swings from side to side. Still, I clung to the aluminum mast and focused on the area I'd seen the color.

There she was. At least, I spotted a yellow dot. She'd moved a long way off, about a quarter of a mile. I took a quick bearing with the sun. She was northeast of *Carina*, and I almost dropped from that height to the deck in my excitement. My logical angel stopped me, reminding me that if I injured myself, it might sentence Amanda to a terrible death.

Once my feet landed back on deck, I scanned the water again. There was no sign of her, and I ran back to the controls. In a second, I had the wheel turned and the throttle all the way down. Not that it got me anywhere fast.

In fact, even with the RPMs revving, it took me thirty seconds to straighten the boat on the new heading.

One hand kept the helm steered in the correct direction while the other held the binoculars up for me to search. I saw the flash of yellow again. She or I had drifted some, and I adjusted my course. As I closed on her location, I could see her floating upright and waving at me.

My heart leaped with relief. She was alive. As the diesel churned us toward her, I detached the jackline from my waist and attached it to the Lifesling I kept on the back railing. Man Overboard drills weren't something I did a lot of. Mainly because I was a solo sailor, so who was I going to save? But I'd done similar drills in the Corps.

I lined up the bow with her and slowed the throttle to a crawl. It kept enough forward motion to keep *Carina* on course, but I wasn't going to run her over. My helm had a lock to prevent the rudder from turning, and I secured it so we stayed straight.

As I passed her, I hurled the Lifesling to her. The flotation device splashed about five feet behind her, and she caught it as it dragged past her.

"Hold on!" I called as I started reeling her in. My foot hooked the throttle, nudging it into neutral. Now we glided forward with only inertia. My hands worked fast, one over the other, as I brought the rope back.

"Grab the ladder," I urged as she almost reached the stern.

Amanda reached out and caught the bottom rung of the swim ladder. She released the Lifesling, and I hauled it in. She held onto the ladder for a minute before she pulled herself up.

"Are you hurt?" I asked, taking her hand and helping her aboard.

She shook her head. "I thought you'd get back faster," she gasped as she panted for air. "What happened?"

"I found Davey," I acknowledged.

"That fucker better be dead," she barked.

"He's shark bait. So is his buddy."

"Dammit, Chase," she groaned, rolling onto her back. The water dripping off her soaked Lou's dried blood, sending streams of pink salt water draining toward my scuppers.

I flopped back on the cushion. "Oh, who doesn't enjoy a day on the water?" I asked.

She lifted her head to stare at me. The icy-stone face cracked with a smile. "What's the saying? 'Any day on the water is better than a day at the office?'"

"Something like that," I agreed.

"We'll have to redeem this one, then," she suggested, sitting up. She glanced at the streams of water and blood, noticing them for the first time. "What the hell?"

"Sorry, that's Lou," I acknowledged. "I didn't have time to clean it up."

She flicked her wrist, flinging droplets of blood and water across the cockpit. "Glad you didn't take the time to do that," she admitted.

I leaned forward and touched her cheek. "Amanda, I'm sorry about this," I told her.

"Don't blame yourself, Chase," she said.

"You could have died out there," I declared. "Do you know how scared I was that I lost you?"

She cocked one side of her mouth up into a half-smile. "How scared?"

"Oh, fuck you," I said, grinning at her.

Amanda leaned forward, grabbed my face with both

hands, and kissed me. When she let go, she said, "Well, I love you."

I hadn't been expecting that, and I responded the only way I could. I returned an "I love you, too" as I kissed her back.

Then a phone chirped.

I pulled away from her and looked at Davey's phone sitting on the helm where I'd left it. "It's Davey's," I explained as I picked the phone up. No notifications showed on the screen.

"What if he has an alarm or alert that his phone got wet?" Amanda wondered.

"Yeah, I don't know how it's working still," I confessed.

"It's an Apple. They can be wet for a bit, although the salt water might cause problems. What are you going to do with it?"

"I wanted to see who used it."

Another chirp. That one didn't come from Davey's phone.

"That wasn't his," she remarked.

"Where's your phone?"

"At home," she told me.

I stood up and searched the cockpit. Stuffed between the cushion and the fiberglass, I found an iPhone. Holding it aloft, I wagged the device at Amanda. She took it from me. The screen had opened to the camera setting, and when she swiped the app away, the phone remained unlocked.

"Bingo," she declared as she opened the text message. "'We are en route to the rendezvous,'" she read.

"What else does the text say?"

She swiped her fingers to scroll up the text. "The message before asked, 'Done?'"

"Of course," I said. "They planned to let the boat drift.

Or they would hoist the sail and set the autopilot and let her wander the sea alone. Whatever they did, they needed a way back to land."

"Someone's going to meet them," she said. "Where?"

I looked over her shoulder. The message had no coordinates. "They must have prearranged it," I speculated.

"What do we do?"

"Send these," I instructed as I found our location on the chartplotter. Tapping the coordinates with my finger, I added, "Tell them the engine crapped out. We need a lift. And tell them we're dead."

Amanda glanced up at me. "We're dead? You and me?"

"Well, pretend you're the bad guy," I suggested.

The phone chirped again, and Amanda read the message.

"They confirmed and said their ETA was an hour and a half."

"Good," I replied. "We have time."

Amanda cocked her head. "I know what we can do with that time," she suggested slyly.

33

"How do you plan to hide?" she wondered.

I motioned to the water surrounding *Carina.*

"What?"

"We don't know what's coming," I explained. "However, they need to find an empty boat."

"What does that do?" she asked.

"Hopefully, it's just a driver coming to pick them up. But we'll prepare for a passenger, too. If they arrive and find *Carina* empty, they'll assume something happened and all four of us are in the water."

"So you and I are going to hide?" she asked. "Under the boat?"

"Not you," I corrected. "Come here."

I led her below deck and took her to the aft cabin. Although I found it nice, it was far from spacious. However, it had a small hanging locker that was a bit bigger than the one I used in the front. I used this one, too, but it only held my Sharkskin wetsuit and some spare parts.

I pulled the Sharkskin out and showed her the cubby.

"What about it?" she asked.

"You're going to hide in here. I doubt he'll check here."

"What if he does, Chase?"

"I'll rescue you?" I offered with a questioning smirk.

Amanda rolled her eyes.

"No, seriously, I put a small twenty-two pistol in there. If someone opens the door, stick the gun in their face and pull the trigger."

She nodded. "Do I have to get in now?"

"No, I'm going to change, so can you go up and keep watch?"

She nodded again, leaving me in the cabin. I stripped down and donned a pair of swim shorts before I squeezed into the Sharkskin. I found one of my dive knives and strapped the blade on the back of my left thigh before I pulled the wetsuit pants over my legs. There was an awkward bulge on my leg, and it wasn't easily accessible. However, if I got to the point I needed the knife, things would be pretty sour.

In another cabinet, I dug a waterproof backpack from a storage locker. I dropped Lou's phone in it along with the M45. When I came back on deck, Amanda was peering across the water with the binoculars. She scanned the horizon.

"There's a big ship to the south of us," she told me. "But it's chugging east. Probably nothing."

I nodded. "Listen, Amanda," I explained. "Once they leave, you'll have to take *Carina* back to port. Can you handle it?"

"I need to dock her?" she asked with wide eyes.

"Yeah, when you get closer, call Randy on the radio. He can help you," I told her. "I've got the Tilly marked on the chartplotter." I tapped the screen to show her how to access it. "Just click it, and she'll give you the route. It's several hours back, so take your time."

"Okay," she agreed. "What are you planning?"

"I'm going to let him take me back to his boss," I informed her.

"You think it's Connors?"

"It seemed elaborate," I remarked. "My disappearance at sea solves a lot more problems than my getting shot on the streets."

Amanda wrinkled her brow. "How does that help them?"

"When people start asking or looking, someone will remember *Carina* heading out. No one will think I'm missing for months unless *Carina* turns up. You're more of a problem, but I guess they are counting on your friends and family assuming you set sail with me. Once they got out far enough, they could sink her, but this is a busy enough route that someone might see debris, and a search starts too soon. Better to set the autopilot on a heading that has nothing in its path. Aim for Britain and let her go with the wind."

"There's something almost poetic about that for her," Amanda noted.

I nodded. "There are certainly worse ways for her to spend her last days. Who knows? Someone might salvage her and give her another life."

Amanda stared at me with wistful eyes. "You realize she's not going out like that now, right?"

I returned her gaze. "Yeah, I was just waxing poetic."

She kissed me. "It was kinda sweet to see that side of you."

I shook my head. "Where's that other phone?"

"Here," she said, handing me Davey's phone.

I dialed a number, and she asked, "How is his phone getting a signal?"

"Probably running off satellites," I informed her.

The phone rang until Rob answered, "Isip here."

"Rob, it's Chase," I said.

"I thought you were going to call me back?"

"I got kidnapped," I informed him. "Twice."

Amanda shook her head, holding up three fingers. I covered the phone, saying, "The first one doesn't count because I told him about it already."

She rolled her eyes at me.

"I tracked down a boat you might be looking for," he told me. "One of Connors's companies, Strickland United, owns a ninety-meter Oceanco superyacht designated *Capitulate*."

"*Capitulate*?" I questioned. "Sounds... I don't know... arrogant."

"I'd agree," Rob replied.

"Fits Connors to a letter," I stated. "That's not what I was calling about, though."

"So, I did that for nothing?"

"No, it was perfect," I confirmed. "However, I am very recently post-kidnapping, and I suspect the people coming to pick me up are going to take me to Connors. Presumably on this stupid boat."

"Not so stupid," Rob corrected. "The fucking thing cost close to a quarter of a billion dollars. I imagine it's pretty nice."

"Great. Can you find it and arrest the guy on it?"

"Me personally? No," he replied. "Do you have any evidence on him?"

"Not yet," I told him.

"Then you already know the answer."

"If he kidnaps me, though?"

"It gives us more leeway," he answered.

"Great. If you haven't heard from me in six hours, start looking for it."

"Chase, I can't really do that," he stated.

"Look, Amanda is bringing *Carina* back to dock. Did I mention they stole her, too?"

"No."

"When she gets back, she'll reach out. If I get there first, I'll call."

"It's not like we're the cavalry," Rob told me. "You don't even know where you are."

I looked at the coordinates on the chartplotter and read them to him. "Wherever they are is within an hour and a half of here. At least according to the guy coming here."

"Wait... you're in communication with your kidnappers, or you're actively kidnapped?" Rob asked. "I'm confused."

"We were taken hostage and transported on *Carina* to the middle of the Gulf Stream, where they intended to dump our bodies and either sink or send *Carina* adrift."

"I'm guessing that didn't happen?"

"Not like they wanted," I said.

"Chase!" Amanda gasped.

I glanced at her, and she pointed at the horizon before handing me the binoculars. In their field of vision, I found a speedboat clipping toward us from the northeast.

"Rob, I gotta go. I'll be in touch," I told him as I hung up.

"Are you sure about this?" Amanda asked.

"I'm never sure, but I think this will work."

"Dammit, Chase," she muttered, and kissed me.

"Go hide," I told her. "Stay there until you are certain you're alone. Then head for port."

"I will," she said, grasping my fingers.

"Don't worry," I encouraged her. "I'll be back."

She nodded and went below deck. When she'd had

enough time to secure herself, I reached into the compartment under the port settee and grabbed a mask. This wasn't my diving one, but my emergency-because-something-is-wrapped-around-the-prop mask. Next to it was a small pony bottle of air. I wasn't a fan of the little handheld cylinders, but they did work in a pinch. This felt like it counted as a pinch.

The speedboat was growing closer, and I needed to be out of the cockpit before we came into visual range. My arms slid into the straps of the waterproof backpack, and I pulled the mask over my head before dropping off the far side of *Carina*.

The water felt warm, and with the Sharkskin, I was quite comfortable. It took another ten minutes for me to hear the roar of the engine over the sea's surface. I stayed on the port side, keeping my head just above the surface. If I situated myself in the right space, I could see past the stern and track the approaching vessel.

It was a white speedboat whose model I couldn't recognize. The boat's operator slowed as he approached my boat. It appeared he was the only one on board. That was a relief.

The engine went quiet, and the driver coasted toward *Carina*. I pulled back out of sight as the driver stood up.

"Cal? Davey?" the man called.

Of course, no one answered.

"Cal!" he shouted.

Still no response.

The engine started up again, and I worried he was just going to leave. In which case, I would miss my ride.

But he didn't leave. Instead, he circled *Carina* at idle speed. As he rounded the bow, I stuck the pony bottle in my mouth and submerged beneath the hull.

The water was crystal-clear, and if he strained his eyes,

he might have seen me. But I wasn't wearing yum-yum yellow. My wetsuit was gray with no bright flair on it. From below the surface, I watched the speedboat move around my Tartan twice before the driver pulled up alongside *Carina*. I could see the twin screws on the powerboat, and I guessed it was a pretty quick little boat.

My arms stroked me underneath the second boat, and I came up on the far side.

"No one's here," the driver was saying to someone.

"No, Cal's not here. No Davey. No one. Not even this Gordon and the girl."

He must have been on the phone, as only his side of the conversation was audible.

"Yeah, I'm tying up, and I'll double-check it... I don't know the first thing about sailing... fine, I'll figure it out."

Then silence, and he climbed from his speedboat into my cockpit. I swam toward the back of his boat, where there was a raised swim platform that sat a few inches above the water. The added height must reduce any drag.

"Hello!" the driver called. I saw him peering through the companionway. "The fuck is everyone?"

The man, a tall blond fellow who looked like he should be an accountant somewhere, turned to look across the sea. He couldn't help it. Before he climbed below, he wanted to make sure he wasn't alone. Or maybe he hoped to spot his buddies bobbing around in the ocean.

They were, but not here.

Satisfied or at least satiated, he climbed through the cabin. I moved fast, grabbing the swim platform and pushing myself up onto it. The interior of the boat was like most speedboats, with a bench along the stern with seats for the driver and two more passengers, and a little cuddy cabin. I scurried along the gunwale to the front of the boat and jumped down.

The hatch slid open, allowing me to crawl inside. I closed the opening and glanced around the hot cabin. There were no lights on, but enough ambient light filtered in to show the area. A twin-sized bed and porta-potty occupied most of the space. A small porthole on either side of the boat gave me a little view.

I sat down on the berth and pulled my gun from the bag. It took him another two minutes to emerge from the cabin. He didn't have Amanda, and he still had his face. I assumed that meant her hiding place worked.

The blond fellow began messing with the lines like he was trying to solve a Rubik's Cube. At last, he figured out which one raised the mainsail. As soon as it started up, the breeze filled the sheet and turned the vessel into the wind. He needed to release the boom so the main would rotate to catch the wind, but he didn't know what he was doing. As the boat spun, he grabbed the helm and fought to straighten it up. Once he had it pointed in the direction he wanted, he bent over the navigation instruments, probably turning the autopilot on.

Carina moved through the water, but even from in here, I noticed she was sluggish. The speedboat on her side wasn't helping, and when he untied it, she might tack the other way. I had to hope Amanda was comfortable enough to handle her. She might not have enough confidence to manage the sheets, but she'd seen me do it. Even lent a hand the last few times we were out.

Blondie jumped back on board the speedboat. He released the lines, and I watched *Carina* veer away. She was trying to sail into the wind, which sent her into a spin as the breeze filled the sails and pushed her around, the autopilot attempting to correct it.

The speedboat's motor roared to life, and we pulled away from my home. I monitored her for the next half minute as we drove away, and then I lost sight of her.

I settled on the bed, soaking the sheets. Already the stuffy cabin was heating up, and the Sharkskin acted like a sauna suit. Although, in this case, it might have been closer to a steam-room suit.

It was going to be a long, hot ride.

34

After forty minutes, I started wishing I'd brought some water with me. My wetsuit had dried in the draftless, hot cabin, and now I was sweating beneath it.

If it took him ninety minutes to reach us, then I hoped we were halfway there. Another twenty minutes passed, and I felt like I'd lost ten pounds of water weight. It wasn't as hot as the desert when I was geared up, but then I always carried around water. I once figured I drank over a gallon or two a day, and I still had days without peeing. Another half hour wouldn't kill me.

Twice, I heard Blondie speaking. The first time, I thought he was on the phone again, and I couldn't quite understand him over the engine noise. The second time, though, he was using the VHF radio. There was a speaker installed below.

"Opening the port garage door," a man stated through the speaker.

Blondie responded, but his voice blended with the din of the motors, which were loud down here.

"Roger. Bring her in. The boss said to find him on the salon deck," the radio voice declared.

Blondie responded with a muffled "Roger."

The powerboat slowed to an idle, and I peeked out the porthole. A massive white yacht loomed ahead. It was difficult from my position to estimate the length, but I would bet it was about ninety meters.

Capitulate. Such a fucking stupid name.

My view was limited to port or starboard, yet our trajectory indicated an imminent collision with the enormous vessel. Almost as soon as that thought crossed my mind, the boat lurched as the hull glided onto the ramp or supports that held the boat in transit. The light outside extinguished as we entered the docking bay.

Someone shouted, "One more time!"

The engine revved, thrusting the speedboat up higher on the supports. Then the motors fell silent.

"What happened?" a voice called.

"Fuck if I know," Blondie said. "No one was there."

"Think the bastard got them?"

"Man, have you seen Cal? Dude's a walking muscle."

"Yeah. Weird, huh?"

"I gotta go up and talk to Connors. Doubt he'll be happy with this."

"What can you do?"

The pair stopped talking, and a thud sounded, telling me that someone had jumped to another platform. With my M45 in my grip, I waited, watching the hatch. Two minutes passed, and no one boarded the boat. I stood up, hooked my arms in the straps of the backpack, and opened the hatch. Despite being inside a massive garage, the air seemed fresher, and relief washed over me.

Before I climbed out, I listened. There was some movement echoing off the interior walls of the boat, and I crawled out of the cabin, staying below the gunwales. Once I was in the open, I lifted my head up to survey the environment.

The garage, or docking bay, wasn't much bigger than a standard carport, but it was on a yacht. There was another smaller Yamaha jet boat parked next to me. A man stood about ten feet in front of the speedboat with his back to me. He bent over a workbench, fiddling with something, and after a second, I recognized it as a carburetor. On the other side of the powerboat, I saw the Jet Ski the carburetor belonged to. The blue personal watercraft had been dismantled.

The rest of the space was empty. Blondie must have headed up to the salon deck, leaving this mechanic alone. I lifted the M45 and leveled it at the back of his head. With just a little pressure on my trigger finger, I could move on. But I couldn't do that.

I jumped onto the polycarbonate deck that resembled a wooden dock. That was a trivial detail to note, because my feet thumped on the plastic, causing the mechanic to turn around.

He stared at me. Or rather, he stared down the barrel of the M45.

"Don't make a sound," I ordered. "And maybe raise your hands."

He blinked twice and lifted his hands up. "Don't shoot me."

"Don't make me," I told him.

He shook his head.

"What's your name?" I asked.

"Antonio," he replied.

"Good, Antonio. I really hate shooting people who I know by name. Are you going to make me?"

He shook his head.

I studied him for a second. "Take off your clothes."

He stared back, and I wagged the barrel at him, signaling him to obey. He took the cue and started removing the blue polo and khaki shorts that must have been the uniform for the crew. Standing in his boxers, he looked at me, hopeful that was the extent of his embarrassment. I shook my head and aimed my M45 at his crotch.

He got the message and stepped out of the boxers.

"Get in the boat," I ordered. "Climb into the cabin."

Antonio watched me with nervous anticipation. I gestured with my head toward the speedboat, and he obeyed, climbing into the vessel and going through the hatch I left open. I grabbed a screwdriver off Antonio's workbench and followed him.

"If someone comes along, I suggest you stay quiet, Antonio. If you don't move from here, your chances of survival increase to nearly a hundred percent."

He nodded with shaky trepidation.

"Don't worry, just tell everyone I held you at gunpoint," I assured him.

"What if they don't believe me?" he asked.

"In about ten minutes, they will," I promised, sliding the hatch closed. I jammed the screwdriver into the track. Not a surefire locking system, but it would contain him for a bit. It wouldn't matter much as long as I had five to ten minutes before the alarm sounded.

Satisfied, I jumped back onto the polycarbonate dock and located the stainless-steel staircase leading up to the next deck. Antonio stared out the window at me as I left him alone in the stuffy cabin. At least he didn't have a wetsuit on, although that was a consolation he might not understand.

I unzipped the top of my wetsuit and slipped the M45

against my chest. It was one thing to wander around the yacht in a wetsuit. In fact, it might help me blend in. But toting an automatic handgun would draw the wrong attention.

Hopefully, I wouldn't need it until I reached the salon deck.

Even the next level up only took me into another crew section. The master of the vessel likely never came this way, or at least rarely.

How many men crewed a yacht this size?

This superyacht appeared to be a newer model, or it had some serious upgrades. I'd seen my fair share of engine rooms, from *Carina*'s to naval aircraft carriers to freight haulers. Next to the naval vessel, this one had the most high-tech gear. The Navy always had the newest technology, even if no one knew it existed yet. But this superyacht had spared no expense, and I suspected, for some instruments, this one had more upgrades.

But it couldn't fire a SAM or send out a squad of fighter planes.

When I stepped through the next door, I amended that last thought. It had an infinity pool, and that seemed as valuable as a nuclear missile.

Especially when I saw the two naked women lounging by the pool, although they looked more like girls. My stomach turned as I thought about Lyla and Diamond. Neither was old enough to be passed around like a joint at a frat party, but Connors and his associates did just that.

One girl, a petite blond, lifted her head and peered at me from under her sunglasses. I must not have been someone she wanted to see because she dropped her head back again.

A man strolled down the steps from the upper deck. Of

course, he didn't have a bit of clothing on, either. He was in his fifties or sixties, judging from the gray in his pubic hair.

"Where did you come from?" he asked, and I couldn't shake the feeling I'd seen his face before. Although it was a challenge to focus on anything above his neck with all his wrinkled bits dangling about in the sun.

"Oh, I went out with Antonio on the Jet Ski," I lied.

The man nodded as if that made perfect sense. "We're going for a dip," he remarked, nodding at the two girls.

"Grant, you were supposed to bring me a drink," the blond who'd appraised me a few seconds earlier declared.

"I forgot," he blubbered with a sheepish grin. "You'll have to punish me."

I gave the girl who could have been Grant's granddaughter an eye. It hadn't been intended as a lecherous stare, but her right buttock had caught my attention. Or, more to the point, the tattoo of a wolf caught my attention.

She caught me staring. "You want to get out of your wetsuit and join us?"

"Tempting, but I'm looking for Clayton," I said.

"Saw him up in the lounge or whatever he called it," Grant told me. He pointed up, indicating the direction I needed to go. "But by all means, come join us." His licentious gaze touched me, and I fought to maintain a straight face.

"I'll be back," I assured him.

As I climbed the steps, this man triggered my memory. Grant Thomas. He was a justice on the Supreme Court—the United States Supreme Court. I glanced behind at the outspoken judge who railed against gay marriage a few years earlier.

The hypocrisy soured my stomach, a feat considering how sick the idea of Grant Thomas with a couple of high-school-aged girls already made me. I wondered if the Coast Guard boarded the vessel now, would underage girls be enough to arrest Connors? Probably not. We were somewhere between the United States and the Bahamas. When Connors returned to the port, he'd be in the United States' jurisdiction. But if he were smart, he'd have someone ferry the girls off the boat before they entered US waterways.

However, I didn't intend to give him advice on how to commit pedophilia. If anything, I might throw him over the side of the boat for it.

The next level had a small bar where two middle-aged men sat with a couple of Bloody Marys. Both wore only bikini-style swimsuits that rarely looked good on anyone. Neither was Connors, and I walked past them without giving them much notice. Both men lifted their eyes long enough to see a man in a wetsuit walk by before returning to their cocktails.

I pushed through a door that led to an ornate salon with several couches and settees in the room. Expansive windows offered a view of the ocean from almost all sides, although the six individuals in the space paid no attention to the seascape. It was a gross, sweaty pile of naked people. I averted my eyes, but not before I recognized Diamond. She was too involved to see me, and I turned away, crossing behind the couches. Not one person paid me any attention. The remainders of a white dust covered a glass-topped coffee table.

At the forward end of this section was a carpeted staircase leading up to another level. I was halfway up the stairs when voices from beyond a door registered to me. I pressed my ear against the wooden door.

"Do you think they were dead?" a voice asked. It sounded like Connors.

"There was no one on the boat." Blondie, I guessed.

"What happened to our people?"

"I don't know," the other responded. "Something must have happened."

"Are you certain Gordon didn't abandon ship?"

"No way to know," Blondie replied. "Why would he leave his boat out there adrift, though?"

"I don't like it," Connors noted. "I don't like it at all."

My hand slipped into my wetsuit and removed the M45. With the gun in my right hand, I reached with my left for the handle.

35

The door opened, and I stepped in, raising my handgun.

"Morning, boys!" I announced.

Blondie faced a seated Clayton Connors, who wore a purple silk robe that he thankfully kept closed. Blondie turned around, spinning on the heel of his right foot. He had a second to see an armed man wearing a wetsuit barge in. The ticker in his brain clicked through an array of possibilities until it settled on the truth.

Then he fucked up. His hand jerked toward a Glock holstered on his belt. He didn't make it. The 45 in my hand fired, and the bullet pierced Blondie's sternum and destroyed his heart. He was dead before the body fell to the floor.

In the far corner, I noticed a man I'd missed when I entered. He had a nine millimeter in his grip, but he hadn't gotten it much farther than his holster. I dove at Connors as the bodyguard raised his weapon.

Connors's eyes widened, and I slammed him in the face with the M45. My left hand grabbed the billionaire by the hair, dragging him toward me like a shield as his bodyguard moved in my direction with his gun at the ready.

"Put down the weapon," he barked, but I yanked Connors up with the barrel shoved against the real estate mogul's temple.

The guard narrowed his eyes and stared me down. I gave him a half-smirk as I whispered in Connors's ear, "Tell him to put it down."

"Fuck you, Gordon," Connors declared. "You won't get out of here alive."

"Pretty sure that was what Cal and Davey told me," I informed him.

The guard's eyes flicked between my face and Connors's. He wasn't sure what to do. The manual would advise him to take me down, but in a moment like this, he had to decide if chancing his boss's life was worth such an attempt.

My head shifted to the side so that it was behind the billionaire's. If the guard tried to fire, he better be damned good, or his boss might lose an ear.

"This is quite a cruise you offer here," I said. "I have to say, this is indescribable."

Connors muttered a "harrumph."

"I take that back—it's describable. It's disgusting."

"You'll never survive this day," Connors stated. He ordered his bodyguard, "Kill him."

The bodyguard didn't comply. He couldn't without risking Connors. Despite the order from his boss, he wasn't making a foolish move.

My left hand still had Connors gripped by the hair. I tugged him back, keeping his mass between me and the shooter.

"What were you?" I asked Blondie. "Navy? Or Army?"

The guard focused on me. "Army Ranger."

"Nice," I said with a whistle on the sibilant.

The man offered a slight nod, and my wrist twisted as I fired. The forty-five caliber round ripped through the guard's face, and he pulled his trigger.

Clayton Connors jerked as his own guard's nine millimeter struck him in the side. "Fuck!" he barked as his legs collapsed from under him.

With a handful of hair, I held the man aloft, and the billionaire mogul who had ordered my murder screamed in agony. The butt of my gun slammed his head, stunning the already disoriented man. When I released his hair, I turned to lock the door. It was possible that no one heard the three gunshots. Unlikely, but possible. The most likely to have heard it were the members of the orgy one deck below. I hoped they'd stayed occupied enough to pay the sounds no attention.

With a flick of the deadbolt switch, I locked the cabin before turning to Connors, who was pulling himself up on the sofa where he'd been sitting. His robe no longer stayed closed as he struggled to pull himself up.

I marched over and thrust the barrel into his face. "Let's talk, asshole."

"You can't do this," he barked as he clutched at his side. The blood bubbling out was dark.

"Right now, you are on a very precarious timer," I warned him. "Pretty sure he hit your liver."

"Don't let me die," Connors begged.

I sat on the chair opposite, holding the M45 in my hand. "I can do whatever I want," I corrected him. "You tried to have me killed. Tried to have my girlfriend killed. That was a really bad idea."

"She was collateral," he stated as if that meant much to me.

"See, there's the problem," I explained. "The thing with collateral is sometimes you have to pay for it."

Connors pressed his left hand against his side. Blood oozed between the fingers. That nine millimeter slug was still in him, but it must have ripped through several organs.

"What about the girl?" I asked. "Did you kill her?"

"Not me," he panted. "Cal did it."

"On your order, though?" I pressed.

He coughed, and someone knocked on the door.

"Mr. Connors, is everything okay?" a voice called through the door.

"I'll kill whoever comes through and let you bleed out," I warned him. "Or you tell me what I want, and I'll allow them to airlift you to the hospital."

"I'm fine," he called back, keeping his eyes locked on me. "Leave me alone."

No one tried to kick in the door, but I kept my ear on it in case he'd given some signal.

"Why kill her?" I asked Connors.

"She saw something. Someone."

"Who?"

He shook his head. "Even that will kill me."

"You're dying, anyway," I pointed out.

"You did this," he complained.

"Technically, you told your guy to shoot me. He just wasn't good enough. That all falls on you."

"Do you have any idea what you're unwrapping here?"

"Considering you have a Supreme Court justice in a pool with two—I'm guessing—fifteen-year-old girls, I can imagine it won't be pretty."

"You'll make some enemies here," he warned, his already pale face whitening more. Blood drenched the cushion he reclined on.

"At least people won't remember me as a child rapist," I pointed out. "In these last few seconds you have left, I want to leave you with something."

"You said you'd get them to airlift me," he argued.

"Tell me who Lyla saw," I demanded.

He stared at me and then looked at the blood covering him. I tapped my wrist, reminding him his time was almost out.

Connors closed his eyes. When he opened them, he said, "The president."

I leaned back in the seat. There was probably a stunned look on my face. I'd met the president before. At the time, I'd just rescued his son, and he seemed grateful. Although I wasn't all that political, in my days in the Corps, I considered whatever president there was to be my commander. Therefore, they received a degree of respect based on that.

"I need help," Connors pleaded.

"So did Lyla," I remarked, standing up. "Hopefully, you'll live long enough to pay for your crimes." My gun lowered as I studied the billionaire. "Although, I doubt it," I commented as I walked out of the room.

The corridor was empty, and I moved forward, avoiding the orgy that sounded like it was still going. The next stairwell led all the way up, and I climbed it to the bridge level. When I stepped onto the yacht's command center, two crew members spun around to see me holding a gun on them. Neither was much older than thirty.

"Hi fellas," I said. "We're going to turn this vessel around and head toward US waters."

Both men remained motionless for a full ten seconds before the younger of the two nodded and turned.

"Are you two aware of what's happening here?" I asked.

The younger one nodded again. His partner announced, "We don't have any part of that."

"You think that it's okay?" I inquired.

He shook his head.

"Here's what's going to happen," I explained. "We're going back to the States, and hell will come down on everyone on this boat. Follow me?"

Both men blinked at me with blank eyes.

"I need a nod or something," I prodded.

They nodded.

"Good job, guys. Now, who's the captain?"

"He's below deck somewhere."

"I need a line out," I told them.

The younger of the pair pointed at a receiver. "You can use that," he said. "It's run off the satellite internet."

"Thanks. When the captain comes up here, you better think carefully about which side you pick."

The two crew members nodded as I picked up the phone. It looked almost like the cordless phone we kept in the Manta Club. I dialed Rob's number.

"Isip," he answered.

"I found the boat," I announced. "Let me give you our coordinates."

My fingers snapped at the crew member, who recited our longitude and latitude. I repeated them to Rob.

"What do you want me to do?" Rob asked.

"Consider this a mayday," I said. "Clayton Connors was shot by his security guard. More importantly, there are at least a couple of underage girls engaged with some powerful political figures."

"What?" Rob blurted. "How powerful?"

"Would you like my suggestion, Rob?"

"What?"

"If you had any idea who it is, you would tell whoever is going to respond, and that might temper what happens."

"You mean, it's that big of a deal?"

"Yeah. Your CO might wish you'd have told him, but if you do, he'll start covering his own ass. These people are engaged in sexual assault against girls who should be in high school."

"Fuck me," Rob growled. "What else do you need?"

"Detective Carlson from Palm County. Call him and tell him what I've told you."

"Is Connors dead?" Rob asked.

"Not when I last left him," I said. "But he will be soon."

"We can dispatch a chopper, maybe," Rob suggested. "Damn, Chase, this isn't my job, you know?"

"You might get a promotion," I offered.

"I don't want to get promoted," he barked.

The bridge door flew open, revealing a man in his mid-fifties with a shaved head and a thick build. "Why are we turning around?" the man demanded.

Both crewmen pointed at me, and I raised the forty-five toward him. "Rob, I gotta go. Get that chopper here. Include someone with handcuffs."

I returned the phone to the cradle.

"Who are you?" the man I now assumed was the captain asked.

"Have you seen that Tom Hanks movie?" I asked. "Hell, what's it called?"

"*Captain Phillips*," one of the crewmen offered.

"Right," I acknowledged. "I'm the captain now, right?"

The same crewman nodded. "What do you mean?" he asked.

"Consider this a citizen's arrest, I guess," I announced. "Your crew has decided to follow my orders."

"You can't do this," the captain stated. "We aren't in American waters."

"How long until we are?" I asked the two men operating the vessel.

"An hour," one of them answered.

I shrugged. "Right now, your boss is bleeding out because his bodyguard shot him. The Coast Guard is dispatching a chopper to airlift him out."

The captain's eyes widened. "We have a doctor on board," he said.

"My guess is that it only buys him time," I informed him. "Of course, when the Coasties arrive, there's going to be some questions for sure. You witnessed what's going on down below?"

The captain closed his eyes in a prolonged blink as he considered his options.

"I'm no lawyer," I said. " But if you wanted to mitigate your potential troubles, I'd suggest preparing to roll over on everyone you can."

"You have any idea how much money and influence Clayton Connors has?" the captain asked me.

"Not enough to stop a nine millimeter bullet," I retorted.

"What about the people onboard?" he asked. "There are some powerful men here."

I nodded. "Yeah, it's going to be quite the show when CNN airs this story."

The color drained out of his face. "Fuck me," he mumbled.

"That's about the way I'd feel, too," I remarked.

"I never touched those girls," he insisted.

Shaking my head, I replied, "That doesn't change much, does it?"

He let his chin bounce against his chest.

"How many people are on board?" I asked.

"Twenty-three," he said.

"Crew?"

"Six," the captain informed me.

"Including Blondie?" I asked. "Or the guy guarding Connors?"

The distraught mariner shook his head. "No, that guy was Connors's man. Who is Blondie?"

"Guy that took the speedboat out," I stated.

"Oh, that was Lucas. He's another one of Connors's guys. He had three."

"Where's the third?" I asked.

The bridge door burst open, and a man in a black t-shirt and white pants stepped through the door with a twelve-gauge Mossberg shotgun in both hands. "Someone killed Connors!" he shouted before he spotted me on the bridge.

In a moment of dawning, he saw the captain standing in the center of the bridge. Then his eyes shifted to me, and I pointed the barrel of the M45 at him. He tried to lift the barrel toward me, but I pulled the trigger.

The last guard fired the shotgun. His blast ripped through the captain's midsection and struck the older of the two crew members.

My round sent him back, and I fired again in case he had enough energy left to pull his trigger a second time. It didn't require a high level of skill to hit something with a Mossberg, and it was best if he couldn't try.

"Fuck, Jamie!" the younger crew member called, dropping to his knees.

I stepped toward the captain. He was dead. Jamie wasn't, though. The blast hit the captain, who'd shielded Jamie from the brunt of the shot. The right side of Jamie's face might have been ground burger. His shoulder and neck looked like someone had ripped him open.

"The captain said there was a doctor on board?" I asked.

The younger man nodded.

"What's your name?"

"Tim," he told me.

"Okay, Tim. Here's the deal. We need to get him some help. Can you find the doctor?"

Tim nodded.

"Where is he?"

"I don't know."

"Can you page him from here?"

Tim's face lit up a little, and he nodded.

"Do it."

Tim grabbed a microphone and flipped a switch. "Dr. Swanson, please report to the bridge for…" he paused.

"An emergency," I finished for him. "No details."

"An emergency," Tim stated.

It took the man five minutes to arrive, and I recognized him from the orgy.

"What the hell?" he demanded.

"You're going to keep him alive," I insisted, gesturing to Jamie.

"What is this?" Dr. Swanson asked.

"It was something of a coup," I said. "We don't want anyone to know about it."

"Where's Clayton?" he insisted.

I rested the barrel of the M45 against his head. "Keep him alive, or I don't need you."

His Adam's apple bobbed as he swallowed. "Okay," he stammered.

36

It only took us an hour to reach American waters. In fact, Amanda wouldn't have covered as much distance as we did. I'd tried to raise her on the VHF radio to no avail. She might have been too far away. Or she wasn't used to listening for it.

Jamie was stable. Dr. Swanson had staunched off the bleeding and tended to him. Twenty minutes after we encroached into US territory, a chopper appeared off our port bow.

Everyone on board realized at some point that things weren't normal. It took about half an hour before someone found Connors.

"You can't hold us," Grant Thomas insisted.

"No one is holding you here," I assured him. "If you don't want to return to the States, all you have to do is jump overboard and swim. It's only thirty or so miles to shore."

The justice narrowed his eyes. "I'll have your job for this," he informed me. "Who are you working for?"

"I'm not sure at the moment," I admitted. "I believe I might be unemployed."

"What are you going to do? You killed these people."

"Technically, Clayton Connors had me kidnapped. It just backfired."

"Who the fuck are you?"

"I'm the guy who can't wait to read the papers tomorrow," I said with a smile.

"This won't make the news," Thomas scoffed.

I chuckled. "Judge, I believe your world is about to be rocked. Now, can you go below deck?"

"You won't get away with this," he declared.

I shrugged, pushing the older man out the door. "Be sure to tell anyone who wants to leave which way to swim," I called to him.

Now the chopper hung over the bow as four men rappelled down. Each man carried an M4 and a Glock 19, except one guy who shouldered a Remington 870 shotgun with his Glock.

"Where is the captain?" the first Coastie asked. I had my hands in the air, and my M45 rested on the floor.

"He is," I told him, pointing at the corpse on the floor.

"Are you Gordon?" he asked.

I nodded.

"Who killed him?" he inquired as the medic came through the door.

"Actually, that guy," I said, pointing at the last guard. "He shot the captain, and Jamie caught the blast."

"Mack, how's he look?" the leader questioned the medic as he looked at Jamie.

"He's bad, but looks like he's stable."

"Thank the doc," I said, directing my head toward Swanson.

The leader looked at Swanson.

"Uh, Lieutenant Commander," the medic called to his leader. "That's Dr. Swanson."

"Who?" the lieutenant commander asked.

"The surgeon general," the medic stated.

"I'll be damned," I whistled. "We have a Supreme Court justice below deck, too."

The lieutenant commander turned his focus on me. "What is this?"

"A floating brothel," I explained.

"You're shitting me," he barked. "Why are you here?"

"Long story, but Clayton Connors had me and my girlfriend kidnapped."

"Where is she?" the Coast Guard commander asked.

"She's supposed to be on the way back to West Palm," I said.

"How did she get away?"

"The two guys who stole my boat and kidnapped us took a swim in the drink. Technically, all four of us did, but I managed to get back aboard."

He shook his head. "That's a hell of a story," he remarked.

"I glossed over most of it," I informed him.

"We have a cutter on the way," he assured me.

"You're Direct Action?"

"Yes. Lieutenant Commander Derrickson."

Two more of his team showed up.

"LT, we need to get him to the chopper," the medic briefed his commander.

"Leake, you help Oscar carry him out on deck. Blake, you man the bridge." Derrickson looked at Tim. "Who are you?"

"Tim," he answered. "I'm just bridge crew."

"You work for Blake now," Derrickson commanded him,

and Tim nodded. "Blake, keep us on course for West Palm." The commander gestured for me to follow him. "Gordon, let's walk."

"Yes, sir," I said.

"You were Recon?" he asked.

"Read my file?"

"No, my commander relayed that to me," he stated. "Where's Connors?"

"I'll show you," I said. "Can I take my gun?"

He shook his head. "I'm sure it will be evidence."

"Terrific," I moaned.

I walked Derrickson down to the level where I left Connors. He was dead. Had been for a bit now.

"Walk me through everything," Derrickson ordered.

I gave him the details, starting with Amanda and me finding the body in the marina. I omitted a few details, such as the hitman in the woods and the fire at the theme park. I brought him up to speed with our being kidnapped at gunpoint from Amanda's apartment and ferried to *Carina.*

"You weren't kidding," he replied. "All four of you went overboard. Smart to grab the line."

"It was the only thing I could think of," I confessed.

"If they let your boat follow the stream, we might never have seen it again," Derrickson noted.

"That's what I thought," I said. "Can you check if anyone has seen *Carina*? I'd feel better once I confirm Amanda is safe."

"I'll put out an alert," he assured me. He radioed the helicopter, asking them to relay his request to all units. When he turned back to me, he asked, "How'd you get here?"

I decided to fib a bit and pointed at Blondie's body. "He came out to pick up the two guys on my boat. I let him take me. I escaped in the garage—which reminds me, there's a naked mechanic in the tender."

"Why is he naked?" the commander asked.

"I figured he'd be less willing to run out and sound the alarm."

The lieutenant commander jutted out his bottom lip as he considered that. He shrugged and motioned for me to continue the tale. I carried him through my trip up to here and on to the bridge.

He clicked his radio. "DAS team, I want all passengers corralled."

I couldn't hear the responses, but assumed they consisted of "Roger that" or some variation.

"Let's go see who besides a justice and the surgeon general you've drummed up," Derrickson said.

When I inhaled a breath, I wondered if I should mention the allegation Connors gave before he died. It seemed pointless, and what would Derrickson do with that information? Had an asset told me in the field that the president killed a girl, I might not have listened to him, either. There was no proof. At least, none that I knew about.

Although, it occurred to me that as this blew up, more details would emerge about Connors. Perhaps that evidence would present itself. I'd wait and share that with Carlson. While he wouldn't be able to do anything, it seemed like he needed to learn what happened to Lyla.

Derrickson and I walked down to the same salon where I'd seen the surgeon general performing acts that should have his own warning slapped on them.

"Not to tell you your job, sir, but we need to split the girls off," I said. "These men have a lot to lose, and those ladies will be the linchpin."

"Good point, Gordon," he agreed. "I want statements. The LEDETs will be here soon."

LEDETs were the Law Enforcement Detachments arm of the Coast Guard. While the DAS or Direct Action Section operated similar to SWAT as the front-line Spec Ops branch, the LEDETs would do the actual investigating.

"If your guys interview the girls, I'd like to know how many are tied to a Haitian gang in Miami called *Les Loups Noirs*," I said.

"That's the gang pimping them out?"

I nodded.

"I'll see what we can come up with. For now, why don't you settle in and wait with everyone else?"

I gave the people in the room a good look and considered suggesting that I wait somewhere else. I'd seen a few of these men bare-ass naked a little while earlier, and if Swanson and Grant were an example of the level of power in this room, I might make a few enemies. However, I complied. After all, I'd run up against an entire Haitian gang. These men might have the power to close down the Manta Club, but Lucien Baptiste still wanted to send a horde of men after me.

"What are you doing here?" Diamond asked, walking up to me. She was now dressed, having wrapped herself in a terrycloth robe.

"Your host kidnapped me," I explained.

"What happened the other night?" she asked. "I'm sorry Loup grabbed you."

I shrugged. "Was that the plan?"

She shook her head. "No, that guy really was hassling me."

"You know Connors?" I inquired.

"Clay?"

"Yeah, he's the one who had Lyla killed."

Diamond let her face sag a bit. "Why?"

"Do you know who some of these people are?"

The girl shook her head.

I gestured toward Grant. "He's a Supreme Court justice. The surgeon general is here, too. I don't know who else. These are powerful men, and Connors catered to them."

"Really?" she exclaimed.

"He probably used it to control them, too, but I have no proof of that."

"Is that why she died?" Diamond asked.

"Before Connors died, he said she saw the president."

Diamond made a questioning face. "The President of the United States?"

I nodded. "I'm guessing she recognized him. Maybe she thought she could get more money out of Connors or the president."

The girl chuckled. "That sounds like her," she said. "Lyla always wanted more."

"That might have made her a liability. This place will be inundated with cops very soon," I warned her. "This isn't going to blow over, either. There will be a scandal like you haven't seen before. Get a lawyer—and not one that Baptiste offers."

"I can't afford a lawyer, and Loup will leave me out to dry," she told me.

"Diamond, call a good lawyer and explain how you are involved. I think you might find some will do it pro bono. Play your cards right, and you should come out much better than your current situation."

"How would I do that? Isn't this illegal?"

I leaned toward her. "You're a victim here," I explained.

"This is your moment to get free. Don't waste it. Save your-self and any of the other girls Baptiste controls."

She stared at me, and I wondered if my words were falling on deaf ears. She'd been a prisoner her whole life. Whatever had spurred her to flee to South Florida and become a prostitute was just the beginning. It would be a hard life to break free from. I doubted Lucien Baptiste or his wolves would allow it.

"Uh, should I ask the judge about a lawyer?" she asked.

"Diamond, no. These men want you to remain silent. That's your weapon. Call the most expensive lawyer you can find. The publicity on this will be enough for them."

"Is that so?"

"I'm no expert," I admitted. "But human nature rarely surprises me. A good lawyer will have you on talk shows and such to make sure your story gets out."

Diamond nodded. "You mean I could be famous?"

"For at least fifteen minutes," I promised her.

And that seemed to satisfy the girl.

37

It took Amanda about two hours longer to make it back to port than it did for us. Detective Carlson somehow got on the cutter with the Coast Guard's investigative team. By the time we reached West Palm Beach, he came up to the lounge and settled in a seat beside me.

"Be careful where you sit in here," I warned, adding the details of the orgy I'd seen earlier.

Carlson curled his lip. "This is going to be a big mess."

"My thoughts, too."

"But none of it connects to the girl," he pointed out.

I nodded. "There's no evidence, but Connors confessed to me. One of the men who grabbed Amanda and me did the deed."

"He say why?"

I told him.

"Oh, shit," Carlson muttered. "You've dredged up something."

"Doubt anything sticks," I advised. "Unless someone else witnessed it, the people involved are all dead."

"Except the president."

"Yep, and I'll let you figure out how to connect that."

Carlson shook his head. "It's all hearsay, and the minute I bring it up, the cover-up begins. Probably will as soon as word breaks about this raid."

"Yeah, it won't be pretty."

"We're docking here shortly. I've talked to Derrickson and the Coast Guard's lead investigator, Nichols. There will be an investigation, and we need to talk to Amanda about the kidnapping. However, you should be in the clear. There's a bit of confusion with the naked guy in the docking bay."

"Antonio," I said.

"Yep, him. But I don't think it's going to be too much trouble. Unless the powers-that-be want to rain hell down on you."

"Detective, that girl Diamond."

"What about her?"

"Really, any of these girls, they're the linchpin in this. But they need more than just protection."

"I'll talk to her," he promised.

"You might hate me, but I told her to get a lawyer."

He nodded. "She should. There's going to be a lot of lies and blame thrown around here."

"This will all be tried in the court of opinion," I stated.

"True. That can make life easier," he reasoned. "At least for me. I wanted to close the other girl's case, though."

"You still need to find out who she is," I reminded him.

"We have some leads. Somewhere, there's a family looking for her, and the only news they'll get is she's gone."

"At least it's news," I countered. "Missing is open-ended. Now they can start to grieve and heal."

"I suppose," Carlson said. "By the way, Derrickson told

me to inform you they contacted Amanda. She's safe, but they dispatched an escort for her."

That was a relief.

"One day, you'll have to tell me all the things you're leaving out," he suggested.

"Why, I do not know what you're talking about, Detective."

"I'm sure," he replied dryly. "We're coming into the inlet. I don't know where they plan to dock this bitch. That's the Coast Guard's problem."

He stood and left me, stopping to talk to Diamond for a moment. She glanced my way, and I nodded to her, hoping that would signal Carlson's trustworthiness. She seemed to take my meaning and answered whatever he asked.

When we docked, they chose the municipal marina of West Palm Beach. Carlson and the Coast Guard investigator Nichols released me. Both reminded me to stay put for a few days until they cleared me altogether.

Even then, Carlson warned me that I should expect to be subpoenaed in the future. The consensus between the two lead investigators was that this would end up in not only the criminal courts, but there would be some Congressional hearings to follow.

Carlson ordered me a rideshare, complaining again that I didn't have a phone. To which I pointed out that even if I had a phone, my kidnappers wouldn't have allowed me to carry it with me. As a general rule, kidnappings were a cell phone-free event. At least for the victim.

I reached the Tilly to find my slip empty. Randy saw me coming down the dock, still wearing the Sharkskin pants. I had the top of it slung over my bare shoulders.

"Chase, where's *Carina*?" he asked.

"Arriving shortly," I assured him. "Think you got a spare shirt?"

"Got a couple of those old Tilly Marina shirts we sold a few years ago," he replied.

I recalled those shirts. Some vendor had offered Missy a deal on the shirts, making them cheap. Unfortunately, when they arrived, the screen printing was already flaking off and the material was almost gossamer. She ended up giving most of them to the marina tenants and taking the loss. At the time, I gave her some crap about getting hoodwinked. Now, I figured it was better than nothing.

Randy ducked into his office and came back with an extra-large shirt.

After I dressed, I hung my wetsuit up by the showers to dry. Once Amanda returned, I'd change.

"Chase, your girl just called!" Randy shouted from his office. "She's coming around the bend."

"Mind giving me a hand?" I asked.

"Already on it," Randy alerted me, stepping out of his office with two sturdy aluminum boat hooks. He tossed one to me, and I snatched it in midair.

As we walked to my slip, I could see *Carina*'s mast as she entered the Tilly Marina's harbor. Amanda helmed the wheel, and she smiled when she saw me at the end of the dock. I waved, and she returned the gesture with ample enthusiasm.

"Chase, I know you have a thing with Missy, but that girl is something," Randy beamed.

"Yeah, I think I agree," I admitted.

Carina banked wide before Amanda spun the wheel. I gestured for her to slow her approach, and she did, pushing the throttle to neutral. Docking required patience, calm, and hopefully no wind. Right now, she seemed to have the ideal situation. The breeze was steady but not strong. That meant she could use inertia to drive the Tartan forward.

Carina's momentum slowed, and Amanda looked to me for guidance.

"You're doing good," I assured her in a loud voice. "Just let her come on in."

"Do I need to hit the gas?" she asked.

Had I been behind the helm, I would have nudged her forward with a burst of throttle that would push the bow forward. Of course, I'd end up counteracting that with a similar burst in reverse. Since Randy and I were here, we could grab the bowsprit and tug her in by hand.

I stood at the end of the finger, extending my boat hook out. The crooked end caught the bowsprit, allowing me to pull her into the slip. Randy reached out and hooked his so I could get another grip. By now, we had *Carina* in the slip. Amanda climbed forward, throwing the bowline to Randy, who secured it with a hitch knot. I snagged the stern line and pulled it to me, repeating the same knot as Randy's on the back cleat.

"Thanks, Randy," I told my friend, signaling him to let us finish up. I handed his extra hook back. "I'll come get my wetsuit after I change. Want your shirt back?"

"Eh, keep it," he muttered, and he gave a little wave to Amanda, who returned the gesture with her bright smile.

I climbed aboard, wrapped my arms around Amanda, and kissed her.

"You worried me, Chase," she told me.

"Same," I said.

Her arms wound around my neck. "I'm hot, hungry, and horny," she whispered. "Which one of those can you fix right now?"

"Get below deck," I ordered.

"Oh?" she replied wistfully.

"Yeah. I think there's a granola bar down there."

She punched me in the arm. "Not what I want," she informed me, turning to climb through the companionway.

I was still standing in the cockpit when her shorts flew out of the companionway.

"Get your ass down here, Chase!"

38

My hand held Amanda's as we strolled back to *Carina*. After the last twelve hours, I wanted to put the day behind me. We walked south on Flagler Drive to Pistache, a little French bistro near the park. After two bottles of Bordeaux and the crispy duck confit, we enjoyed the evening together.

Tomorrow would offer plenty of fresh problems. I needed to check in with Missy. We'd left a lot of loose threads dangling between us, including my current employment status and our personal issues. Those would fix themselves over time. I knew Missy better than most people, and she'd come around.

There would be the inquiry with the Coast Guard and the follow-up questions from Carlson. Those would be tiring and intense.

But tonight, pure bliss washed over me, enhanced by a delightful tipsiness. The aftermath of today's events should be wide-sweeping as the investigation started identifying some of the passengers on Connors's carnal cruise. The news had picked up the reports, and by now, journalists had swarmed West Palm Beach and the Tilly, something that Missy would be grateful I'd made happen. This might even overshadow the shooting in the Manta Club, or it could just be icing on an already salacious story.

It was probably the Bordeaux, but I didn't notice the Suburbans until they pulled up beside us. The black man popped out of the back seat, holding a MAC-10 automatic rifle pointed at us.

"Damn," I muttered.

"Mr. Gordon," Lucien Baptiste ordered from the back-seat of the Suburban. "Why don't you come with us?"

"You're just going to kill us," I commented.

Baptiste leaned forward so that I could look into his face. His right index finger pointed at a group of teenagers strolling through the park to our left. "If we kill you here, then I have to kill them, too."

I glanced at Amanda. Her face was stoic, and I realized she had faced a lot of danger in the last twenty-four hours.

"Leave her," I ordered.

Baptiste shook his head. "I can promise I'll make it quick —for her."

"Just do it," Amanda urged. Was that resignation or trust that I'd get her out of this?

I wasn't sure. Adrenaline coursed through me, sobering me up. In my inebriated state, I didn't believe I could take a guy with a MAC-10. Although the automatic often jammed, its nickname as a spray gun existed for a reason. When he pulled the trigger, the MAC-10 would pepper everything in sight with forty-five caliber bullets. While its accuracy was shit, the sheer speed it spewed ammo could empty the magazine into us before I made the three steps toward him.

"Cuff him, bitch!" Baptiste demanded, and the gunman threw a pair of handcuffs on the ground in front of Amanda.

She stared at the restraints on the sidewalk. "Do it," Baptiste reiterated. "We aren't giving you an inch."

Resigned, I extended my hands in front of me and presented them to Amanda.

"Behind the back," Baptiste instructed.

I rolled my eyes and turned. He wasn't kidding. They weren't giving me much to work with.

"Lucien, the police already know about you," I informed him as Amanda slapped the cuffs on my wrists.

"If they had proof, they'd come for me," he barked.

"Not necessarily," I suggested.

"We'll find out," he remarked with no concern in his tone. "I'll take my chances."

I shrugged as the gunman grabbed me by the shoulders and pushed me toward the Suburban.

"Put her in the other one," Baptiste ordered. "If he causes any problems, kill her."

The gunman nodded and waved at the other Suburban parked in front of Baptiste's.

"Tell them to make it hurt, too," Baptiste added as he locked eyes with me. "Don't cause me any problems, and she'll be okay."

"Until you kill us both," I amended.

"What can I do?" he asked nonchalantly.

"This won't end well for you," I told him, although I doubted my own words. The binding of my hands limited my options.

There were plenty of people who were able to escape handcuffs without a key. Unfortunately, I wasn't one of them, and certainly not when they were behind my back. If I had ten to fifteen minutes with no one bothering me, I could free myself if my hands were in front of me. As it was, I would not escape without breaking my hand. That was not as easy a feat as the movies might show.

I watched one of Baptiste's men escort Amanda to the lead SUV.

"Listen, we don't have to do this," I urged him. "It was Clayton Connors who killed your girl."

"I heard you killed him," Loup noted.

"He had you under his thumb," I pointed out.

"It was a very profitable thumb," Baptiste rebutted. "I didn't like the man, but he paid well for the girls."

"You'll rebuild that."

"And the heroin?"

"What heroin?" I questioned with a look of innocence. At least, I hoped I made it look innocent.

"I know it was you," he remarked.

My brow furrowed. "What are you talking about?"

"Colin?" Baptiste spoke.

For the first time, I recognized the guy in the passenger seat as he turned around. Smoky.

"Fuck me," I muttered.

"It would seem so," Baptiste stated. "You misread my men's loyalty."

"I guess I did," I confessed. "In fairness, you tried to kill me first."

"That was business," Baptiste told me.

"So I shouldn't take it personally?"

"Take it how you want," he said. "You can't hit me without me hitting back."

"Colin, you're going to end up dead," I told the kid.

"Better than being a snitch."

"Fine. How can we make this right?" I asked. "There has to be something you want."

Baptiste pursed his lips. "Nothing you can offer."

"I have money," I lied.

"So do I," Baptiste explained. "It was the lack of respect you displayed that has to be punished."

"Of course. You don't want to look weak in front of your men, do you?"

"I'm not weak," he told me.

"Except you jumped when Connors called," I added.

"Again, that was only business," he informed me.

"How about influence?"

"What do you mean?"

"How much money could you make if you worked with someone like Julio Moreno?" I asked.

"And you can make that happen?"

"Julio and I are friends," I exaggerated.

"When I'm done, I'll put Julio Moreno in the ground and take over his business," Baptiste stated, adding, "Without your help."

"At least that's something," I said.

"What?" Baptiste asked, confused.

"At least I know Moreno will kill you," I quipped. "That comforts me. Pretty sure Scar will cut your heart out."

"Who?" Baptiste asked.

"You'll find out eventually," I replied. "Not today, but soon enough. Moreno controls this area, and you're encroaching. All you are is a mosquito. Julio is the fucking alligator."

A forced smirk crossed Baptiste's face. This wasn't something new I was telling him, and he was already worried about it. Sure, he boasted he'd take out Moreno, but that was just for show. Baptiste realized what he was up against, but he'd been promising his Wolves that they'd get more of the pie.

"At least killing you will send him a message," Baptiste announced, deciding that there was a positive angle.

"Not really," I said. "Julio Moreno couldn't care less if I was killed."

He shrugged.

I looked forward to see we were heading out of town. "Taking us back to Swampland?"

"Seems appropriate," he answered.

"Colin, I bet you don't leave there, too," I told Smoky.

The kid turned to glare at me. "*Fèmen bouch ou!*"

I didn't know what that meant, but his tone conveyed the sentiment. Settling in my seat, I considered how to get out of this situation without getting Amanda killed. There were four men, including Baptiste, in this SUV. Five if you counted me, but I didn't. It was safe to assume the same number in the forward vehicle.

Eight men against me and Amanda. I had no weapons. Carlson or the Coast Guard still had my backup M45. *Should have kept my dive knife strapped to my thigh.* Not that I could have reached it now, though.

Behind me, a man sat in the third row, and while I wasn't positive, I suspected he held a gun ready to blow my brains out if I attacked Baptiste. In the confined space, there was nothing I could do before one of them shot me. My best course of action was using my feet, and that would be futile now.

Once we reached our destination, my time would be limited. I didn't think Baptiste would stretch this out long. Maybe he'd make me watch Amanda die, but I figured that would be fast. He had no plans to extend my life longer than necessary.

I thought about the layout of Swampland. Baptiste had

probably abandoned the theme park now that the police had responded to the fire.

"Loup, we might have a car behind us," the driver announced.

Baptiste twisted to stare out the back. "There's nothing there," he said.

"When we turned off, there were headlights, but they are gone."

"Keep a lookout for them," Baptiste ordered. He turned to me. "Who's following us?"

I shrugged. "Might be the police? But I didn't know anyone was following us."

"You seem to be some super-spy," he commented sarcastically. "How did you miss them?"

My head shook. "I didn't," I denied, adding, "Although I didn't spot you."

"We had one guy sitting on your hotel," Baptiste admitted. "When you went out, he followed you and called us in."

"Maybe the cops did the same thing," I suggested. My eyes tried to glance at the rearview mirror, but I only saw the edge of the driver's face.

"Lights!" the driver announced. Everyone turned around to watch as a pair of headlights appeared in the distance behind us. The two round lights zoomed toward us.

"No blue lights," Colin, AKA Smoky, remarked.

"Cops often run silent," I pointed out.

In only seconds, a Corvette raced up on us. My hopes sagged as the sports car passed us. I caught sight of the bright yellow blur as it flew past us. The Corvette whizzed by both SUVs and sped ahead, the taillights vanishing a few seconds later.

"Not a cop," Baptiste declared with a satisfied smile.

"All clear behind us," the driver informed Baptiste, who only nodded.

It was a few minutes later when we turned into the parking lot of Swampland.

"This is good enough," Baptiste declared. "We don't need to go in. Kill the lights."

The driver obeyed, and the Suburban in front followed suit, plunging all of us into darkness. With no moon out, only the stars provided any ambient light. Colin was the first one out of the car, followed by the gunman with the MAC-10. Both held their weapons on me as I got out.

"Lucien, if you'll please spare the girl," I pleaded. "She didn't do anything."

"It will serve as a lesson to others," he advised.

"You don't have to do this."

The Haitian's white teeth flashed in the darkness, and I never saw his fist. He slammed his knuckles into my jaw. Unprepared, I toppled over like a bowling pin. As I rolled to my side, the gang leader kicked his right foot out. A red Nike trainer struck my torso, knocking the air out of my lungs. My feet kicked at the asphalt as I tried to scoot away from my attacker. It was pointless, and he delivered another kick to my chest.

Pain rippled through my torso. He'd broken a rib with that blow.

"No!" Amanda screamed from somewhere in the dark. "Leave him alone!"

I heard the slap as someone struck her. My body twisted as I pushed my right knee under me, trying to get to my feet without the use of my hands.

Something hit me again, and I flopped down to the asphalt. My face scraped across the rough, tarred surface. A foot slammed down on my back, flattening me to the ground. Another came from somewhere else, kicking me in the face. Blood spewed from my nose and covered my face. I tasted the coppery fluid. My head turned away as another foot hit me on the side of the head.

Pebbles, dirt, and grass filled my mouth as my face planted into the surface of the deteriorating parking lot. Laughter filled the darkness as the *Loups* enjoyed tormenting me. Amanda's sobbing filtered through the jovial sounds of murderous fraternity.

Beams of headlights suddenly illuminated the area, but all I could see were the feet of the Wolves still kicking at me. The barrage ceased for a second, and the overall aura of the group shifted from maniacal laughter to whispers of worry.

With the assault paused, I struggled to my knees. Blood filled my vision, and I blinked to clear my eyes before it began to coagulate and crust over them. Six headlights aimed at the group from the darkness. I lifted my head to see the man who stood closest to Amanda had a gun raised toward the lights. Baptiste, too, had a .357 Magnum in his hand, raised at the lights.

Slowly, and with pained movements, I pivoted my head in the direction of the lights. A shape behind the lights was barely visible. My eyes darted from the blinding lights to the ground in front of them. A pair of colorful boots stood just past the beams.

Les Loups Noirs collectively held their weapons toward the lights. I pushed my right foot down, pressing my sole down as I sprang to both feet, charging at Amanda. In a split second, I saw only her face, and her eyes widened.

Gunshots exploded in the darkness as I hit her like a linebacker running a blitz. My shoulder collided with Amanda, lifting her off the ground and driving both of us to the asphalt.

"Stay down!" I shouted, trying to cover her with my body.

It seemed like an eternity as the Wolves unloaded their weapons at the lights. Glass shattered, tinkling shards over the parking lot. Metal pinged around us as bullets peppered the Suburbans behind us. Amanda wrapped her arms around my neck and pulled me tight against her.

The entire gun battle lasted twenty seconds. Cordite filled the air, and it grew silent except for the persistent ringing in my ears. Amanda's breath blew into my ear as she panted. I stretched across her as the still Florida night flowed in where the gunfire had just been.

It took a second for me to recognize the clopping of feet across the pavement. I rolled off Amanda to see a figure looming near us. Amanda sucked in a breath as he stepped closer.

"Gordon, you dead?" Scar asked, staring down at me.

"Esteban, nice to see you," I remarked.

"*Señor Moreno* thought this *hijo de puta* would come after you again," he stated, bending over to grab my arm and pull me to my feet.

"You were following me?" I asked as Amanda stood up.

"Not me," he admitted. "You'd have seen me."

"Are you okay?" I checked with Amanda.

She nodded without a word.

I looked at Scar. "How, though?"

"Baptiste was making moves to move in on *Señor Moreno's* business," he explained.

"Who are these people, Chase?" Amanda wondered.

"You might be better not knowing everything," I suggested. "I think we're safe now."

I gave Scar a questioning stare. He rolled his eyes and nodded.

"Any chance you can get these off me?" I asked.

Scar gave me a sly grin. "I don't have a key," he admitted.

I walked over to Baptiste's body and nudged him with my foot. "Someone has one," I pointed out.

Scar waved one of his guys over. "Ernesto, see if you can find a key in there," he ordered, waving his hand over the dead bodies. "Don't leave any evidence, though," he warned before leaving us standing in the dark.

Ernesto found the key on Baptiste. Once I had my hands free, the beating I'd just taken caught up to me as the adrenaline subsided. My chest hurt more than my face. Every move I made sent streaks of agony through my body. Amanda must have noticed, and she stepped up beside me with her arms around her.

"I'm so sorry," I told her. "You shouldn't be with me. I've almost gotten you killed too many times."

"Don't tell me what to do," she ordered.

"Seriously, Amanda, they were going to kill us."

"You got us out of it," she noted.

"That wasn't me," I reminded her.

She shrugged. "Good enough for me. We need to get you to a hospital."

"Can we go to your place instead?" I asked.

She leaned over and kissed my cheek. I winced, realizing my face was battered as badly as my ribs.

"Sorry," she whispered.

"Gordon, if you want a ride back, we're leaving!" Scar shouted.

"Can we trust them?" Amanda asked.

I nodded. "Right now," I qualified.

She helped me hobble toward the headlights, leaving the corpses of the remaining Wolves scattered across the Swampland parking lot.

Grab a special epilogue here
Click here
https://dl.bookfunnel.com/ghomtp7i8o
Or scan theQR code